C000002602

STOLEN CHILDREN

David Wickham

2QT Limited (Publishing)

First Edition published 2016

2QT Limited (Publishing)
Unit 5 Commercial Courtyard
Duke Street
Settle
North Yorkshire
BD24 9RH

Cover design: Charlotte Mouncey
Additional images from iStockphoto.com

Printed in the UK by Lightning Source UK Limited

Author/Publisher disclaimer:

While historical details are believed to be accurate, all the characters and
names in this book are fictional, and have no relation whatsoever to anyone
bearing the same name or names.

A CIP catalogue record for this book is available from the British Library

ISBN 978-1-910077-97-9

For Pam
who always knew
and for all the stolen children who have
been reunited with their proper families
and for those who have yet to be found

By the same author

More Than a Game (with David Teasdale and Sebastian Coe)

How she would have loved
A party today! –
Bright-hatted and gloved,
With table and tray
And chairs on the lawn
Her smiles would have shone
With welcoming... But
She is shut, she is shut
From friendship's spell
In the jailing shell
Of her tiny cell.

From 'Lament' by Thomas Hardy

Between 1976 and 1982, the Argentine military government killed about 30,000 people who they believed were enemies of the State. Around 12,000 simply disappeared; they were murdered in captivity after being tortured for information. Among the missing were at least 500 pregnant women who were allowed to give birth to their children in prison and were then killed. Their children were given to military families, or friends of the military regime, to prevent the rise of another generation of subversives.

CHAPTER 1

1977

The rain on the corrugated iron roofs of the outbuildings sounded like the stamping of the crowd at the Bombonera football stadium in Buenos Aires when the home team scored. The ground shuddered in the same way but there was no joy in the ceaseless vibration. On the rounded Spanish tiles of the main block, the noise was more muted but it still threatened disaster.

At midnight, most of the windows were in darkness save in the guardhouse and the prison hospital. The young squaddie in the sentry box heard an occasional, muffled scream between the thunder claps, but people screamed in their sleep here. And the dogs were never silent, barking at their own shadows, leaping across the wall with every flash of lightning.

Inside the building, in the prison hospital, a young woman prisoner was giving birth and dying. She could see the doctor's grey eyes over his white mask but they never looked at her. The pains were coming more quickly now. Between the spasms, she drifted in that half world between awareness and near death.

Sometimes she thought that she was already dead and suffering in hell for her sins. The darkness, the fire, the pain, the terrible noise, they were all there just as the priest who had heard her confessions since she was a little girl had said they would be if she did not behave. In the last few years she had been less honest with her confessor and this was clearly her punishment. More fire, more noise, more pain, and they did not bother with confessors in this place. Another spasm caught her. She was sure there would be worse in the afterlife.

She pulled against the manacle which chained her to the operating table. She was trapped. She had seen other women go off to have their babies and assumed that the guards took the manacles off. The women never came back so she could not ask.

All the pregnant internees were kept at one end of a long corridor, their torture over for the moment. They were the only ones who stayed for long in the prison; others would come for a few days and then not return to their cells.

What would become of her baby? Until now, Caridad had never given up hope, never stopped praying for a miracle. Maybe if she had been more honest with God He would have come to her and her baby's aid.

Caridad had tried to stop her baby coming, to delay the spasms, to prevent her child being born into such a world; now it was too late.

'Please!' she screamed.

'Shhhh. Be calm.' The doctor was stern and he gripped

her leg hard.

She had only seen one doctor at San Juan, when she was first arrested and they realised she was pregnant; subsequently she was seen twice more. She remembered when she, or rather her jailers, had dislocated her shoulder after hanging her up by one arm. Two of them held her down then and the doctor yanked her arm back into position. Since she had arrived here, she had never felt a soft hand, never a hand at all unless it was beating her senseless or squeezing the life from her.

'Please!'

Who was she pleading with? What was she asking? She didn't know any more. For five months Caridad had screamed and no one had heard. She remembered what a women in the next door cell had said when she first arrived: 'Tell them what they want to know. Everybody does in the end.'

After two or three days she had told them but still they tortured her: beatings, near drownings, sleep deprivation, the *picana* – a prod they moved cattle with which gave her electric shocks – and rape. She had lost track of how many times she had been raped and by how many people; her only solace was the knowledge that they could not contaminate her with their sperm because she was already pregnant. Sometimes one of the soldiers or policemen would wander into her cell, slap her hard across the face, rape her and leave, without saying a word. Sometimes two or three or four men would come in, rip from her body what passed for clothes and pass her around, spinning her from one to another and raping her, laughing and talking as though she were not there. Sometimes they raped her with the *picana*.

That went on until about four months ago, when the doctor said that she would lose the child she was carrying if they continued. The men had smirked and warned her not to regard it as a reprieve but 'just a little pause in our activities'. And then one had squeezed her nipple hard to show he outranked the doctor. Since then, they had taunted and cajoled her but didn't physically abuse her. They moved her to a cell in the special corridor, gave her proper food to eat and a mattress to lie on.

She had been pretty before, even beautiful. The hair which used to spring from her head was now lank and thin. The once full lips had narrowed; now they were rigid and pursed with pain. Her quicksilver eyes were dull; once indigo and as wide as the pampas, they had retreated behind her high cheek bones. Her face already resembled a skull.

Now her baby was coming and there was nothing she could do to stop it. The pains were coming every two or three minutes but, after the pain of the *picana*, she could bear them. She dragged her wrist against the manacle, braced her knees again and arched her back.

'Push!' the doctor said. 'Just push ... and relax. And push!'

There was no pethidine, no epidural, only oxygen to keep her alive long enough to deliver. She drew on the mask but it did nothing to ease her pain. She pushed.

The nurse was more excited now. 'It's coming.'

'Pushhhh!' said the doctor.

Months of agony and brutality the world had not yet heard about were fused in Caridad's single scream and the child was born.

'*Bueno!*' The woman was aware of someone saying that above the cries that announced her baby's first breaths. She tried to raise her arms to the child but one was shackled to the bed and the other could only wave weakly in the air. The doctor finished wrapping the child in a white linen cloth and passed it to a nurse, then it was gone in an instant. They did not tell her whether it was a boy or a girl.

She tried to scream, 'My baby!' Her mouth moved but emitted no sound. She had no more fight left and anyway, she was already being wheeled out.

CHAPTER 2

The outer door of the operating theatre swung open and a wavy-haired man in a police captain's uniform entered. The doctor, swathed in surgical cap and gown, glowered at Captain Raul Martinez but reluctantly accepted his authority. It was dangerous to appear disinclined to do one's duty.

'I was about to call you,' the doctor said.

Martinez did not need to be called; he saw everything, knew everything. He only ever needed confirmation. His own question, barked rather than spoken, ignored the doctor's remark. 'The child?'

The doctor handed over a piece of paper with the infant's details. 'Perfectly healthy,' he said.

'I shall inform the commandant.' Martinez nodded to another policeman hovering by the door. 'We've finished with the mother.'

The words were delivered without emotion. It was an execution order and the young policeman accepted it without question. It was not the first time, nor would it be the last, that he must kill for his beloved country and he knew the woman deserved to die. She was a proven enemy of the Motherland.

Captain Raul Martinez marched out, the echo from his boots on the stone floor a chilling, thumping base line to the rain.

* * *

The phone rang shrilly in the commandant's office on the first floor, waking him up.

'Yeah!' An arm jack-knifed the handset towards an ear, bruising it.

'She's had the baby.'

The commandant put down the phone carefully. It had not been a good week; come to that, it had not been a good month or a good year, though soon things would be different.

The pretty, dark-haired woman in the photo frame on his desk smiled at him. Opposite her was a picture of the Shrine of Our Lady of Lujan where they had married. How had he ended up here? He was the most eligible man in the village, not rich but with the promise of a solid future. And she? She was the prettiest girl in Cordoba, who had eyes only for him.

Of all the nights to be delayed – but Army Command were sticklers for procedure and he had already been warned once about his sympathy towards the prisoners and the poor results his interrogation team were getting. Besides, he knew he could not trust everyone here. Ambition, he decided, was more dangerous than terrorism, and just as bloody.

* * *

The young policeman thought of none of these things as he took charge of the trolley outside the operating theatre. He was scarcely more than a child himself, perhaps seventeen or eighteen years old. The medical staff returned to their duties and he to his.

On his way to the prison block, he collected a short canvas strap with a buckle. It was a standard Army-issue strap which could be tightened and locked to any length; normally it would have been used as a child's belt, or an accessory for a hiker's rucksack. Now it was placed around the woman's neck and buckled tight. Sometimes they took the prisoners to an aeroplane and threw them out over the sea, thus saving the trouble of a burial. Sometimes prisoners were shot but, most often, they were despatched in the way that he now despatched this woman.

The new-born child was already sleeping comfortably in a nursery, geographically adjacent but already in another world. Here the steel and stone of the prison hospital were hidden by the benign atmosphere of a fully equipped maternity ward. Tiny hands and faces wriggled their way through eating, excreting and sleeping, oblivious to the tortuous route to the maternity clearing house.

Baby Number 46, born 10.4.77, was placed gently in a cot alongside several others. Each cradle bore a neat label at its foot with the only details that mattered: number, sex and date of birth. In the military parlance of the day, it was known as 'transfer' and no one involved in the process found it strange. It was renaissance at the moment of death, a beginning with no past.

Numbers 43 and 45 had left that morning, one with a Navy lieutenant, the other with an Army general and his young wife. The general had sent his driver and one of the nurses travelled with the baby forty miles to the *estancia* outside the capital. The family welcomed the child as their own; it was theirs to cherish and love and imbue with Christian virtues.

The only nurses on duty were bottle feeding their charges as Number 46 was placed in a cot, a temporary station before being transferred to a grander residence with a family already anxiously awaiting their baby's arrival.

'Who's beautiful!' cooed the nurse, her doe eyes brimming with tenderness. 'Where are you going?'

The baby's passage into the world, the journey through the glorious moment of conception to the trauma and torture of confinement and delivery, meant nothing to the nurse. Or rather, she gave no thought to them. That the baby was here, briefly in her charge, was enough. Soon she would shepherd the infant on its way to a new beginning in a politically acceptable home.

* * *

The commandant had finished his log for the day and written a letter. The first he locked in the safe; the second, he stowed carefully in his briefcase. He had chosen his words concisely, measuring them onto the page with a slow two-fingered rattle of the ancient typewriter. He had only to add his signature and that was an end to it.

He cast a look around the office, a standard military office with a steel desk, chair and bookcase. There was not much of himself in it. The bookshelf was full of files and the odd tome on police regulations or the law. The pictures on the wall were Army issue: a map of the Malvinas, of course, and another of the province; a portrait of President Videla. The Argentine flag hung from a pole with an ornate brass cap which stood in a rack behind his desk. The picture of his young wife on his desk was all that distinguished his office from a thousand, perhaps ten thousand, belonging to other factotums across the country, assiduously doing their duty and staying out of trouble. Next to the photo were a telephone, an ink stand with pens and clips and rubber bands spilling from it, and two filing trays. In the top one was a file marked 'BIRTHS' and inside it a neatly typed paper headed 'OFFICERS AWAITING CHILDREN'.

The commandant looked at the files. He had awesome power but he felt ashamed at the way that power was abused. He was the jailor but now he felt as much of a prisoner as his charges. What had started as a dream profession and a magical posting to the city and this place had become torture as the Dirty War progressed. He wanted out and he hoped the day of his exit was fast approaching.

His boots crunched on the gravel outside until the

sound was drowned by the laboured groans of an eight-ton truck. A constable was reversing towards the hospital block. By the time the commandant reached his car, the truck driver and another militiaman had carried the naked body of a young woman across the yard and loaded it into the back of the truck. As the commandant drove out, his headlights caught sight of a long white leg sticking out from the tarpaulin. For a second it was almost theatrical: in the night-blackened auditorium, a vision of hell centre stage. The mask-like features of the militiamen were rimmed by soft smoke from the truck's exhaust. One of the men forced the leg back inside and, as the car turned it snapped the stage into darkness. The commandant drove off, glad to be away from it all.

CHAPTER 3

Six years later - 1983

Guillermo Haynes cut across the square on his way back to the office, another deal under his belt and far bigger deals awaiting him in the future if he played his cards right. It was not worth having the driver wait and then crawl round the perimeter when he could stroll back in his own time and smile at a girl or two on the way. The girls were out in force now in the January sun, sandaled, short-skirted, scoop-necked. The Malvinas War was over.

It was well after lunchtime. If this were Boston or New York, he could have picked up a sandwich at a corner store; here in Buenos Aires, he was cutting lunch altogether. Fast approaching his mid-thirties, he was too vain, though he would not admit it, to lose his lithe stride and taut frame without a fight. Besides, he had a particular new restaurant in La Recoleta in mind for a particular lady that evening. He would not deny he valued, even thrived on, the commotion he could sometimes create in certain members of the opposite sex.

He walked taller than he really was – he was, perhaps, six foot one in his socks. From the back he had the stance of a soldier. From the time he could walk it was impressed upon him by his father, and beaten into his shoulders whenever he hunched them or his neck when he hung his head, that he should be straight-backed, like a man. So now he walked tall and straight and, if his head did not move much, his eyes took in everything across a hundred and eighty degrees, particularly if what he espied was female and pretty.

Guillermo did not hurry although he never dawdled. The walk into the Plaza de Mayo and then down the Avenue Rivadavia to the office was to get some air and some exercise, to take in the sights and save time. For Guillermo very few things had a single purpose; business could always be combined with pleasure.

A clock chimed three o'clock and suddenly there was movement in the square. The Mothers of the Plaza de Mayo, a mass of mostly middle-aged women who had been standing alone or chatting in groups of twos and threes, started to process around the square. Like a choir without a conductor, it was unclear who was leading and who was following. In formation, five and six across, they paraded in a circle in front of the Pink Palace, as they had done every Thursday afternoon for the last six years. Dignified but defiant, they unfolded posters and collections of photographs, holding them high on poles. Many of the women wore white triangular headscarves.

Some passers-by stood and watched, others joined in; it was safe now, or at least safer. Last year, when the mothers were demanding information about their 'disappeared' children, they might easily have disappeared too. The verb became a noun and few had taken much notice, until now.

The war over the Malvinas Islands, what Guillermo's British friends called the Falklands, freed Argentina from the weakening grip of the military. Guillermo's grandfather was British and, as an Anglo-Argentine, he had found the war difficult at first but he stood full-square behind the military and was deeply shocked at their mauling by the British. It was an inglorious defeat for Argentina; however the military junta had fallen and the country enjoyed its first genuinely free elections for seven years. Those elections produced a government with plenty to say but little experience in turning their words into actions.

The not-very-secret police in their not-very-well-hidden Ford Falcons had not completely disappeared but there was less truck with the old order, particularly the military. There was a sense of expectancy; people still remembered the dangers of the past but increasingly railed against everything that had gone before.

Guillermo could feel all that; he sucked in the differences with every breath and he was rich enough and confident enough to eschew those bits he did not particularly like. He and others of his class were still changing their money as quickly as they could into American dollars as a hedge against the galloping inflation of the peso. At the same time, Guillermo could see how a well-placed law firm could benefit from the changing times. He was determined that *his* firm would benefit; he, Guillermo Haynes, was the man to bring that business rolling in.

A new group had emerged from among the Mothers. They styled themselves the Grandmothers of the Plaza de Mayo and were looking not just for their children, but for their children's children. They wore white scarves on their heads as a distinguishing uniform. These women were the same as the Mothers in that they had daughters or sons who had been abducted by the military – but they accepted that their offspring had been murdered. Now their task was to find their grandchildren who had been born in captivity and sentenced to a life with another family.

Guillermo was spellbound by the latent power of the procession. The unflinching mass protest, unleashed by a clock striking three, would melt away as miraculously as it had started, to be re-formed the following week. No one who witnessed it at first hand and with an open mind could doubt its force. Guillermo visualised a team of heavy horses pulling effortlessly at the plough. As a small boy, before he had mastered the art of riding horses without saddles or reins, he liked to walk alongside the ploughmen as they controlled their teams of two or four great beasts with the lightest touch on the reins. The team in the square had no reins but they pulled together in time. Their quiet power had already helped see off a dictatorship as strong as any in South America.

Guillermo moved across the square and his eye alighted on two children, one perhaps eleven and the other five at most, walking purposefully hand in hand towards the Casa Rosada, the President's Pink Palace, presumably to watch the guard change. The older child, her mind already fixed on the scarlet coats and the shiny helmets, was hurrying her small sister. They were such a pleasing picture and Guillermo was tempted to watch the guard himself but business beckoned. He bought an evening paper at the newsstand at the edge of the square.

* * *

In the square, the circle of marchers moved seamlessly. Clara Silva held her banner high and the white woollen baby bootees pinned to the bottom of it by their laces dangled in the breeze. They were the only tangible link with a grandchild she had never seen.

Although she'd been mysterious, her daughter Caridad had been so happy that day at the clinic when it was confirmed that she was pregnant. In her mind Clara was knitting before she was off the bus, and one tiny bootee was finished before supper, even if supper was a bit late. Not that Jorge minded. They sat there after the meal in their neat apartment on Quilmes Street, each sipping a small brandy and talking of their daughter and her unknown lover.

A couple of weeks later Caridad was a Disappeared and the shock of it killed the old man. Clara never lost hope, but she never took up her knitting again.

She walked now as she had then, with her belief in humanity unshaken. Small, fragile, her brow furrowed and her frame bowed, she gripped her banner and marched like a storm trooper. If Boadicea had not fallen in battle, if Cleopatra had not succumbed to a snake, they might have grown old like Clara Silva.

Certainly Clara drew the troops to her by the way that she held her head, her small nose pointed forward, her lips pursed but not set hard. Determined, rather than dictatorial, Clara would march towards victory no matter how long it took.

* * *

There was plenty to praise in Guillermo Haynes. A lesser man might have been turned into a dilettante by the advantages heaped on him but Guillermo worked hard and played hard, usually in that order.

He was entering a Baroque phase, which was reflected in his office in the grand *fin-de-siècle* mansion block which housed his law firm. A large mahogany bookcase, intricately carved and heavy with legal volumes, dominated one wall. The angular rosewood desk that he had favoured previously had recently been replaced with a huge antique, said to have belonged to the *Libatador* himself. At the office Guillermo was allowed to give free rein to his own fancies. There was no accord to be struck with his wife, Pilar, or his mother, and no discussions about price. As a newly promoted senior partner, he was spending his own money and redecorated his office every three or four years when it suited him.

Later in the afternoon he took some papers from the

desk and settled onto one of the sofas, flicking on the television as he sat down. The news was predictable. The US grain deal would push prices up, so that was good, but there was no mention of the figures which showed the economy plummeting out of control. The one thing the television broadcasts and the newspapers did not headline was inflation but Guillermo was constantly reminded of the need to change every available peso into dollars as soon as he could; tomorrow, inevitably, the peso would be worth less. The fate of the national economy mattered less than the economy in your own pocket.

The Malvinas war had changed Guillermo's mind about politics and it had opened his eyes. The Malvinas Islands were lost and the Army sent back to barracks; the treaty with Chile had been ratified; friends had changed places with enemies. The radicals were in disarray, even though their chosen president was now in office. Or perhaps it was *because* he was in office?

The television news reflected that disarray; it was not jugular-hunting journalism but at least it was more honest than the sanitised diet fed to the population under the military junta. The rest of the bulletin was just as predictable as the economic news: another delay in the trials of the junta members; another military demonstration against the trials; another parade by the Mothers and Grandmothers of the Plaza de Mayo, followed by library pictures of bodies of the Disappeared being dug up from a Buenos Aires market garden, which had apparently been shown first a couple of days before. Guillermo saw a skull unearthed from the ground and the camera zoomed into it. Guillermo saw the groups of women with their triangular headscarves. He saw the banners and the photographs held high. He saw Caridad's face and sat bolt upright, dropping the file of papers to the floor.

He knew that face; he had loved it, betrayed it, forgiven it, lost it, but he had never forgotten it.

'My daughter, Caridad,' Clara Silva was saying to the television reporter, 'had a child in prison before she was murdered. There were many like her. We cannot bring our children back to life but we can find *their* children, many of whom have been illegally adopted. We can bring them home!'

It was Caridad speaking; an older, frailer, more earnest Caridad, weighed down with the problems of the world, but the sentiment, the passion, the strength were the same. Caridad could not be anyone else's daughter. And Guillermo was beginning to understand that Caridad's child could not be anyone else's but his child too.

He had asked her, all those years ago, in the tea shop in Olivos, Caridad's hand in his, her face serene. Moments before she had rushed off to the lavatory and been sick. He had asked her if she was pregnant. Those wide, dark, innocent eyes he could never forget shone back at him; surely they could not have lied to him?

He would have whisked her away to Europe or America immediately had he known that she was carrying his child and they would still be together now. Their love was all conquering; there were no limits and no secrets. At least, there should not have been. He had never lied to her, he had been scrupulous in telling her the truth even when it hurt. But thinking about it, he knew that his whole relationship with her was founded on half-truths.

'Of course I'm not,' she had replied, perhaps too quickly. 'I would tell you.'

Guillermo had wanted to believe her; he *did* believe her. They had talked about it before. She was in the middle of her studies and too young to have a child and he was— Well, how could he? She said she understood but that was only the half of it. God, he had screwed things up.

Now Guillermo was a drowning man and he clutched for air. Somewhere, behind his eyes, he saw stark, unconnected images. The detail in the centre was brilliant and vivid but the edges were blurred. He could see Caridad's teeth and her eyes, pearlescent in the moonlit water; oiled fingertips in a circular motion against her back; the rise and fall of her breasts as she slept; her smile and her screams.

'Christina!' Guillermo shouted for his secretary. He leapt towards the desk and hit the intercom button. 'Christina!'

'I'm here, Señor.' She was already at the door.

'Get me Channel Five!' And then immediately 'No … forget it.' His mind was racing ahead. 'I'll do it myself. Sorry.'

Christina paused and he waved her away impatiently. She had been a faithful servant to her master for nearly eight years, from the day he first came to the firm. She was ready to do his bidding now or later.

The television news was still playing. Guillermo could

see a man with a spade carefully separating earth from the bones buried in a mass grave. Could those bones be Caridad's?

Guillermo picked up his private phone then put it down. He dived into a drawer for papers which were not there. He looked around the office for inspiration which was not there either. He could see that life again, or part of it, stretched before him.

If he had thought about the Dirty War then as he did now, much would have been different. Caridad always said that was his problem: he never thought about things. But he was thinking about her now; he could feel her skin, he could hear her breathing. He thought about a life that might have been.

Guillermo had the same square jaw and wide forehead as his father and dark hair, like Caridad's. His brother, Horacio, had fair hair; all were now dead. War had claimed them all and left him unscathed. Where was justice? Guillermo's eyes and his wit were inherited from his mother. He and Horacio had spent a strict but happy childhood; secure, pampered sometimes, and always loved. Until Daddy died. The blinding flash and the deadening thud, and the still, white shape.

War changed things all right, but not the things you wanted. First there was the Dirty War, the very dirty war, which took his father and then Caridad away from him. Now, after the Malvinas War, Horacio was dead too. The junta was gone, and the Malvinas still were not Argentina's. What was the point of it all? And Caridad, where was she now? Was there some corner in heaven for those who gave everything and asked for nothing?

The voice on the television said: '...*the Presidential Spokesman added that more than four thousand people had registered denunciations at the National Commission for the Disappeared since the doors opened on Monday...*'

The camera caught Clara again with the picture of her daughter held high. Guillermo saw Caridad's face and the way she carried her head, just higher than demure, just lower than haughty. He saw her at the cottage at Tigre, engrossed in a book at the library, lying in the bath, smiling, naked on his bed after they made love, just looking at him.

The tears trickled down his cheeks. What a mess he had made of things. He was in the prime of his life and he had everything he could possibly want: a beautiful wife and home, a good job, good health, horses, boats, holidays, a rich circle of friends. And yet...

If the pain of Caridad's absence had ever receded, Clara's appearance on the television brought it sharply back into focus. It was a pain as physical as any Guillermo had suffered: the double burden of betrayal and guilt.

CHAPTER 4

It had been an awful week; even Pilar had noticed. Guillermo had rung the TV station; the manager was officious and demanded to know why he wanted the information. Guillermo summoned the full authority of Berruti, Pasquale and Haynes but then backed down. He decided to go to the Plaza de Mayo the following Thursday and see if he could meet Clara.

In the intervening week, he introduced the news broadcast into conversation at various times in the office, at parties, at home. Few of the people he spoke to had registered it; fewer still were interested. The war was old news.

Guillermo talked about it one lunchtime with Mercedes during a rendezvous they had arranged. The restaurant was not that good and he seemed to have lost his lust for sweet talk and what might follow. Mercedes was pretty enough but Guillermo's mind was elsewhere. He promised to ring her but he knew he would not. He vowed he would never ring another woman again. Could Caridad still make him feel like that six years later?

That night he woke Pilar with his tossing and turning. He reached out and touched the silk of her nightgown, and beyond, and she drew him to her, but soon after he tossed and turned again and withdrew to the far side of the bed while she retreated into sleep.

He went to the central library and searched through the *La Presna* and *Nation* files. The Mothers of the Plaza de Mayo, The Grandmothers of the Plaza de Mayo, The Presidential Commission for the Disappeared, Amnesty International, The Catholic Institute for International Relations and on and on. Some of it he knew; most of it he found unbelievable. He felt now that all of it was true, just as Caridad had said.

On the Saturday, he and Pilar went to the opera. The Colon Theatre was at its most splendid, effulgent in red and gold and the myriad reflections of the nation's finest jewels: diamond tiaras, sapphire chokers, ruby bracelets and rings and studs and clasps. Silk and satin gowns billowed like sails, galleons loaded with treasure on the arms of their captains. The fading daylight outside still lit the magnificent stained-glass dome over the vast foyer which was already tightly packed with people. The sparkle of the conversation eclipsed even the jewels until everyone settled down in the red-plush auditorium and the music took over.

Guillermo always looked upward at the Soldi frescoes for that fleeting moment of silence as the lights dimmed and the glow from the central chandelier, fully thirty feet across, floated in the air before all was dark and the orchestra burst into life. But tonight the sparkles were razor cuts and the rose hues were puce coloured.

Four friends had joined them in their box for a gala performance of the new production of *Fidelio*. Beethoven might have completed it in 1805 but it was new to Guillermo and he squirmed as he read the plot before the lights went down. The secret prisoners of the State, the tyrant governor Don Pizarro gloating with a long dagger in his hand; even worse, the brave and devoted Leonora risking her life to save her husband. The irony was inescapable; the triumph of individual effort over authoritarianism, of simple love over the massed forces of evil.

Throughout the performance Guillermo saw nothing but the shocking television news pictures of skeletons being removed from the former market garden in a Buenos Aires suburb. 'One of a number of mass graves ... hundreds of "no-name" victims...' The reporter's nasal tones were replaced by the throbbing prisoners' chorus, but Guillermo could still hear the scraping of the spades in the hard earth; the sharp sound cut through all the percussion and brass of Beethoven's score. When the orchestra was quieter, with the strings leading Leonora's lament, he heard the dull crunch as steel dug into bone. Caridad's face and the crashing chords fused together. The lyrical majesty of the music, the physical power of the television pictures and the shameful memory of his own self-preservation... No!

No one else in the party seemed to be affected by

that news footage. Perhaps it had simply had passed them by, just as the original disappearances of so many of Argentina's students and trade unionists had passed them by during the Dirty War. They had enjoyed the music; such an interesting performance. And for heaven's sake, Guillermo, stop being so miserable and cheer up.

There was champagne in the Gold Room for nine hundred 'Friends of the Colon'. Guillermo looked at the gathering that stretched the hundred metres length of the room. He saw the guests and himself with mounting loathing, caricatured in the mirrored walls. The shawl-collared, anthracite-black jacket; the winged tie, blacker still. Black for death. Against it, the bright, white shirt. In the mirror he saw it stained with blood, red spreading from the centre and growing darker, until it was as black as the rest of him. He shuddered.

He was beginning to feel faint and looked sufficiently flushed for the others to be concerned when he said he had to leave. He insisted he would be all right if he had some air. If Marco would not mind running Pilar home, everything would be fine.

Guillermo did not go straight home but drove to Palermo and parked the car. For an hour he sat, watching the moon. At any other time, had he escaped from Pilar, he would have gone to Recoleta to see who was eating there; perhaps an old flame or a possible new one would have caught his eye. Now the thought filled him with revulsion. Eventually, drained, calmed but still deeply troubled, he drove home, grateful that Pilar was not already back.

Sunday was, if anything, worse. Guillermo drove out

to Tigre, to the tiny A-framed house on the banks of the river that he used as an escape from the city. On that terrible night when Caridad had nearly drowned, they had become really close; there was a spiritual meeting as well as a physical one. And after the storm, after the television news had infiltrated the calm of the evening, after the stinging, hurtful words they hurled at each other, something had happened between them. When they had sat huddled together, soaked but alive, he had resolved to leave Pilar and make his life with his lover.

Chapter 5

1976

'I took you at your word,' Caridad said. 'You said that if I ever needed a lawyer...'

Her unexpected arrival at his office caught Guillermo off guard. He had met her some days before at a restaurant, but then he had been in charge of their time together. He had approached the table where she was sitting with a group which included two people he knew, one a friend from college and the other a new business acquaintance. Ostensibly he went to see them, but it was obvious that he had eyes for her – and who would not have? She shone! Tall and conspicuous, elegant in an angular sort of way, relaxed and yet throbbing with life. It was her energy which was the source of her magnetism. And that's what it was, magnetism. She drew people towards her and Guillermo was no exception.

At the table, his friends joked that his earnings would soon outstrip even his wife's fortune; everyone in Argentina would soon need a good lawyer and he was the best there was.

'For company law, perhaps,' he interjected modestly. With an exaggerated flourish he took a slim, silver case from his jacket pocket and extracted some business cards but only gave out one, to Caridad.

'I'm sure I'm never going to need the services of an expensive corporate lawyer,' she said, looking at the card before placing it in her bag.

'Don't believe what my so-called friends tell you,' said Guillermo. 'We cater for our clients' every whim and we scarcely charge them at all!'

There was a raucous howl of protest from the table as Guillermo returned to his own group.

In the flirtatious atmosphere of the restaurant, heady with the perfume of people, cooking and cigarette smoke, the real world was easy to forget. Now, in his office, things were rather different. Caridad looked out of place in her casual clothes: a T-shirt and cotton skirt, bare brown legs and sandals. She looked as if she had dressed for the beach; it made Guillermo feel stuffy and put him on his guard, as did her demeanour.

'I know you're not a criminal lawyer,' Caridad said. 'Anyway these people haven't committed any crimes. But when you gave me your card, you...'

'I meant ... I don't know, traffic violations, smoking dope, perhaps.'

'But nothing political?'

Her long neck excited him, the way she carried her head, erect, confident. He was thinking more about what she would look like without her clothes on than what she was saying.

'There is a state of emergency. That makes some things a little difficult,' he said.

'Students are being arrested. No one will say where they are. People are disappearing!'

She was not in the least bit overawed by him; why did he feel at such a disadvantage? If he had met her in court, he could have demolished her simplistic arguments.

'I'm sure the authorities will advise the families in due course.' As he said it, Guillermo thought how pompous he sounded.

Caridad looked genuinely aghast. Her eyes burned with anger, her nostrils flared. Then she subsided. If the frontal assault was unsuccessful, a subtler move to the flank may be more appropriate. 'You must know what's going on?'

It was so obviously a question. There was the faintest contraction of her eyebrows, a hint of mocking perhaps, or was Guillermo imagining it? Whatever it was, he was uncomfortable again. 'I'm not sure what you mean. What have your friends done?'

'They haven't *done* anything. They've just *disappeared*!' She said it quietly. For her, the interview was over but for some reason she kept the door open.

Guillermo's pride was a little dented and he felt distinctly uncomfortable. He had not been able to win her over intellectually but he was desperate not to terminate their discussion. He made a final attempt to convince her that terrorists were causing chaos; that the Army needed to be tough.

'We don't arrest people for nothing. They must have done something,' he ventured.

'*We,*' she mimicked. 'Are you in league with the authorities or somehow connected to them? You should be asking yourself what you are doing as a lawyer. If my friends are terrorists, they should be tried in a court. What is the law doing?'

'If I took statements about certain offenders who might have disappeared ... if I tried for writs of *habeas corpus,* the chances are that I and half your witnesses would disappear as well.'

'So you *do* know what's going on!'

'The country is fighting a civil war!'

Politically they were Achilles and Hector but he was still drawn to her.

'So why all that guff about the "precision" of the law?' She was getting agitated. 'Why did you give me your card in the first place?'

Because you are the most exquisite creature I have ever seen and I want to make love to you. He could scarcely admit that. And all he had wanted was a harmless affair. That was true, and yet it wasn't; there was much more to this young woman than bed and goodbye. Even here in his office, she stirred emotions he had forgotten existed.

'This is very po-lit-ic-al,' he enunciated finally, 'and I don't deal with these kinds of cases.'

'In other words, you're not a real lawyer. Thanks a lot.' This time she prepared to leave, civilised, controlled but disappointed. She went before he had a chance to change her mind. All that was left was the faintest hint of a perfume and an image in his mind that he would never forget. She was gone, for good.

CHAPTER 6

'Señor Haynes, it's Caridad Silva on the telephone. She says it has nothing to do with the meeting in your office last week.'

It was almost five o'clock, almost time to go home. Guillermo was surprised; in fact, he was astounded. He thought that Caridad had flown away, never to be seen again. She reminded him of a bird, soaring effortlessly through the sky, a coscoroba swan, not normally seen this far north. When she extended her arms they looked like the wings of the swan, although instead of black wing tips she had bright red nails. In a moment, she had been up and gone; now she had flown back.

'I took a chance that you would be here,' Caridad said, when she was put through.

'What a pleasant surprise.' Guillermo could scarcely contain his emotions; this woman, this swan with red wing tips and wide eyes, had had a dramatic effect on him. 'I honestly didn't think I'd hear from you again. I'm very

… honoured.'

Guillermo knew that he was pushing his luck but he had to hang on to her this time. He could not let her escape again. So far he'd had a great day. In the morning he had completed a case very satisfactorily for his client and early in the afternoon he had gained a potentially lucrative account through someone with whom he was at Harvard. He was feeling heady, if not reckless.

'I was probably a little rude last Wednesday,' she said. 'I didn't mean to be.'

'Not at all! I rather think I was being a bit of a stick in the mud.'

'Well...'

How strange life was. Yesterday the week had seemed perfectly ordinary yet nothing had gone right. He had not lost any business or injured one of his polo ponies or rammed the car, but nothing had gelled; it had been dull. Last weekend had been no better, particularly as he had lost at polo, had a pony go lame and then lost heavily at poker.

Now things were looking up. For a start, the weather had improved; it had been unseasonably grey but now the skies were rich blue again. A chance meeting with an old friend at an otherwise tedious dinner party looked as if it would lead to some lucrative work. Then there was this morning's deal which earned him the praise of old man Berruti, the senior partner. A celebratory lunch at *Au Bec Fin* had been confirmed. Now there was another telephone call from Caridad. But how to hold on to her?

'It's certainly nothing we couldn't sort out over

lunch,' he blurted out, hoping she could not sense the desire in his voice.

She would not have lunch; she had told herself she would not do anything except apologise. She wondered why she had telephoned; this was not a relationship that was destined to go anywhere. On a personal level there was nothing in it for her, even though Guillermo was undoubtedly attractive. She remembered the quick smile and the bright, piercing eyes which took in everything.

Eventually, perhaps inevitably, she agreed that they could meet for a coffee.

'This evening,' Guillermo said quickly. 'Or have you other plans?' He immediately regretted his haste.

They met the following day. After work Caridad and Guillermo sat outside the little cafe in Florida Street that she visited sometimes with her mother. Caridad sipped coffee, Guillermo his usual iced tea.

The evening sun cast lengthening shadows across the bright shop windows. Two or three of them always had a sale running and, no matter how good or bad things were in the country, business always seemed to be brisk. Harrods even had a 'bomb damage' sale; two of their windows were still boarded up, presumably from the effects of the explosion. There was a steady parade of passers-by: shoppers, browsers, promenaders, couples arm in arm, mothers with chattering children, old men taking the evening air. Only the regular patrol of soldiers in full battle kit suggested that all was not perfect. They were always in pairs or threes, machine guns or automatic rifles pointed arrogantly at anyone who came into view.

'That doesn't seem very democratic,' Caridad said, gesturing at the soldiers.

'Oh, come on,' Guillermo laughed. 'Would you rather we had armed...' he searched for the word '... insurrectionists roaming the streets, killing and maiming anyone they chose?'

It wasn't the most effective argument against the military government that currently ruled Argentina, which everyone in the outside world and half the people inside the country called a dictatorship. Caridad did not respond but she raised her eyebrows and looked at him, quizzically.

'You're right,' Guillermo conceded. 'A military government is not the best outcome for a democracy and their methods are often a little ugly. But we are safe in our beds.'

'Provided we don't speak too loudly,' Caridad replied, as quick as lightning though without malice.

Guillermo had hoped to stay off politics and Caridad partly obliged. She told him about her parents, her university course, her ambition to travel. There was something childlike yet mature about her, which made him feel both very young and very old. She was only twenty but she had the composure of a city elder in the body of a young fawn.

Guillermo didn't mention his family, except to admit that his father had been a commodore in the Navy, seconded to the Foreign Office for five years, and had been killed by terrorists.

'Tell me what happened, if you can,' Caridad asked.

As he paled and pursed his lips, she realised how painful this would be for him. 'Not if you don't want to,' she said quickly. 'You can tell me another time... I mean—'

'It's OK,' Guillermo interrupted. 'Why shouldn't you know?' He did not speak for what seemed an eternity then he said: 'Last year, terrorists planted a bomb in his car. My dad was killed, instantly we think, but his driver was terribly injured and died in hospital two days later. He left a wife and four small children. Another woman was hurt. My father was waiting for me. I was about to get in the car. It was horrible.'

'I'm so sorry.' Caridad squeezed his hand and then drew back.

'It kind of explains what I meant just now. My father may or may not have been fighting the Montoneros but what had the driver done?' Guillermo paused for a moment. 'What made it much, much worse was that my father and I had argued the day before about the Army's tactics. I said they were acting like bully boys; he said they were trying to stop innocents being killed.'

'I'm so sorry,' Caridad said again. There wasn't much more she could say.

'My dad was a good man. He wanted me to go into the Navy. I chose the law but my younger brother went into the Navy, so the family honour is satisfied.' Guillermo laughed; the moment had passed. He told her about his polo ponies, which were his passion, and his job. He did not mention that the law practice had been set up by his wife's late father and that his wife, Pilar, sometimes reminded him of it.

'How long have you been married?'

Guillermo was surprised by her question, though he did not show it. He had avoided mentioning being married and he did not wear a wedding ring, but now he did not try to hide it. 'Nearly four years,' he answered.

'Children?'

'No children.' He hoped there wasn't an edge to his voice. 'I'm ... well, I'm not in any hurry.'

Caridad did not respond and they never mentioned children again until much, much later during that time in the tea shop in Olivos.

Caridad was quite tall, about five feet six, with long arms and legs and elegant fingers. She looked at him over the top of her cup as she took it to her lips, her dark hair swept back and her eyes alight. With a little more weight and a different mouth, she might have been a Greek goddess. She wore soft cotton slacks, sandals and a T-shirt; maybe it was standard student garb. He noticed that she had lovely feet, her toenails painted a pale, pearly pink. When she laughed, which was often, her whole face lit up.

'What about coming to Tigre on Sunday? For an *asado*? I have a cottage there…' It was suddenly an urgent appeal, like a 'man overboard' cry from a ship. Guillermo almost regretted saying it. Almost, but not quite.

She was hesitant, partly because he was married, although she had guessed that earlier, partly because of their different backgrounds and partly because a barbecue at a secluded weekend cottage with a handsome man was too exciting a prospect.

'There's a crowd of us going, we won't be alone,' he lied. 'Bring some friends.' Now he sounded calmer, more casual; the request had become more of a throwaway line than a formal invitation. That informality was all she needed.

She wondered later why she had given in so easily but Riaz had been rather tedious recently; in fact, she was often bored by the men at the university. Besides, she had never been to a private cottage at Tigre and a lunch party sounded thrilling.

'A group of us are going,' she told her mother, not sure why she was being so unspecific.

Guillermo phoned her on the Friday to ask whether she had invited anyone else. 'Not yet. I thought I might, perhaps, tonight...' She had, in fact, asked Lizabet, who could not come. Caridad did not want to be alone with Guillermo for the afternoon but somehow she did want to share him either.

It was a dilemma which Guillermo solved for her. 'Well, let's just leave it at us. A couple of my friends can't come.' He said it causally but clenched his fists and held his breath as he spoke.

'If that's all right with you?'

'Of course! It'll be fun on our own.'

Caridad spent much of that night pondering the merits of going. She knew for certain that he was married, which meant he could only be after one thing and she was not prepared to give that to him.

The next morning she wanted to phone him then realised she only had his office number. She resolved to tell him when they met but somehow she could not bring herself to do so when he picked her up to drive to the boat station. She was glad he met her at the university and not at home, where she would have had to introduce him to her parents.

It was only their fourth meeting but it felt as if they had known each other for weeks. He greeted her like an old friend with a non-committal kiss on the cheek and a gentlemanly flourish as he took her basket. He had insisted that she bring nothing.

'This is my treat and I will bring the lunch,' he had said when they last talked. 'Just bring your swimming costume.' And then added, wickedly, 'Or not!'

But she had brought her swimming things: a cerise bikini she had bought last summer and the big beach towel her mother had treated her to one day when they were shopping together before the start of the university term.

'I'm going to university, not on holiday,' she had protested at the extravagance.

'You'll be wanting to go on holiday soon enough,' her mother Clara said, adding it to the day's purchases. They had gone home, laden with bags and boxes, giggling like two schoolgirls.

Later that night, as the three of them sat having dinner, her father forecast a brilliant future for her. And here she was, three weeks into her second term, speeding along in a car driven by a married man, inhaling the rich warm smell of leather and walnut and a hint of expensive aftershave. She was pleased that their afternoon with lots of friends had, without effort, metamorphosed into a more private arrangement, although the thought made her vaguely uncomfortable too.

She imagined herself adrift on a desert island, her toes lapped by warm water, the smell of frangipani wafting through the air. It was about as far from reality as she could ever be.

Guillermo parked in a side street behind the boat station at Tigre. Because of the camber of the road, Caridad could not open her door. Guillermo bent down and pretended to lift the car level.

'What are you doing?' she asked.

'It's no good,' he said, struggling. 'I'll have to move the car!'

She giggled. 'Don't be so silly,' she said, as she slipped over the central console and allowed Guillermo to help her out of the other side. 'But it's just as well I am wearing slacks!'

It had rained heavily overnight but now the sky was set in a glorious blue for the day. They picked their way around the potholes towards the shops where Guillermo filled his basket with steak and wine, some tomatoes, fruit and a cherry cake. The river-bus station was already crowded as they clambered aboard the ferry for the twenty-minute journey up river.

The skipper exhibited the same skill as the driver of a double-decker bus with a vehicle three times as long. He took the ferry zig-zagging across the river, sweeping in towards each stop before slamming the engines into reverse at precisely the required moment to push the stern-side steps tight against the landing stage. Boat and stage merely kissed; if there were only a couple of passengers disembarking, the ferry did not actually stop. The mate helped the passengers ashore before the forward gears re-engaged and the boat drew away gracefully.

'This is ours,' Guillermo told her as the river bus rounded a long bend. On the right-hand bank, the triangular roof of a Swedish-style chalet on short stilts showed from behind the grass.

'It's beautiful,' she said as he helped her onto the landing stage and the ferry continued on its way.

They walked into the front garden, a dark green lawn of rich, close-cropped grass and neat flower beds bursting with foxgloves and irises on either side. Dark red and purple bougainvillea ran riot around the windows, over the door and one side of the roof; a fig tree threw a shadow over the other side. Underneath were two sun loungers, a couple of chairs and a table and, close to the side of the house, an *asado* and a pile of wood. Beyond the flower beds, the grass was left to grow long before the next owner a couple of hundred yards away carved his little piece of garden from the *campo*.

Guillermo left the baskets by the *asado* and took Caridad round the side of the house. He dug in his pockets for the key and opened the back door to let her into the kitchen.

'It's beautiful,' she repeated. 'It's just like a doll's house.'

'I'll show you around as soon as we've opened the windows.'

Guillermo unbolted the wooden shutters on the wide

windows at the front. Smooth Scandinavian austerity and rich Indian colours and textures combined to give the room an expensive but homely feel. All the light came in from the gable ends; between them, the steeply pitched, A-shaped roof reached almost to the ground. The effect was a paradox of space and intimacy. A large open fireplace with a long plush sofa opposite, a couple of smaller easy chairs and a low table covered with books and newspapers filled the living room.

Caridad admired it all. Guillermo came back from the fridge with two glasses of wine, handed her one and raised the other. 'Cheers, and don't you dare say it's beautiful,' he warned.

She laughed. 'But it is.'

'And so are you,' he said, intoxicated before his lips touched the glass.

'Cheers.'

There were pictures on the walls, sculptures dotted about and a large bouquet of fresh lilies and roses on the table in the middle of the room.

'How did you organise the flowers?' she asked him. 'They are beau— lovely.' They both laughed. 'I came here early this morning,' he said straight-faced, 'especially to arrange them.'

'You liar! But they are magnificent. Thank you.' She raised her glass.

'Make yourself at home. Go and sit in the sun, relax! I am going to set the fire for later.'

While he busied himself with the charcoal, she insisted on helping with the lunch and chopped up the tomatoes and doused them with dressing. Then Guillermo announced that they should go for a swim before cooking the meat.

'Sounds good to me,' she said. He pointed her up the stairs to where she might change in private. There was just one bedroom, with a double bed draped with a fine Indian tapestry, and a bathroom. Small windows in each gable cast shafts of light into the room and gave a cooling draught. On the walls were pictures of horses, a small oil painting and an old-fashioned barometer; on the bedside table was another bunch of fresh flowers, this time a mixture of marigolds and little purple flowers Caridad could not put a name to. She was enchanted.

In truth, Guillermo had tried harder for Caridad than he normally did for his trips to Tigre. Late on Friday he had telephoned Bianca, the woman who cleaned the house and watched over it for him. He begged her to find some flowers for the main room and the bedroom, and to make sure that everything was perfect. Bianca, a woman of fifty who cleaned a number of weekend retreats, had to journey miles to find the lilies but Guillermo was always kind to her and paid her handsomely. Like most of the women in Guillermo's life, she would do anything he asked.

After the rain, the river was the colour of mulligatawny, but no less inviting for that. The sun was beginning to burn and, when they splashed about, the water droplets shone like diamonds.

They swam again after they had eaten canapés and then sat together in the hammock, watching the boats go by.

'Doesn't your wife ever come here?' Caridad asked.

'She hates it. It's far too small and grubby for her. She prefers the luxury of Punta del Este and I prefer it here. And before you can say it's beautiful,' he laughed, 'I love it, and come here often.'

'With a different girl each time, no doubt?'

'Of course!'

It *was* beautiful. The lushness of the countryside after the rain; the sparkle of the trees as the wind turned their leaves; the pageantry of river life. On the opposite bank, a grey stork lifted itself into the air in slow motion and glided off downstream.

Guillermo caught her gaze. 'It's miraculous, isn't it, that a bird that size can fly?' *It's like you,* he thought, *up and away without a care in the world.*

'It's wonderful being able to watch it. It is so different here from the city. There's no sense of ... of...'

'Of what?'

'...of the torment.'

They had promised to stay away from politics, but it was never far from the surface.

'What torment?' he asked.

'We shouldn't start, otherwise I will regret coming and I don't want to do that.'

'Nor do I,' Guillermo countered. 'But I enjoy talking to you, even if you don't think so. You're so interested in everything, always asking questions. You should have been a lawyer.'

'My mother wanted me to be but I thought it would be rather dull. Besides, there is no law in this country.'

'As a lawyer, you could fight for it.'

'Then why don't you?' Caridad was as quick as a cobra; if she had bared her fangs he would have been dead. Instead, her smile and her eyes neutralised the attack.

Guillermo said quietly, 'I do my bit, you know. I try to uphold the law. Sometimes I think I should leave Argentina altogether and settle in America or Great Britain. That's where my grandfather came from. But then I think it's better to try and improve Argentina from within.'

'And how far have you got?' It was a serious question but Caridad curbed its sting by laughing.

'Time for the *asado*,' Guillermo ventured. 'As Marie-Antoinette would say.'

He made a joke of it but the political differences between them were starkly obvious. He was a child of the rich, cosseted by servants, urbane and comfortable in his own skin. Caridad was from what his mother still referred to as the 'labouring class', what the English termed the 'working class', the Soviet Union as the proletariat; life was always a struggle for them. Surely that had all changed now. Harold Wilson, the British Prime Minister, was working class. Jimmy Carter, the new American President, said he was born 'dirt poor'. But in Argentina?

Guillermo busied himself preparing the *asado*.

After they had eaten, Caridad was pleased to get out of the sun and they sat on the sofa opposite the unlit fire. She admired the Indian rug from Mendoza with its rich, angular design.

'I picked it up on a hunting trip. Hunting for wine, that is,' Guillermo told her as he rubbed cream into her reddened shoulders. 'A little too much sun, I think.'

'I'm OK, really,' Caridad said. She was hardly burnt at all but the cream was Guillermo's excuse to touch her. She knew it too, and she did not resist when he pushed the straps of her top away to apply the cream more widely. He kissed her on the nape of her neck and then, turning her, full on the lips.

She was not sure why she did not object but she did not, not then. But when he undid her strap on the back of her bikini top she clamped her elbows together and pushed him away. 'I think we've gone far enough, don't you?' she said, more sharply than she had intended.

Guillermo raised his head slightly and said, 'Whatever you say.' The moment passed.

Guillermo thought about that moment constantly over the next few days. She had sought his lips, hadn't she? It felt as though he were falling in love but this time it was different. Did she feel the same about him?

He was quiet on the way home, holding Caridad's hand on the ferry and in the car, kissing her gently when they parted. But he was slightly troubled.

CHAPTER 7

Guillermo spurred his pony up to the ball and swung his stick for a shot at the goal. The ball went wide and he cursed himself. It was the fourth or fifth he had missed that afternoon and there were still two chukkas to go. Pilar and a group of their friends were watching from the clubhouse lawn, laughing and chatting about who was sleeping with whom, who had bought what, and which plays or films they had seen. The back of the building, ivy clad from ground to gutter, was cast in shadow, but there was still a good crowd drinking champagne and cheering.

Guillermo wished they were not watching and he was not playing. For the first time that he could remember, he would have forfeited polo for an afternoon elsewhere. His mind was focused on a woman considerably less beautiful than his wife, a woman who shared none of his aspirations, who mocked his class, rejected his values, teased his macho image and only half-welcomed his touch. Expressive but malleable, responsive but also headstrong, rather like the pony he was astride. Should he have pushed her? Would she have succumbed to his overtures? Better to leave it where it was.

He tried to cast Caridad from his mind and concentrate on the game but, as he squeezed his legs and felt the mare surge forward, the analogy between the girl and the pony grew stronger. The same butter-soft mouth and steely spirit; the same suppleness and strength. He had heard of girls getting excited by their saddle horns but never men. Yet, as he galloped towards the ball, braked and turned his body for the swing, the rise and fall of Caridad's hips was uppermost in his mind and Guillermo missed another easy shot at goal.

Although he could not see her that weekend, he was desperate to hear her voice. She was out and he had to wait until Monday.

'I just wanted to speak to you,' Guillermo said, when Caridad returned his call. 'Will you have a coffee with me this evening?'

'Maybe,' she replied, mischievously though her heart was pounding. She was cross with herself for going home for the weekend and missing his call; she knew she could not call him at his house. 'Same place?'

'Same place.'

That evening they had coffee and iced tea, pretending to be casual acquaintances. Guillermo asked Caridad to go away with him for the weekend. 'I've got to go to a conference in Rio,' he said. He did not *have* to go, and if Caridad had not been there he would not have gone, but he wanted to take her. 'I'll hardly go to the conference.

We'll have two whole days together. Please come.'

Caridad thought about the proposal. 'If we can have separate rooms,' she said, determined not to be the pushover she thought every girl would be with Guillermo.

Guillermo, surprised, agreed instantly without revealing his annoyance.

* * *

Caridad had needed little persuasion to make the trip. She had planned to go home to her parents for a long weekend and only had to ask them if they minded her going away instead. Clara did not press for details when Caridad told her it was with 'someone she had known a while.' Her daughter would tell her everything in her own good time.

Caridad reasoned with herself that she had known Guillermo for a while, if she started counting from the time of their first meeting in the restaurant. But she could not explain her reluctance to share this man with her mother; normally Clara was her first *confidante*. Perhaps it was simply that he was married and she was slightly ashamed.

She already recognised that Guillermo was someone important in her life; she was drawn to him despite his arrogance. He disguised genuine compassion as if it were a weakness; his upbringing gave him a blinkered view of justice but he could – and did – argue passionately about fair play. He obviously had an eye for women but when he was with her, she commanded his absolute attention.

So she was persuaded and they spent the two-hour flight engrossed in conversation about military heroes. St Martin, Napoleon, Winston Churchill and Che Guevara were curious bedfellows but the years and the battles flashed by with the journey. Soon the plane was above the sandcastle city, almost level with the huge, floodlit statue of Christ on His mountain top. Beneath them, the most beautiful bay and the most hedonistic streets in the world lay cheek by jowl with the worst slums, sweeping down from Christ's feet across to the Sugar Loaf.

Guillermo had been uncharacteristically nervous as they checked in for the Aerolineas Argentinas flight from Buenos Aires but, once on the plane, his mood relaxed. By the time they disembarked in Rio he was laughing and teasing her.

The broad, white, colonial hotel was a refuge from the beach opposite, which was still bustling with life. At the Copacabana reception it was Caridad's turn to tease him. This was her first time in Rio; she had only got her passport the year before, when she and two friends had flown to the Iguazu Falls, and she spent a weekend spellbound by the power of the water as it plunged down the ravine on the border with Brazil. She giggled now and shamelessly examined her ringless hands as Guillermo leant over the reception desk to ask the concierge to ensure that the two rooms were adjoining.

'Aren't you afraid of being seen here?' she asked as they waited for the lift. 'You may be spotted.'

'In Punta del Este maybe, but not here.' Punta Del Este was the fashionable beach playground of the Argentine rich, just a hop across the River Plate from Buenos Aires. Guillermo and many of his friends had beach houses there.

He smiled, that warm, sly smile he seemed to keep only for her. 'Here is your key,' he said, as they walked to the lift.

'Is this why you don't have conferences in Punta del Este?' She was enjoying herself, even though she had been nervous about coming and about what she might tell her parents.

The following day, after Guillermo had made a brief appearance at the conference, they walked across the road to the beach. Near-naked women of all ages sprawled everywhere, flesh bursting out of tiny bikini tops and even smaller bottoms. Men lounged or did press-ups and pressed weights on the machines on the beach, their muscles rippling in the sunshine. Every skin colour was there, from anthracite black to the purest milk white. Vendors wandered along the sand laden with baskets of food, fake watches and trinkets. There were several beach volleyball games in progress and a stream of men and women were running in both directions on the running track between the beach and the road. Everyone was oiling themselves or admiring themselves and each other. Caridad was almost embarrassed as she laid down her towel and eased herself onto it in her bright cerise bikini.

'It's all so different here,' she said as they sipped *caiperenhas* in the shade of their beach umbrella.

'You mean it's beautiful?'

'No,' she began. 'It's beautiful of course. But I mean ... I almost feel we shouldn't be here.'

Guillermo knew she was not only talking about a possible – probable – affair between a young woman and a married man, but an affair between two people from opposite sides in a war. He refused to be drawn but in the afternoon, when they returned to their space on the beach after drenching themselves in the Atlantic rollers, she began again. 'It's wonderful here, and so ugly at home.'

'Would you prefer the politics here?' he asked. 'A country with more natural resources than the rest of South America put together that can't even feed itself. Ninety million people and ninety *billion* dollars in foreign debt.'

'All you think about is economics. What about freedom?'

Guillermo dug into the sand with his fingers. 'Freedom from what? Corruption, crime, unbelievable squalor? Step off the beach and let's go have a look! We're not safe in half of this city to go and have a look. Would you prefer that? There's a benign dictatorship here that can't even manage a racial policy that's fair to most of its citizens. There's a...'

'And what have we got?'

'Well, we haven't got the racial problems that Brazil has. It's true we have a military government but it's hardly a dictatorship.'

'Of course it's a bloody dictatorship!'

Guillermo looked around at the other couples soaking up the sun, every one of them smiling. He would have to buy her a tanga, he thought, and imagined the thin string of material resting in the crease of her beautiful backside. But Caridad was more intent on arguing with him.

'Is there nothing in between,' she asked aggressively.

'Of course there is.'

'What?'

'I know you didn't promise this time, but can we stay off politics?'

'Why? You seem quite able to discuss the internal affairs of a foreign country, and with some knowledge too.' Now there was a touch of sarcasm in her voice. 'Why can't you discuss your own country with the same degree of interest?'

Her words were earnest and, above all, truthful. He wished he didn't feel so uncomfortable disagreeing with her. 'I think things are getting better in Argentina. You must see that. Things will be back to normal soon.' It was an asinine comment.

'How can you say that?' she shot back. 'You told me how your own father was blown up in the street. How is that *getting better*?'

'These things take time.'

'You're just like *my* father.' Ernesto Silva had been tamed and smoothed by Clara's love and care. A small, wiry man from the foothills of Tucuman, he idolised his daughter and had given her the roots of her belief in natural justice, but he never had Caridad's stomach for a fight. 'He thinks I'm exaggerating when I tell him what's going on. The whole country is blind!'

Guillermo prided himself on his adversarial powers. 'Why should you have a monopoly on far-sightedness?' he asked. 'The junta is making progress now, real progress, getting a grip on things at last.'

'A *grip*! What an unfortunate choice of words with more and more people disappearing. And we're just lying here, pretending it's not happening.'

'No one is forcing you to stay.' Guillermo said it quietly; he meant it to be conciliatory but Caridad reacted angrily.

'Too right! I'm going back to the hotel.' She was up, plunging her feet into her sandals, grabbing her shirt and shorts and flicking her towel across her shoulders. Before he had brushed the sand from his eyes, she was striding across the beach.

He watched her go; calling her now would do no good. After a while, he got up and collected the rest of their things before walking down to a beachfront cafe for a cold drink. He sat in the shade of a sun-hat tree and watched the girls go by, stunning creatures poured into cut-off denims and tight cotton tops. It was difficult to separate the hookers from the holidaymakers; had he been here alone, he would have had fun passing the time of day with some of them, trying to guess before they gave the game away.

Almost unconsciously Guillermo returned the smile from one black beauty queen strolling past, arm in arm with an equally glamorous white girl. Some minutes later, on their way back up the boulevard, they joined Guillermo at his table. 'English?' the white girl asked.

'No, but I speak English.'

'This is your lucky day,' the black girl said.

'Because?' asked Guillermo, intrigued.

'Because we are going to buy you a drink.' The white

girl joined in, summoning the waiter.

'*You're* going to buy *me* a drink?' Guillermo was disbelieving. 'I thought it was usually the other way around.' His eyes moved from one to the other; black-and-white chess queens with bobbed hair, perfect features and, he noted, perfect breasts bursting out of their bikini tops.

'OK,' said the black girl, 'you win! You can buy us a drink.' She ordered them from the waiter. 'You going to have one too?' she asked sweetly.

Guillermo smiled at the well-rehearsed routine. More fun than a scam, and the dollar he would get no change from was well worth the sight of the two of them sitting close.

'You want to fuck us both?' asked the black girl.

'Together!' Her friend underlined the point, in case it was not clear.

Guillermo was not at all sure he did not want to, but he knew it was time to go. 'I'd love to,' he said with feeling, 'but I've got someone waiting for me in my hotel.'

'Have the three of us,' and they all laughed.

'No thanks,' Guillermo said, as he stood up. 'But it's been nice talking to you.'

'Another time perhaps,' the black girl said.

'Another time.'

The sun was casting long shadows down the Sugarloaf Mountain by the time Guillermo reached the hotel. He went into the lingerie shop in the hotel lobby to look for a gift for Caridad, and also bought a large bunch of flowers from the booth next door. He knocked quietly on her room door and heard her call, 'Who is it?'

'It's a very sorry and very lonely man,' said Guillermo.

A moment later, the door opened. Caridad was wearing one of the hotel's embroidered dressing gowns, without the belt, and she held her arms across the front to stop it opening. The drapes were drawn and the room was streaked with warm shadows.

Guillermo offered the flowers and the elaborately tied box. 'Peace offerings,' he said.

Inside the box was the tanga he had bought her, a sliver of material smaller than her folded handkerchief, joined by strips of string covered in silk. He wondered whether she'd be brazen enough to wear it on a deserted beach somewhere. He hoped the gift-wrapped box might break the ice; perhaps he could look forward to a private showing.

'I don't need peace offerings,' she said, as she walked back to the bed. 'But these are lovely.' She inhaled the scented bouquet, then peered into the box and laughed.

'I'm really sorry,' he said.

'I'm the one who should be sorry. I've been abusing your hospitality and been a bore into the bargain.'

'You haven't and that's not possible.'

Then they were kissing. The gown slipped off her shoulders as she lay down on the bed, and then she was naked. Her breasts shone white against the rest of her body. Their bodies were lunging and plunging, probing with fingers and tongues, holding and caring and sweating and coming.

He had never been so sexually satisfied before; with

Caridad there was an excitement and a tenderness he had not ever experienced with a casual lover or a constant one. For days afterwards, for weeks, months, even for years, Guillermo thought about that time when his relationship with Caridad changed. It was not like a normal 'conquest', the scalp on his belt. It was not a conquest because she had not given in to some wild impulse or to his pressure. Surely she had wanted him as much as he wanted her?

He felt differently about Caridad than he had about any other person he had ever known. He had been attracted to her immediately in the restaurant that very first evening. When their lips touched a flood had swept across his brain, cleansing it of every thought – his marriage, his career, his very soul. The space that was left was filled with one thing only: Caridad Silva.

All too soon the holiday was over, and the hedonism of Rio was exchanged for the sombre reality of Buenos Aires. In Rio there were no clocks to watch, no shadows to creep into and no excuses to be made. Guillermo remembered with tenderness the thrill of having Caridad to himself for the night and the morning, free of the fear of discovery and full of the joy of a normal relationship.

Guillermo was in love. Normally he could allow these flights of fancy, imagining himself in another relationship and yet knowing that he would always return to his wife. But this time it was different. Caridad had unlocked something in him.

CHAPTER 8

After polo on Saturday evening, Pilar invited a group of friends to the house for an *asado*. It was a couple of weeks after Guillermo had returned from Rio; before he met Caridad he would have been thrilled at the prospect of an *asado* at home, with good friends and convivial conversation about the polo, or soccer, or the latest art exhibition or opera. In the past he had always found parties at home quite convivial. He could focus his attention on one or two women and enjoy an evening of harmless flirting. Now it was a party to endure, a duty to be borne. It could not compare to Rio, nor with the *asado* that he and Caridad had shared in Tigre.

Pilar looked as beautiful as she always did but more and more she resembled an ice queen. She had none of Caridad's warmth and spontaneity. Guillermo realised he was no longer in love with his wife, if he ever had been.

'You look as though you spent most of your time on the beach!' Felix said, clapping Guillermo on the shoulder.

'You're still sporting a tan!'

Guillermo had never really liked Pilar's elder brother, Felix, and his attempt to be amusing now was particularly unwelcome. It was not just Felix: his old friends bored him. The usual entertainment, the routine of drinks and dinners, theatre, polo, tennis, swimming, always with the same acquaintances, was a merry go round which was no longer so merry.

He had never been one to discuss his affairs, even with his closest friends. Sometimes, of course, he could not keep them a secret and occasionally he needed help to prevent Pilar from finding out about them. But, unlike many of the people he knew, he did not need to broadcast his conquests to confirm his masculinity, and he kept his affair with Caridad very close to his heart.

Tonight was particularly trying. The guests included Felix, his wife and two of his Army officer friends, as well as a dozen other people. In the small garden where everyone was jammed together, it was impossible to avoid close-quarter fighting with guests whose political opinions he had once thought he shared. And it was not just politics.

'Well, come clean, Guillermo. How much time did you actually spend at the conference?' It was Felix again, trying to unnerve him. Coming from one of the most boastful philanderers in the country, Guillermo found the constant innuendo irritating.

'I spent Friday and Saturday morning at the conference, Saturday afternoon on the beach and came back on Sunday night.'

'And you missed polo for a day on the beach? You sure there wasn't something else there?' Felix and the others roared with laughter.

'If I thought for a moment there was,' Pilar began with mock severity, 'I'd cut his balls off.'

They all laughed again, Guillermo the loudest. He had been tempted, upon his return, to own up to Pilar. Their marriage had been moribund for months. He suspected that she might be having an affair with Marcus. Marcus was here tonight; there always seemed to be a reason for him coming. The dreadful thing was that Guillermo did not know if he cared. Once he had believed he was in love with Pilar, and he had been the envy of all his friends when they married. The most beautiful girl of her generation was how someone had described her.

Pilar certainly turned heads and she knew it. Tall, slender, proud, every inch the Spanish queen she claimed she was descended from. When she was not playing the queen she played the gypsy, with heavy colour on her eyes and lips and blood-red flashes on her nails. Pilar glided rather than walked, her long, black hair billowing like a sail. Sylphlike, she would stand naked in front of the mirror, caressing herself. She was adamant about not having a child too soon for fear of ruining her figure. Her breasts were erect without the help of corsetry or surgery. She ate frugally and exercised regularly. She was an accomplished tennis player, a strong swimmer and rode at least as well as Guillermo. In bed she was as athletic as she was on the tennis court.

She had adored her father and now adored her brother

and her uncle. At one time she had adored Guillermo but he was more difficult to control. The very unpredictability which Caridad found so engaging, Pilar found infuriating.

The rattle of machine-gun fire, not very far away, brought the conversation to a stop. The three soldiers strained their ears and affected knowing glances.

'You'd better go and check the radio,' Felix told one of his comrades, showing off his authority. Distant gunfire was all too familiar these days, even in the smarter areas of Buenos Aires. The Dirty War had no boundaries; it seeped into everyone's lives at some level however much you chose to ignore it. The sound of gunfire was usually the military shooting at unarmed civilians.

'How can anyone justify a campaign that will kill and maim innocent people?' said Felix. 'Women and children, for God's sake. It's obscene.'

He looked straight at Guillermo; it was an unspoken challenge for Guillermo to answer. Felix and others were concerned that during the last few weeks Guillermo had suddenly started questioning, challenging and even contradicting views that were obviously true. In the ensuing arguments Guillermo was usually trapped in a corner and Felix enjoyed scoring the points. Not that he did not like Guillermo; his only sister's husband played a cracking game of polo, so he could not be all bad.

'No one can defend it,' Guillermo countered. 'But innocent people are killed on both sides.'

'It's a war we're fighting and war is not for the squeamish. And the Americans can sound off all they like.'

Pilar added her voice. 'President Carter should put his

own house in order before interfering with ours.'

'Human rights has become a catchphrase for the left; it means nothing.' A young major, not very bright but well connected, reflected the mood of the majority of middle-class Argentines, living daily with danger and feeling bitterly hurt that their old ally, the United States, had pilloried them on the world stage.

Felix gave his brother officer a warm smile. 'When we have peace we can have human rights.'

'When will we have peace?' Guillermo asked, returning to the fire with more meat. 'When we've all disappeared?'

The Disappeared had become an issue for Guillermo since Caridad had come to his office complaining that two of her fellow students had gone missing and he had failed her so lamentably. He had read a lot and made discreet enquiries, very discreet, about students disappearing without trace.

'Not until we've got rid of every communist in the country.'

'And their sympathisers!' Pilar's *sotto voce* produced an immediate change of mood: more intimate, more conspiratorial, more menacing.

'I'll tell you what my boss said yesterday,' Felix began, drawing his audience towards the innermost secrets of the Army High Command. Felix's boss was the governor of Buenos Aires, a fact which always gained Felix special respect at parties. 'This is a *policy* declaration, confidential by the way, for the time being.' He underlined its importance with his hands, holding them like a preacher. 'In fact, I helped St Jean write it.' That was not true but it did not matter; the audience was spellbound. Felix stood up, both arms holding an imaginary podium as though he were delivering the very speech General St Jean would shortly give.

'First we will kill all the subversives, then we will kill all their collaborators, then all their sympathisers.' He was getting louder. 'Then all those who remain indifferent, and finally,' his voice dropped so everyone craned forward, 'we will kill the timid!'

He looked straight at Guillermo. Years later Guillermo read that speech, credited to General Iberico St Jean and infamous across the world as the despotic scream of an unimaginably cruel regime. It horrified him to reflect that he had first heard it around the *asado* in his own garden. It horrified him even more that he did not, at that moment, stand up and strangle it at birth.

'That's the most disgusting thing I've ever heard,' he managed, and went back into the house.

A few minutes later he was back with the party, having been dragged from his study by Pilar's old school chum, Marie, who accused him of sulking. She pressed herself against him and gave him a kiss to tempt him outside. He rubbed her backside and reluctantly agreed. His return coincided with that of the captain who had gone to find out what was happening. The coincidence served only to re-open an old argument.

'It's a house raid,' the major told them, scarcely hiding his excitement. 'Everything's under control. Nothing for us to do.'

They seemed almost disappointed. Felix looked at

Guillermo. 'I suppose, Guillermo,' he asked, 'you'd prefer us to go in unarmed so we don't wake up the neighbours.'

There was a ripple of laughter. Guillermo knew he should let it pass but he could not. 'Why doesn't the Army just round them all up and shoot them?'

'Well, why not?' asked someone, not seeing the irony.

'We're picking them up as fast as we can,' said Felix. 'But I'm afraid things will get worse before they get better.'

'I really don't see why you should object to that, Guillermo.' It was Marie, still clinging coquettishly to his side.

'General Videla himself said when he was appointed, "As many people as necessary must die in Argentina so that the country will again be secure." That is absolutely true.' Felix stared hard at Guillermo, daring him to contradict what the commander-in-chief had said.

'Guillermo feels the Army is being too hard on the communists,' Pilar answered, smoothing her skirt across her knees and smiling at Marcus.

'I did not say that. But—'

Felix cut him off. 'If we don't kill them, they'll kill us. Jesus, you should know that!'

'No one's objecting to you killing terrorists,' Guillermo countered. 'But why should people just disappear? We have due process and we should use it.'

'We are fighting a war! We haven't always got time for "due process".'

'Every civilised country should have time for due process.' The lawyer in him was angry now and he snapped back at his brother-in-law. 'If we don't maintain the law, if we don't operate within civilised constraints even in wartime, we're no better than terrorists!'

'Jesus, Guillermo! You are amazing. Your own father was killed by terrorists. There was nothing civilised about that!'

'I haven't forgotten.'

The reminder brought an uneasy pause. Marcus suggested they change the subject but, having been brought back into the fray, Guillermo was spoiling for a fight.

'Sometimes, Felix, I think you and most of the rest of the Army are bloody fools. If we resort to the same tactics as terrorists, how are we different? No one's saying you shouldn't kill armed terrorists but you shouldn't be picking up unarmed civilians, who may be innocent, and making them disappear. What's wrong with admitting they've been arrested? Bringing them to court? What's wrong with evidence, for Christ's sake?'

Caridad could not have put it better except that when she presented such a view Guillermo had always become an apologist for the junta. Now here he was, making an impassioned speech against everything he had stood for in the past.

There was an embarrassed silence around the *asado*, before Felix asked sarcastically, 'And how many innocent people do you know who have disappeared, Guillermo?'

Guillermo did know one: a lawyer who had applied for a writ of habeas corpus on behalf of a client. The lawyer was an idealist, not overtly political but certain of the sanctity of the law. The day after he delivered the writ, quietly and without publicity, he disappeared. *Pour encourager les autres?*

'Felix told me to advise you to be careful,' Pilar told him later that night when they were getting ready for bed.

'About what?'

'About voicing some of your opinions in public. He said it could be dangerous.'

'It could be dangerous because I disagree with your brother?'

'It's got nothing to do with my brother! I don't know what's got into you. This liberal view is a big act, and a dangerous one. Be careful!'

Guillermo tried to reason with his wife, to make her recognise what was happening to them, their lives, their country. It was a speech he had learnt from his mistress but he thought it might save them. 'Look, Pilar, today the communists are arrested. Tomorrow people we *think* are communists are arrested; the day after that people who other people *say* are communists are arrested! That's what Felix was talking about. Don't you see where it could lead?'

Guillermo was looking at Pilar but he saw Caridad's face. It was Caridad's argument, her view rejected by him and now regurgitated word for word. He believed them wholeheartedly. *Why didn't he believe them before?*

'I don't see any alternative,' Pilar said. 'I want to sleep safely in my bed at night. I don't want to be blown up by a bomb!'

CHAPTER 9

General-of-the-Army Hector Fernandez Felix Horloz watched his favourite niece. She looked even more radiant than the bride, but then she always did. None of the two hundred women present could match her.

Pilar Pasquale-Haynes could have married any man in Argentina but she had chosen Guillermo Haynes, an up-and-coming lawyer who worked in her father's legal firm, now one of the largest and best in the country.

'When are you going to give me a grandchild to rock on my knee?' Horloz made it sound like an order but he was smiling warmly.

'We shall see.' Pilar's eyes shimmered as she passed him.

Horloz had been fond of the girl since he first saw her after a tour of duty in the United States. Three years later, when his wife had died in childbirth and the baby had not lived more than a few hours, he looked to his younger sister and her daughter for solace. Pilar had grown up with an adoring uncle who showered her with gifts. When Pilar's father died, the adoring uncle helped fill the void in the young girl's life.

When the band started to play a tango, the bride and groom led the guests to the floor. It was time for Horloz to go and leave the evening for the young people. He nodded a greeting to a couple here, smiled at someone there, and watched Pilar glide in Guillermo's arms. A fine boy, Guillermo, Horloz decided. He had missed his vocation, perhaps, but he was a fine boy nevertheless.

By the time he got to their table the dance was over and Pilar and Guillermo were arguing. Pilar's mood changed the instant Horloz came into view; she kept her warmest smiles for him. 'Uncle Hector, you're not going? It's so early, and you haven't danced with me yet.'

'Dance with her, General. She's cross because a waiter spilled some champagne on her dress.'

Horloz took a step back to look at the dress. 'I'll have him shot!' he said with all the authority of his rank, and then smiled. 'One dance with the belle of the ball, but I can't say it too loudly in case we upset the bride.'

Uncle and niece made a handsome couple and Guillermo marvelled at the way Pilar's mood changed. The Latin in her made her hot-tempered but the fire was extinguished in the arms of her uncle.

Except for the champagne spillage, it had been a good afternoon. Pilar was the centre of attention so she was happy. Some of Guillermo's oldest friends were there and Horacio, his younger brother, was on leave from his training.

'You don't know what you're missing, Guillermo,' Horacio had told him after they stopped hugging. Eight years his junior, Horacio was half an inch taller and beaming in his new cadet's uniform. 'Lots of people knew Daddy, and everyone has been marvellously kind.'

'I'm glad you're enjoying it,' Guillermo said. 'I knew you would. Mama is missing you. Daddy would have been so proud.'

'I have at least six months in Bahia Blanca but then I might be posted to the capital for a spell. That's the fast route to the top, of course.'

'You'll be a captain before you're thirty, I'll put money on it.'

'A full lieutenant before I'm twenty-five anyway.'

Horacio had the same idealistic zeal in his eyes as Caridad and Guillermo worried suddenly that his brother was closer to her age than he was. He had to ring Caridad, just to hear her voice and confirm that she had not slipped away with a more suitable suitor. Pilar and her uncle were still on the dance floor so Guillermo felt safe to slip away and find a phone booth.

He heard the phone ringing in the corridor outside Caridad's room. Someone must be there. If not, he would leave a message to say he had telephoned, to show her that he cared. 'Just say a man phoned to say he was thinking of her. She'll know who it is.' He thought it would be more romantic like that and, anyway, he never liked leaving his name.

He felt the same unease when he went into the

university. Partly it was the sneaking about; he felt old and out of place among the posters of Che and the Peronist slogans on the walls. And partly it was because he knew, deep down, that the authorities kept watch on the university.

His unease spoiled their lovemaking. He had never been able to come properly in her room. He started off all right, but...

The music stopped and Horloz led Pilar back to her husband. 'Look after her, my boy.'

'I will, sir. We're seeing you next week, aren't we?'

'Yes, Uncle. Don't you dare not come.'

Before the general could answer there was a crash of broken glass and the start of a commotion. People stiffened and some moved to see what was going on. Then someone shouted, 'It's a bomb! Get away, it's a bomb!' and they started screaming.

There was a small wooden box the size of a couple of bricks on the floor just inside the broken window. The people nearest made a run for it and suddenly there was nothing between Pilar and her uncle and the box.

It was Guillermo who saved them; perhaps he was moved to inhuman effort by memories of his father and another bomb. He threw his wife and the general to the floor, sliding them towards the wall and shielding them with his body. There was a hiss and then an explosion which ripped across the room, breaking the windows and throwing the furniture around like toys.

'Let's get out of here,' Guillermo yelled, his voice barely audible above the pandemonium. He dragged his

Pilar and his uncle by marriage towards the door, looking around and calling for Horacio.

'Keep away from it,' someone shouted. 'It's still live.' There were more screams and a police siren shrieked outside. Sweat was pouring from the general's head and he was holding his arm which was either badly bruised or broken in the fall.

'Your arm!' Guillermo cried. 'Are you all right? I'm so sorry...'

'Don't say that, my boy. You saved both our lives.'

Just then, Horacio and a couple of other soldiers staggered out of the door, followed by two women, dazed but apparently uninjured. Horacio shouted to Guillermo, 'You get out. I'll see to these people.'

A truck load of soldiers drew up as Guillermo helped the general, his arm held gently across his chest by Pilar, into his car. The driver had already pulled over towards the exit and in moments they were away from the mêlée and into the calm of a normal city. The spectre of death was as far from them now as it would have been in Los Angeles or London. But a bomb at a society wedding in the middle of the capital was a reminder of how close the war was to them all.

'Do you think we should go abroad for a couple of years?' Guillermo asked Pilar later when they were driving home. The general's arm had indeed been broken and they had waited at the hospital until it was X-rayed and plastered. They drove with the general back to his house and then had the driver take them back to collect their own car. 'We could go to New York if you like, or to Europe.'

'Do you want to go? What about your work?' Pilar was not being selfish when she replied; she seemed genuinely to be thinking about Guillermo's future.'

'I don't know what I want any more. To get away from all this for a while. I keep hearing that things are going to get worse before they get better. You remember what your brother said?'

'Isn't that running away?'

'Is it?' If it was, Guillermo wondered what he was running away from. He had not felt fear when he saw the bomb, and he did not normally feel fear in his day-to-day life, at least not the dry-throat, knot-in-the-gut fear he had felt when soldiers asked him for an ID last week outside the university. Was he trying to run away from Caridad, recognising her as a genie who would eventually entrap him in a devil world where everything was dark?

'Look, we were all bloody lucky tonight...'

'I know you must be thinking of your father,' Pilar said. She was as tender as he could ever remember, even holding his hand on top of the gear lever.

'Are you afraid?' he asked. Pilar had been badly shocked by the bomb and, unusually, she was happy to follow rather than lead. 'We've been talking of setting up a New York office. It fits quite well into the company's business plans.'

'I am afraid, sometimes. I was tonight.' They drove on in silence for a while before she added, 'It's not much fun having armed guards everywhere. It's hardly the atmosphere in which to bring up children.'

'We haven't got any children yet.'

'No, not yet.'

It was the first time since their honeymoon that they had talked of children, of raising a family and planning a future. The golden couple would have glittering children, of course, but until now they had not been spoken of. Pilar had certainly not felt motherhood gnawing at her as she clutched her uncle in the hospital, but she remembered his plea to her about children.

Guillermo had often thought about children, more than Pilar he suspected, but he had been content to wait and see what transpired, to get his job established, his wild oats sown. Now he felt a nagging doubt; it was creeping up on the outside, like a racehorse waiting for a gap before an extended gallop to the finishing line. Guillermo was not sure which horse he was riding but he was thinking of Caridad, wishing she was sitting with him in the car, that she had been next to him at the wedding breakfast, that she had been the woman he had thrown himself over when the bomb fizzed. Maybe then she would understand.

The gateman was dozing when they arrived their house on Marcello T. Alvear Street. The conversation had run out and both Pilar and Guillermo were lost in their own thoughts.

'Thank God you're all right, sir. And you, madam,' said the gateman. 'I heard about the explosion.'

'Not much of an explosion, as it turned out.'

'Just imagine what could have happened.'

'I think Señor Haynes would have saved our lives and been blown to pieces.' Pilar was already leaving the car for their door but there was no denying the pride she took in her husband's action.

Guillermo was almost embarrassed by the praise. 'Thank you,' he muttered, and then, 'I shall want the car at a quarter to eight tomorrow, Alphonse.'

'Very good, sir. Good night, good night, madam.'

Pilar's heel tips clipped across the marble tiles. She dropped her gloves on a heavily inlaid hall table and studied herself in the mirror above it. Later she looked at herself, almost naked, in the long mirror upstairs in her bedroom. She ran her hands past her waist to make sure it had not changed.

As Guillermo came in, she stepped out of her knickers and walked to the bathroom. By the time Guillermo got into bed she was ready to make love. Perhaps the shock had quickened her blood. Perhaps the bomb had added a new dimension.

Guillermo wondered if there would be a spate of pregnancies among the wedding guests. Drunk with danger, had they returned to their beds all over the city for nights of unaccustomed passion? He wondered what sort of world the post-wedding generation of Argentina's finest would grow up in. Would the freedoms he had enjoyed as a child be denied them as they marched towards the citadel in battledress?

He realised he was desperate for a child, but not with Pilar. Guillermo spent the moments before he fell asleep wondering how he could tell his wife. And then he dreamt of Caridad.

* * *

It was a week before Guillermo could see Caridad, a terrible week in which wanted only to be with her. He fantasised and he schemed and he dreamed. He and Pilar would move to the United States and have children; he would come back to Buenos Aires every fortnight or so, because he had to keep in touch with the office and there were things to do, and he and Caridad could be together. He would ensconce Caridad in an apartment on the Avenida Sante Fe, they would live there in some splendour and she would have children there. Then, in another scenario he and Pilar moved down to the farm, he continued to work in the capital during the week and lived with Caridad in her Sante Fe apartment. In one dream the women would never meet, never know of each other's existence; in another they would become the best of friends. They would all live in a mansion in Palermo and share their lives, with Guillermo moving from bed to bed and sometimes sharing the bed with both of them.

He would live in a world without politics and there would be no arguments about anything. He would ski with Caridad and go to the beach in Punte del Este with Pilar. He would dive in Cancun or Brazil with Caridad. All of the children would accompany them on holiday and Guillermo would teach them to ride and play polo and cycle and swim. He would teach them about art and music, listen to them at their school concerts. The family would have a bigger box at the Colon and go regularly to the opera. They would all go to Europe together, to Paris to the Tuilleries Gardens and to Florence to marvel at the statue of David and dozens of newly restored Raphael paintings in one room, to the Taj Mahal, where Shah Jahan's love for his wife was manifest in sculptural magnificence forever. They would go to Africa, on a game safari, mountain trekking in the Himalayas, to the outback of Australia to hunt crocodiles and onto to New Zealand to swim with dolphins; it would be paradise. Sometimes he would rush home from work for a quiet dinner with Caridad; sometimes he would enjoy a riotous party with Pilar. But he would always have quiet days with Caridad at Tigre, where he would make an *asado* for them on a Sunday, alone or with a small group of real friends, who would whisper to themselves that Guillermo Haynes had really worked out his life.

If he left Pilar could he remain at Berruti and Pasquale? He could get another job as a lawyer in Buenos Aires. What would his friends think when he pitched up at the polo club with Caridad, a girl from the wrong side of the tracks? To hell with them!

More importantly, how could he and Caridad resolve their political differences? They could go abroad, to the United States or Great Britain, but he would have to study again if he wanted to practise as a lawyer, and Caridad was in the middle of her university course. Or they could go to Chile but the situation there was surely as bad. Or Brazil; he thought longingly about Brazil, about Rio de Janeiro and that long weekend at the Copacabana. But then he would have to learn Portuguese properly and anyway, Brazil on holiday could not be the same as Brazil in real life.

Guillermo and Caridad met in the tea shop in Olivos. Guillermo arrived hot and sweating but carrying, as usual, a bunch of flowers. This time the roses were dark red. He had been playing polo and been thrown in the third chukka, which gave him a good excuse to leave after the game finished and not spend an hour or two drinking and talking.

Six months ago, when he was having an affair with Luciana Perez, he was much less coy unless Pilar was actually at the club. Señora Perez was a wealthy widow in her early thirties who had helped a number of Guillermo's polo team – and others besides – through 'problems' with their wives. Not that she was a loose woman; far from it. She just loved life and lived it to the full.

'You don't flirt with me any more,' she had told Guillermo that morning before lunch.

He laughed and whacked her on the bum. 'You've no time for me.'

Luciana was one of his crowd so during their affair Guillermo had felt he could be more indiscreet. Now things were different; he was moving in uncharted waters.

'It was as close as that.' He stretched his hands apart, as they swallowed a lightning-fast dinner.

Caridad was listening breathlessly to the story of the bomb. She was worried enough about his fall at polo; the news about the bomb made her feel quite ill. 'You could have been killed. Why do you have to be a hero?'

'Some women like heroes.'

'Not dead ones!' She tightened her grip on his hands. 'I'm proud of you though.'

Guillermo was not proud of himself. Since the bomb he had become morose, and it was not because he was afraid of dying. That, he thought, might be the best way out. 'I wish you could come with me on Saturdays,' he said. 'I'd like you to watch me play polo.'

'It's only you that says I can't.'

'You know what I mean.'

Caridad said nothing but she squeezed his hand and smiled. There were worlds she could not share. More important to her was Guillermo's wish to inhabit her world, if not in person then by proxy. He was jealous, suspicious, of her time away from him.

Guillermo found his own possessiveness hard to deal with but he could not deny the feeling. If this was what real love felt like, he was certain he had never been in love with Pilar.

'I wish I could share everything with you,' he said. 'I want to, but … it's difficult.' He had been looking at her slim, delicate hands; now he took in her bright, strong eyes. 'I've always tried to be honest with you about that.'

'Don't worry. I'm not a little girl.'

'You are a little girl. And I suppose you should be looking for a little boy, instead of spending your time with me.'

'Would you like that?'

'You know I wouldn't; that's the trouble.' Then more softly, so softly it was as if he did not want her to hear, 'Just don't get too fond of me.'

He wished he had not said that. He wanted her to fall completely in love with him. Why he could not simply leave Pilar? But he did not have the courage to cut the cord.

They checked into a telo, a pay-by-the-hour hotel, and scrambled out of their clothes and into each other. Afterwards Caridad felt cheap and Guillermo felt dissatisfied, though neither said a word.

Caridad paused momentarily as she got out of the car, kissed her finger and planted it on Guillermo's cheek. Guillermo held her hand briefly before releasing it. She deserves better than this, he thought.

CHAPTER 10

Sundays had become their day. They spent it at a museum in the morning and then Tigre in the afternoon, or sometimes lunched at a small restaurant out of town and out of sight. But mostly they went to Tigre, where they could spend the day together, swimming, eating and making love. Sometimes they met after work in the week for a drink or dinner.

As the weeks went by, their meetings became less furtive. One Sunday morning they went to the Museum of Modern Art in San Martin. Guillermo spent most of the time looking at Caridad rather than the paintings. She stood, her long hands clasped behind her back, her long neck arched slightly forward, and peered at the pictures by Antonio Berni and Walter Kandinsky and exclaimed, 'Brilliant.' A half smile on her lips, she turned to him. He watched her breasts rise and fall with her breathing and wanted to make love to her there and then.

He knew deep down that this dual existence could not

last. One life had to go, and soon. He knew which one. When they reached the cottage that afternoon, Guillermo told Caridad how much he loved her. He wanted to ask her to marry him but wondered whether he should meet her parents first and speak to her father. Would that not be more traditional? And he was already married so he would have to free himself of Pilar.

Guillermo was a cautious man. He needed to be certain that Caridad would accept him before he committed himself. He was certain that he wanted Caridad but, until he asked her, he could not be sure of the future.

He decided that he would buy a ring, not with diamonds like the British and Americans favoured, but a simple gold band that Caridad could wear on her right hand before the ceremony and then transfer to her left. He would ask her to marry him and hopefully she would say yes. He would visit her father for his permission. He would tell Pilar and leave the house; then he would get a divorce.

Life was simple when you sorted it out. He imagined living with Caridad, having lots of children and never wanting for love again. He could see the rest of his life mapped out, and it was wonderful.

He was especially attentive to Caridad that evening before they left the cottage and made their way back to the capital. She lay, snug in his arms after they made love, and talked of holidays and heroes and movies and magic.

'It would be magic if we could go to California,' she said. 'Or London.'

'Maybe I can be a fairy godmother and take you.'

'And what would your wife say?'

Maybe she won't be around to say anything, he thought. 'Maybe she won't say anything,' he said.

Caridad let his reply pass without comment. Was he making jokes or plans? She felt a warm glow; maybe he was being serious.

'Before that, though, I think we could manage a holiday in Rio,' Guillermo said as he stroked her hair. 'I'm sure I can get away for a long weekend.'

'That would be wonderful but it will have to wait until the end of term. I have important lectures to attend on Fridays.'

'I think a lot about Rio,' Guillermo said. 'I think I nearly lost you and that would have been a tragedy.'

'It would have been a tragedy for me,' Caridad said, and then a little later she asked, 'What would you do if I was arrested, if I disappeared?'

Guillermo thought for a while. 'That's not very likely, is it?'

'No,' Caridad replied. 'But hypothetically, what if I did disappear. What would you do?'

Guillermo was silent then he replied, 'I would go immediately to the police, to the head of the police, to the head of the Army. If necessary I would bang on the president's door until they let you go.' He meant it.

CHAPTER 11

On the following Saturday it was dark by the time Guillermo reached the landing stage at Tigre. As the river taxi reversed its engines and slowed to a crawl, he jumped off. He had had a busy week during which he had not seen Caridad at all.

From the front, the A-frame cottage looked deserted but at the side there was a light and the shape of a hunched figure sitting at the table. The table was laid for two but had not been touched and the barbecue had gone cold. There was a bottle of champagne in an ice bucket but the ice had long since melted away.

Caridad, her legs pulled up underneath her, sat slumped in the chair. She had been upset, then angry, then livid; now she was resigned. It was to have been a special day for them, a Saturday at Tigre.

'I'm really sorry I'm late,' he said, as jovially as he could. 'I really am sorry. I got delayed...'

'Delayed? You said you were not going to play.' Caridad

had clearly been crying but now she was calm. Her voice was soft but she could feel the anger welling up again.

'I know, I know, but I had to go.'

'I'm always the last in line, aren't I?'

'You know how difficult it is for me to get away sometimes. I can't just lie. I don't like lying.'

'You lie to me.'

'You know that's not true. I've never lied to you. I may have done every other awful thing, and maybe lied to everyone else, but I have never lied to you.'

Guillermo pulled up the other chair as close as he could to Caridad then he got up and fetched a blanket from the cottage and slipped it around her shoulders. She pulled the blanket towards her but did not look at him. Instead, she hung her head and looked away when he touched her cheek.

'I did tell you it would be like this,' Guillermo said softly.

'I can't manage on once a week,' she almost shouted. 'You promised we would have dinner this week. You said we would meet for a coffee – and then you have to play polo. What about *me*?' She could not bring herself to demand that he leave his wife; he was not yet ready to commit.

'I know, I know, I know,' was all that he could say.

'After last week...' She could imagine the fear Guillermo must have felt when the bomb exploded. 'I just wanted...' She couldn't finish and the tears she had thought were spent trickled down her cheek.

Caridad was finding their relationship increasingly

difficult. Perhaps she had misplayed the moment. Perhaps she should have been angrier with him, forcing him to consider her as a person, to put her at the front of his life as she did with him. Perhaps she should have demanded that he decide.

Guillermo took a handkerchief from his pocket and dabbed her eyes. 'Can I shush you now?' he asked her.

'Why?'

'Because I'm in love with you.'

'Now you *are* lying to me.'

'I am certainly not lying to you.'

The anger passed. Guillermo scooped her up in his arms, carried her inside and laid her down on the sofa. 'Let me get you a large whisky,' he said.

'No,' she said. 'Just come here.' They had shed most of their clothes by the time they got upstairs to the bed. Their lovemaking was furious and fast.

The clock in the sitting room chimed nine o'clock. Outside the rain had started and a clap of thunder shook the A-frame; moments later a bolt of lightning flashed across the sky. The wind rattled the windows.

'I want to watch the news,' Caridad said suddenly.

'There's nothing but doom and gloom, best to ignore it. Besides, I'm not sure we'll have a signal with this lightning.'

Caridad was determined. Naked, she leapt from the bed and strode downstairs to switch on the television. 'Bring the blanket, please,' she called. 'I'm cold.'

Guillermo came downstairs as the newsreader gave details of another murderous incident at another wedding party.

'Christ,' said Guillermo. 'Another...'

'...among the dead was the bride, Miss Maria-Eleanor Nicholson...' the newsreader said.

'Jesus Christ,' Guillermo mouthed. 'I know her. I knew her.'

Caridad shuddered but was silent as they watched the screen.

'...at least four Montenero terrorists burst into the reception this afternoon and sprayed guests with machine-gun fire...'

'Jesus Christ,' Guillermo muttered again.

'...Maria-Eleanor Nicholson was twenty-one. She had just married Captain Jorge Videro, who was seriously injured. The other dead...'

Guillermo swore, more loudly. 'I knew them both.'

'...and the bride's father. Four serving Army officers were also killed. They were Colonel Miguel Astanti, Captain Roberto Myers and Second Lt. Robledo......'

'If that bloody box had gone off that could have been me.' Guillermo was angry now.

Caridad could scarcely watch the screen; she hung her head, peering through her fingers. 'I'm so sorry. It must be awful.'

'Because I knew her? I knew half those soldiers as well, or at least their families. Does that make it worse?' He started to shout. 'Does it? Or can you only kill people you don't know?'

'Don't be so crass.'

'Those are the people you're supporting, those fucking

maniacs...'

'I'm against *all* violence, you know that. But you're only against violence by one side. You can't see anything wrong with the State. What about *their* violence? What about the people who are disappearing?'

'Don't start that again, for Christ's sake.'

Guillermo stomped around the room and then he switched off the set. The cottage was plunged into silence until he spoke again. 'This is the world we are living in now. It's not make believe. It's not a game.'

'I'm going!'

'Caridad!' He was shouting again. 'Why don't you try to see things from my point of view for a change? Why don't—'

'Why don't I? Why don't I just wash you out of my life? What have we got to hold us together? You despise almost everything I stand for. And what's more, you're a coward!'

Guillermo drew himself up. 'I've never denied that I'm a coward but at least I'm a realist.' His voice softened. 'You need more than ideals to change an imperfect society.'

'Well at least I try.' Caridad was pulling on the clothes she had shed. 'What do you do? Nothing!' she spat. 'Except sneak around with your "chums".'

Guillermo tried to stop her as she gathered her things together but she shook him off angrily. He was taken aback by her fury. 'I'm sorry you find my lifestyle so disagreeable but you're stuck with it for one more night because there's no river bus until the morning.'

'I wouldn't spend another night with you if you were

Che Guevara!' As an insult, it was not very successful but Caridad was crying now, tears running down her cheeks.

Guillermo tried to stay calm. 'And how do you propose to get home,' he asked quietly.

'I'll *swim*.' She couldn't look at him. She slammed the door of the cottage behind her and strode off into the night, the rain immediately soaking her, the mud ruining her shoes, the thunder bellowing in her ears.

For a moment, Guillermo did not move. Lightning lit up the sky and thunder shook the windows and the door. On the floor he saw a teddy bear, a toy he had given her some weeks before, which usually took pride of place on the bedside table upstairs. Suddenly he leapt to his feet, grabbed the bear and opened the door.

'You forgot your bear,' he roared. He threw it towards the pontoon at the end of the garden. He was about to slam the door shut when he saw Caridad in the rowing boat tied up at the side of the pontoon. He saw her release the line; the boat was immediately swept downstream and he heard her scream. He watched for a second before he bolted across the garden, shouting, 'For God's sake, Caridad, you'll drown! You'll bloody drown!'

He ran to the riverbank, vaulting over his neighbour's fence and across to the next pontoon. The boat was turning rapidly and Caridad was unable to get the oars out to control it. She was heading in the wrong direction, out towards the mouth of the river, out eventually into the River Plate, then the South Atlantic and eventually the black, icy waters of the Antarctic.

Guillermo knew that there was a weir about half a

mile down the river, if the rowing boat could stay afloat that long. He ran faster but the boat was getting away from him, sometimes lost from view in the blackness and then illuminated by a flash of lightning or the glow of a pontoon light. Caridad had the oars now and she steadied the boat, slowed it, but she could not turn it towards the bank. Guillermo splashed through the water at the side of the river, gaining on her, but still fifteen or twenty yards away. The stones cut his feet. The weir was getting nearer.

'Jump, darling. For Christ's sake, *jump*,' he screamed.

Caridad seemed to notice him for the first time but didn't understand what he was shouting. She struggled with the oars but they were having less and less effect and the boat gathered speed as it was drawn towards the weir. She couldn't see the navigation channel to her left; it was too dark and she was facing the wrong way.

Guillermo plunged into the water and struck out for the boat. He swam as hard as he could, forcing himself through the water. This was not an afternoon dip to cool off in the tepid waters at Tigre after a lazy *asado*.

He heard the boat crash into the railing at the top of the weir and Caridad scream as it tipped up. She was clinging to the railings as Guillermo, swept along by the current, crashed into the railings about ten feet from her.

'Hang on,' he shouted. He inched his way along the barrier towards her. Neither of them spoke as he crept, hand over hand, alongside her. Releasing one of her hands from the barrier, he enveloped her with his arm. Then, hand over hand again, they crawled their way back towards the bank, inching past the point where Guillermo had hit the railings. The current pulled their legs down but somehow they reached a ladder at the end and pulled themselves up onto the bank.

Finally safe from the water, they lay down, exhausted. Caridad was crying softly; Guillermo was unsure whether it was from exhaustion, relief or frustration. He held her body close to his and they lay without speaking. Caridad was shivering and Guillermo held her very tightly, before finally pulling her to her feet and leading her back towards the cottage. The full moon cast shadows across the water which flowed like black ink past the A-frame cottage.

'I thought you said you weren't a strong swimmer,' Caridad said.

'I thought you said you weren't going to stay the night.'

Guillermo wondered what he would tell Pilar in the morning and why he was bothering to hide this affair from her. He was in love with Caridad, he knew that now.

In the days that followed, he resolved to leave his wife and start a new life. But telling Pilar turned out to be more difficult than he had imagined.

CHAPTER 12

Guillermo had to buy a ring. He was old fashioned enough to want to make an honest women of Caridad. He was sure her parents would appreciate it, even if she did not care for the formalities. But first, he had to ask her to marry him.

'No politics. At all!' he said to her the following night. They had arranged to go out for dinner and she had arrived at his office late, when everyone else had gone home. They were about to leave but then she was in his arms and they were making love on the leather sofa in his office. The smell of the hide and of her were intoxicating and he became very sleepy.

They both dozed off and when he suddenly came to, two hours later, she was snuggled against him, wide awake but quite still. 'Why didn't you wake me?' he asked. 'Look at the time.'

'You were tired and it was nice lying close to you. I don't often get the chance.'

'You've missed dinner, I'm afraid.'

'Soon the junta won't allow us onto the streets at all.'

'We agreed: no politics.' He pushed her away and searched for his clothes. Putting them on took rather longer than taking them off had done.

'That's not politics,' Caridad said, pulling on her slacks. 'It's just recognising what is going on around us.'

'I'm not looking around us, I'm only looking at you.' It was now too late for his plans. 'We must have dinner tomorrow night,' he said, then laughed. 'And we'll meet at the restaurant.'

'Tomorrow as well? Two nights running,' Caridad said. 'That is really lashing out. Are you sure we should?'

'I'm very, very sure.'

Next evening Guillermo met her in a restaurant just off the Plaza Britannica where he was sure he would not meet any of his friends, and where he was certain that they would not be side tracked. Being recognised didn't really matter now; he just did not want any interruptions.

A huge fire burned in the window, stoked by a gaucho in a leather apron and a black hat. With a six-foot iron prong, the gaucho deftly pushed and pulled meat onto the grill, constantly turning and testing it. His face was as red as the embers. At various stages of cooking he thrust the meat nearer or further away from the fire; angling, turning, placing and retrieving. Every so often he wiped the sweat from his brow with the back of a leather wristband, then whisked another portion of meat from the fire onto the platters. No orders appeared to be written down, yet a queue of waiters delivered the right mountain of meat to the right tables at a run.

The restaurant was packed, as always. Meatless days had done nothing to the national consumption figures; the population just demanded more meat on the days when their staple food was available. In the warm glow of the candle on their table, the cooking fire flickering behind her, Guillermo thought Caridad had never looked prettier.

They ordered a traditional mixed grill, knowing that the huge plate would be more than enough for both of them. Every bit of the cow was on offer, from *bife de chorizo* to *vacio* to *matambre* to *costillar* to *lomo* and on through the body: steaks, sweetbreads, intestines, kidneys, blood sausage, everything.

Guillermo poured some wine from the carafe into their glasses. He double-checked that the ring was in his jacket pocket. He was just about to speak when there was a clattering from the doorway. The people closest suddenly fell silent.

The silence crossed the restaurant like a wave as three armed militia made their way towards the centre of the room. It was obvious who they had come for and the wretched man tried to make a dash for it. The first militiaman blocked his path easily, striking him viciously with his gun barrel. The man dropped to the floor. Two militiamen hauled him to his feet and half-dragged, half-walked him away. There was no struggle; further resistance was futile.

The diners were silent, the waiters motionless. Near the entrance, the man suddenly yelled out in a last, desperate attempt to remain part of the world. 'I'm Miguel Roberts! Miguel—'

He was prevented from shouting his name a second time when one of the gunmen jammed a rifle barrel into his gut. There was a retching sound which hung over the restaurant like distant thunder. Then the militia and their prisoner were gone.

They all knew that the man almost certainly would never be seen again. His family, perhaps, would search for him. They would ask at the police station or the Army barracks or at the courthouse, but nobody would have seen him. There would be no record of his arrest, his days or weeks of detention, his certain torture for the names of his friends and associates and his probable death, no matter what he revealed. There would be nothing to mark his grave. There were rumours in the city that there was now no room to bury the bodies at ESMA, the Naval Mechanical School, so there was a daily bonfire to burn the dead.

Slowly the restaurant awakened; the waiters resumed their duties, tentatively at first, as if worrying that any sudden movement might bring back the devil-men. But otherwise they behaved as if nothing had happened.

Guillermo was white with shock and Caridad ablaze with anger. 'They were not ERP. They were not...' she exclaimed.

'For God's sake be quiet,' Guillermo cautioned.

'They were not Monteneros. They were the police, or the Army, or the Navy!'

'Hush!'

'Don't tell me to hush!' She was shouting now. 'You should listen, for a change.'

'Alright, I'm listening. But be quieter, for God's sake. You'll get us both killed.'

'That's not law! That's...'

'Caridad, listen, please.' He gripped her hands; she was almost incoherent with rage and fear. 'There is a war on,' he told her. 'A civil war! Things happen in war; they have to happen. Once the terrorists have been controlled...'

'Controlled,' she shrieked. 'How do you know that man was a terrorist?'

He did not answer.

When she was quieter, she asked again, 'Was he a terrorist? How will we ever know? He won't have a trial. The authorities will deny all knowledge of him. Tonight never happened. He will never be seen again. He will *disappear!*'

Caridad's voice was rising again and she pulled her hand away from his. At first his grip stayed tight, then he allowed her to go. As she rose from her chair, she lifted her hand, forbidding him to follow her. Her other hand momentarily touched her lips, whether to blow a kiss or to bid him to remain silent was unclear.

'Maybe tomorrow you'll feel differently about all this,' she said. Guillermo was not sure whether 'all this' was them, or everything that was happening in the country. Without allowing him to respond, she joined the throng of diners who, at an unspoken signal, had decided that it was time to leave.

Guillermo, forced to wait for the bill, watched her go.

He had no answers. How did she know the man was *not* a terrorist? Who was to say Miguel Roberts had not killed a dozen innocent women and children and washed the blood from his hands moments before sitting down for dinner? Only he could say, and he had disappeared.

Later that night, as Guillermo replayed the evening's events, he resolved to thrash things out with Caridad, emotionally and politically.

In the morning he had Christina, his loyal secretary, rearrange his diary to clear the afternoon. He would drive Caridad to Hurlingham; they could ride there. That would put him at an advantage. Better, they could fly down to the *estancia*. It was close to his mother's house but not too close; he had been many times before without seeing her. And if things worked out as he hoped, if Caridad said yes to his proposal, perhaps they would go and see his mother together.

He had business down there and none of the farm hands would reveal that he had brought a young, dark-haired woman that he was obviously in love with. And Caridad would be thrilled by the flight, the first time she had been in a private plane. The country never looked more peaceful than when you viewed it from a light plane. Jet airliners flew too high and flattened the earth and everything on it, but the Piper Cherokee that he piloted himself cruised at eight to ten thousand feet and gave a view one could cherish forever. The world below was part toy land and part dreamland, but the essential details were never obscured.

When he phoned Caridad, she sounded very tense.

Guillermo had expected that; he was tense too. Before he could outline his plans for the day, she interrupted him. Another two university students had been picked up by unknown armed men.

Guillermo was suddenly alarmed by her talking on an open line.

'Surely your line isn't tapped,' she protested.

'I hope not, but yours might be.' His mind was racing. Of course her line was tapped, he thought. 'Anyway, I've told you that there's nothing I can do.'

'What would you do if it was me?' she shouted, and slammed down the phone.

All his plans to talk to her, to tell her how much he loved her, to plan a future, to move somewhere else if they could not live together in Argentina, evaporated.

To spite her, he flew down to the *estancia* anyway. A long horse ride alone would sort out his thoughts. He spent an hour with the manager before getting a groom to saddle a horse and find him some chaps; before five o'clock, he was cantering across the grassland of his youth. He had not gone far when he decided to head for his mother's house. He had thought of driving over later but a destination would give the ride more purpose.

It was a long way, almost twenty miles across the *campo*, and it would be dark in less than two hours. With the wind in his face and his mount pushing at the bit, Guillermo started to feel more at ease. The power between his knees, the regular slap of leather above the horse's easy stride and the smell of the pampas acted like a tranquilliser, as they had so often before. The world was very different here and watching it go by from the back of a horse always gave him a feeling of strength. 'The view through a horse's ears,' his father had always told him, 'is the best view in the world.'

The *campo* stretched before him like a magic carpet, with every shade of green and splashes of bright colours interspersed with browns and blacks. The setting sun turned everything orange and red; already it was glistening off the lake far to his left. He breathed long and deep and felt better. At first he had to hold back the horse, a spirited mare, from exhausting herself but she soon settled into a comfortable trot.

By the time Guillermo saw his mother's house, the sun was half obscured by the horizon. Great black fingers, tinged with red, crossed the sky. He had ridden this way with Horacio many times when they were children, hurrying to get the horses back before dark without too much of a sweat. The city never saw such colour; nor, it seemed, did the sun drop with such speed.

Moments later it was quite dark. His horse was exhausted. Guillermo dismounted. Having loosened the girth and hoisted the stirrups, he draped the reins over his shoulder and led the horse, snorting and tossing her head, for the last half mile or so.

His mother was surprised but pleased to see him; Guillermo did not visit as often as he should. She spent more and more of her time away from the capital; sometimes she heard that he had been at the farm and had not come to see her.

She sent the maid to find the gardener who could bed

the horse down for the night, told the cook there would be one more for dinner and waved Guillermo off for a bath. Two brothers, a husband and two sons who all lived in the saddle had not immunised her against the smell of horse sweat.

'Make sure you change your clothes too,' she called as Guillermo made his way to the room which had been his since childhood. Then she went to the kitchen to ensure that dinner was underway.

The farmhouse was very English: cosy, comfortable, a bolt hole from the rigours of Buenos Aires. In the family flat in the capital the chairs were less commodious, the furniture more ornate, the atmosphere more structured. Here he could sink into an old leather armchair, or lie on the sofa with one of the dogs, and ignore the world. It had been his grandfather's farm when he first came to Argentina from England with his English wife in the late 1800s.

His grandfather never spoke Spanish and Guillermo supposed that his father would not have done either, had he not married a Castilian nobleman's daughter. His father was the first of his family to have been brought up as an Argentinian but his children, Guillermo and Horacio, still spoke English at home. There were countless families in the country who did the same, just as there were thousands of Welsh families further south in Patagonia who spoke Welsh as their first language and poor Spanish as their second.

Before dinner, Guillermo went into his father's old study to smoke a cigar and to make three telephone calls.

The first, to the farm manager, outlined his plans for the following day. The second, to Pilar, was brief. He would stay the night here and fly back first thing tomorrow. He would be in the office by nine and would see her at dinner. The third, much longer, was to Caridad. First he apologised, then he told her how much he had missed her, how much she would have enjoyed the flight and the horse ride.

'I'd have been very welcome at your mother's,' she laughed, her anger from the morning spent. She had been cross that he had gone but sweetened when Guillermo promised to make the same trip next week. She was careful to make no mention of the disappeared students or the man in the restaurant, and he made no mention of what he had wanted to ask her; he wanted her in person for that, to look into her dark eyes and see them sparkle.

'I have something to ask you,' Guillermo said, 'but it can't be done over the telephone. This must be done in person.'

Caridad was intrigued and excited, and they arranged to meet when he was back in the capital.

'I can't make tomorrow night,' he said resignedly, 'but it must be the following day.' He was consumed by impatience, desperate to tell her but certain he must ask her to marry him in person.

Over dinner that night, Guillermo confided in his mother. She had asked about Pilar and about his work and she could sense his unease, but she did not press him. Since William had died she had become closer to Horacio than she was to Guillermo, but she was always pleased to see him and ready to listen to his tales of triumph or of woe.

Dinner passed effortlessly enough with talk of the farm, wheat prices, the latest scandals in the capital, polo, which had always interested Señora Haynes even though she didn't ride. Guillermo didn't mention Caridad until after the maid brought in tea and then, stirring his cup intently, he suddenly let fly a confession. 'I am in love with someone, Mama,' he said. 'And I want to leave Pilar.'

His mother was shocked, though she did not show it. Francina Haynes was a wise woman and had lived in Argentina long enough to know that men and women had affairs. That did not mean they needed to break up their families. 'Are you sure that is what you want Guillermo? Does Pilar know?'

'She doesn't know yet, but I am certain. I just need to know that…' he struggled to find the words '…that … Caridad wants me. I think she does. I definitely want to spend my life with her.'

'And what about your job. Would you throw that away?'

'Yes. Yes, I would if I had to.'

'I think you would have to and you should think very carefully about that before you do anything rash.'

'I love her, Mama. I really love her.' Guillermo looked as though he might cry. He had never mentioned Caridad to anyone else, not even his brother Horacio.

His mother said nothing for a while, and then, 'You loved Pilar once.'

'No, I have never loved anyone like Caridad.' Guillermo's response was immediate. 'This is different. I realise now that I never loved Pilar, not in this way, not...' He trailed off.

'I would think very seriously before you commit yourself.'

'I am already committed,' Guillermo said. 'Whatever it takes.'

Señora Haynes knew that Pilar came from a very wealthy family, much wealthier than her own. True, her son Guillermo would inherit the farm with Horacio but his share would be chicken feed compared with the wealth of the Pasquale family, with only Pilar and her brother to inherit. She was sure that Guillermo's job would not survive a divorce.

Later, as Guillermo left the table and kissed his mother goodnight, she spoke again. 'Sleep well, my son, and remember what I have said. You have a lot to lose if you leave Pilar.'

Guillermo thought not about Pilar but about Caridad that night, tossing and turning on the bed he had slept in as a boy. He knew what he must do.

The following morning, one of the farm hands was waiting outside the house at six and another was already taking the horse back. Guillermo climbed into the passenger seat of the Jeep and the driver hurtled off towards the airstrip. The morning was as grand as the evening had been; the sky was already shining light blue, a huge Argentine flag draped across the world. They passed two gauchos on the road, employees looking for stray cows or itinerants, perhaps, looking for work. They saw no one else until they reached the farm entrance where two old women sat in the shade of the trees, waiting for heaven knew what. They nodded their heads respectfully as the Jeep shot past. There was no hostility here, no dissension, no questioning of authority and therefore no abuse of it. There was an established order, in which everyone knew their place. It worked and everyone was happy, or so Guillermo supposed.

Things were no different at work. Guillermo had changed at the airstrip. Less than two hours after he breathed in the sharp morning air on the *estancia*, his secretary was arranging breakfast in his office and going through his appointments. The first thing he did was to send some flowers to Caridad; she would appreciate that, he thought. He dictated the note to the florist: 'I'm sorry. I love you very much. G', and established that they would be delivered immediately.

There was a studied order about the day, about the office, about everyone there. The turmoil of the Dirty War had not yet had any noticeable effect on Berruti and Pasquale – Attorneys at Law. Before Caridad had come into his life, there was no doubt that it would have soon been Berruti, Pasquale *and Haynes* – Attorneys at Law. Guillermo had grand plans for the business and they depended on people knowing what was expected of them. He had a lot to live up to, taking on Pilar's family firm. Perhaps one of the nephews might come in due course but Felix had abdicated in favour of the Army. Some of the profits would always go to him, of course, but the management and direction of the business would increasingly be Guillermo's. He would make the firm the biggest and most profitable law practice in South America, as well as the most fashionable. Now he was thinking of giving up all of that.

By the time he arrived home that evening, he was tired and, for all of his preparation the night before, unprepared for Pilar.

'How do I know you spent the night at your mother's?' She had been unusually inquisitorial when Guillermo phoned the previous night. Now she was downright disbelieving.

'Because I phoned you from there.'

'You could have been anywhere.'

'Well why don't you phone my mother and ask her?'

'And have her think I can't tell whether you're lying!'

Guillermo almost told Pilar there and then that he wanted to separate and marry Caridad but, as so often before, he hesitated. He had to ask Caridad first. He had spent nights away before, some innocent, some not, but Pilar had been satisfied with his reasons. He remembered the nights he spent at Tigre with Caridad, when Pilar had not batted an eyelid. Maybe she was winding him up now because of what she had been up to last night.

'Have you seen Marcus recently?' he asked her.

'Don't change the subject.'

CHAPTER 13

Caridad was seething when she arrived home from the restaurant. The name 'Miguel Roberts' hung round her neck like a huge cross, big enough to crucify a man; there was a man who would never be seen again, she was convinced of it. And the man she loved had seemed unmoved by the events in the restaurant.

The silence had shocked her when the militiamen walked into the room, as diners fell speechless until there was absolute quiet. She could still hear the thud of the gun barrel hitting the man's guts; she could see him crumple to the floor. The sound of the gunmen dragging their quarry out of the restaurant deafened her now, and she trembled.

Caridad flopped down on the bed; she didn't even take off her coat. She closed her eyes and tried to shut out the evening's events but Miguel Roberts kept shouting at her. She could not forget that name; it was stamped into her mind by the jackboots of the military, and yet Leo – her pet name for Guillermo – was apparently not suffering any anxieties from the events at all.

Leo was a decent man, was he not? She knew that he had been born into a different world from the one that she inhabited; twenty years ago they might not have spoken and he would never have troubled her. If her parents had been even poorer, she might have been a chambermaid or a prostitute and then he might have noticed her, as an aside, a distraction for a moment. But, as a lower-middle-class woman elbowing her way towards a better future than her parents, he would not have given her a second glance.

The world had changed in twenty years; now he saw her for the woman she was; even if he had rejected her, he would still have seen her. He had caught the fire in her eyes and the spring in her step; he saw a woman wanting to be somebody, waiting to discover a constituency beyond the confines of the neighbourhood she was born into. She saw him, through his arrogance and suave certainty: a man with a loud voice but a soft smile and gentle hands; a man who, despite his upbringing, had a social conscience and a respect for people. A man she had fallen in love with.

A knock on the door interrupted her thoughts and Caridad cursed silently to herself.

'Caridad, are you there?' It was Lisabet, her best friend at the university with whom she shared everything – except, for some unaccountable reason, the details of this affair. Lisabet sounded worried.

'It's open,' Caridad called out, raising herself on the bed as Lisabet burst into the room.

'You haven't heard? You don't know?' Lisabet asked.

'Know what?'

'Two boys from Quinta Block were arrested tonight, or at least taken away. It's all over the university.'

'Oh my God.' Caridad burst into tears.

'I don't think we knew them, they were final year…'

'No, it's not that.' Caridad told Lisabet about Miguel Roberts. 'It was horrible, horrible.'

They hugged each other for several minutes in near silence. Caridad wanted to tell her friend about her lover but she could not. She needed to organise her thoughts in her own mind first.

Caridad was still thinking about it when Guillermo telephoned her the next morning. She blurted out the news of the two students but, instead of sympathy and understanding, he transmitted nothing but irritation and then fury down the phone. All her romantic thoughts vanished as the icy *pampero* wind whistled through her brain.

'What would you do if it were me?' she screamed at him, and then slammed the phone down. And then she was sick!

Caridad struggled into her lectures that day but her mind was elsewhere. She was sick again in the night and in the morning, and she felt weak. She dissected her arguments with Guillermo: that first day in his office when she had stormed out but not quite closed the door; that time in Rio when he would not be drawn into politics; Tigre, when she could so easily have ended it forever, and her life with it. Was she regretting it now?

If she convinced herself in the morning that she was regretting it, by the middle of the afternoon she had changed her mind. Leo, she reasoned, was a decent man. She would have to convince him that she was right about the junta and that they did have a future together. Then, and only then, would life be worth living. She had always thought it would be possible but now it was getting urgent; she had something of him growing inside her and soon she would have to tell him.

He would have to decide which life he wanted and, if necessary, she would live out her life alone. Well, not quite alone. She was desperate to tell him she was pregnant, but first he had to decide between her and his wife.

After she had been sick three times in one day, she went with her mother to the doctor and he confirmed it: she was two months pregnant. Caridad had not told her mother who the father was. She wanted so much to introduce Leo to her parents and for them to love him as much as she did.

When Guillermo phoned her from the *estancia* that night, he was tender and said how much he would have preferred to go down to the farm with her. She confessed how exciting it would have been for her to fly in his small plane, watching her country unfurl beneath her. She was intrigued about what he wanted to ask her; she knew what she hoped it would be, and she knew her answer.

In the morning Guillermo phoned again and a short while later a bunch of red roses arrived at her room. In the afternoon Caridad worked in her room but was distracted by thoughts about Guillermo. Lisabet knocked on her door again that evening, asking whether she wanted to go down for dinner.

'I think I'll have a shower and go to bed,' Caridad said. 'Maybe tomorrow we can have a late breakfast together.'

About an hour later, Caridad sat on her bed wrapped in a towel. She looked at the roses, large red blooms, and the simple message: *I'm sorry. I love you very much. G*.

She pulled on a nightshirt without moving from the bed. Her head was still inside the shirt and she did not see the door open. She heard a crash as something fell on the floor and was aware of heavy boots pounding towards the bed. She saw the faces of the two men as they grabbed her arms and pinned her to the bed. She screamed before one of them struck her hard across the face and then stuffed a cloth into her mouth and tied it behind her head. She was kicking now and one of the men punched her hard in the stomach.

They flipped her over on the bed and tied her hands together. One of the men sat on her while the other yanked the drawers out of the bedside table and her desk. They scattered the contents over the floor, picked up a few papers and then hauled her out into the corridor.

By this time two or three of her neighbours had come to find out what was happening. Caridad saw a girl about to raise her voice in alarm then one of the men grabbed her by the throat and pushed her against the wall. 'Be quiet, or we'll take you as well.'

Caridad caught sight of Lisabet and two other people down the corridor. The gathering crowd was hushed into submission. One man bundled Caridad into the corridor, bruising her arm on the door handle and tearing her nightdress at the shoulder. She tried to resist but the second man took her other side and they marched her out, her feet scarcely touching the ground. She tried to scream through the cloth in her mouth and one of the men slapped her hard across the face, smashing her lips against her teeth. She whimpered after that, all the way across the quadrangle and through the gates to a waiting car.

In a few moments it was over. The door to Caridad's room swung on its hinges, papers were scattered across the floor, the chair was kicked over. The corridor was now full of people but they were silent, numbed with shock or fear. A bunch of roses lay scattered on the floor beside a shattered vase. A small toy bear sat alone on the rumpled bed.

CHAPTER 14

Guillermo had phoned Caridad in the morning to tell her he loved her and to apologise again for his outburst. And to send her more flowers. But the phone in the hallway at went unanswered.

He was worried but he was interrupted by two of his colleagues bragging about the previous evening's football. Before work got underway, he leaned back in his chair with his feet on the desk, a cup of tea in his hand; two colleagues slouched on the sofa in front of the desk. The morning's newspapers, with stories of the results and pictures of the goals and the saves, were spread over the desk and the side table. There was plenty to talk about. Boca Juniors had scored a narrow victory over their rivals, River, to win the national title in a replay soccer match that had electrified the whole of Argentina. The Bombonera stadium was full to bursting; the roars of the crowd could be heard all over the city. The streets around the stadium were still littered with the red, white, blue and yellow streamers of both sides. The rain thudding down against the window did not dampen the atmosphere in Guillermo's office as he, Santo and Henry relived every moment of the game.

Then the telephone rang. Guillermo picked it up and heard Christina on the end of the line telling him there was a young lady who refused to give her name but seemed anxious to talk to him. 'Put her through,' he said, scarcely pausing in his argument with Santo about Ruben Sune's winning free kick. Then he said: 'Guillermo Haynes, can I help you?'

'It's Lisabet Orlandi. I'm a friend of Caridad.' The voice on the other end was choked with tears. 'She's disappeared!'

Guillermo sat upright in his chair. 'Er, hang on a moment,' he gasped as he gestured to his friends to leave him in private. They didn't understand at first but when Guillermo furiously waved his arms they left the office.

'Please close the door!' he yelled at them.

As the handle clicked, Guillermo clenched the phone and pressed it tighter to his ear, as if to block anyone listening. 'Where are you phoning from? We can't talk now.'

Lisabet said she was phoning from a telephone box near the university. The whole corridor had seen it, she told him. Caridad had fought and screamed but no one had dared help her. Two men, not in uniform, had ransacked the room, searching for incriminating evidence. They took away some notebooks and books and threw most of the contents of Caridad's desk onto the floor.

After Caridad was dragged away, Lisabet had decided

she must get hold of Caridad's new boyfriend, whom she knew was a lawyer. Caridad had proudly shown her Guillermo's business card, which he had given her at their first meeting. The card would certainly have been gathered up by the police if it were still in Caridad's room. Lisabet could remember the company name, Berruti and Pasquale, because Caridad had told her that it would soon be 'Berruti, Pasquale … and Haynes'.

She had trudged the streets around the university for most of the night after the police burst in. Too frightened to go back to her room, she had found some shelter in the porch of a block of apartments. Every time she saw a Ford Falcon, the car of choice for the security police, she turned her face to the wall. She thought of getting on a train and heading out of the city but she had nowhere to go.

By the time she made it to a telephone in the morning, she was rain-soaked, cold, hungry and deeply worried. The telephone kiosk, an inverted U-shape scarcely large enough for her head, offered no protection from the inclement weather. The rain lashed against her legs and soaked her shoes.

'You must do something, Señor,' she cried desperately. 'Or Caridad will never be seen again. You know what they'll do to her. She'll give them all our names, yours too.'

Lisabet was hysterical and it was all Guillermo could do to calm her sufficiently so that he could interrupt her. 'Lisabet, listen!' He was shouting now. 'Don't do anything. Leave it all to me. Go back to the university and act as though nothing has happened. That's important. Do you understand?'

'Yes.'

'Don't tell anyone anything, and don't tell anyone that you've talked to me. Do you understand?'

'Yes.'

'OK, leave it to me.'

Guillermo was white with fear and anger. He put the phone down slowly and kept his hand on it, almost daring it to ring again. God alone knew what Caridad would say about him; God alone knew what he could do for her.

'What a fucking mess,' he said as he paced around the office, trying to think through some kind of strategy. He must have a strategy; that's what his father had always told him. Well, now he really needed one, where the hell was it?

He turned over what the police might know, or find out, about his relationship with Caridad. How did she know him? Where did they meet? Did they discuss politics? He racked his brains. He remembered giving her his business card and wondered if it had been in her room. If so, there was an easy – and true – answer: he had given it to her at a restaurant where he had met her one night.

Had she ever been to his office? He desperately tried to remember. That first meeting at his office must have been recorded and logged onto the card index system by the receptionist, and then possibly added to by his secretary. Every minute of the day could be accounted for, but, but … no, he could fix that.

He opened his door and called to Christina. Christina was perfectly up front about her role: to protect her charge against all comers. She was a short, rotund woman with curly black hair and glasses, about ten years his senior, not quite old enough to be his mother. She was only a competent secretary but she was always completely loyal and discreet. She had rather slow shorthand but her short fingers raced across the typewriter and spat out words like rapid gunfire. She was always chirpy and polite, but her stare could stop a man instantly if he appeared to be heading for Guillermo's office without passing muster. With every woman, she presented herself as an equal and an ally unless they upset her master, in which case her fury knew no bounds. Guillermo rightly spoiled Christina at Christmas and birthdays, and at other times passed her tickets to the Colon or the theatre or the polo. He was always lost when she took her annual leave and tried to time it with his own absence from the office.

Guillermo thought quickly; he had to, his life might depend on it. He knew that he must not, under any circumstances, burden Christina with information that she might not feel happy relating to a policeman who came knocking at his door; at the same time he had to trace that record of Caridad's visit to his office months before. He was certain that no other meeting had been recorded.

'If I wanted to mark a record card with a letter which I forgot to write, to someone who came to see me about six months ago, how could I do that? Without making a big fuss, of course,' he asked when she sat down, notebook in hand.

'If you tell me who it is, I could access the cards and mark it without a problem and put a copy of the letter in the file, in the appropriate place. I also have a copy of all your clients' letters in my filing cabinet.'

'The cards are all down in the vaults, are they?' Guillermo asked as though the matter was unimportant.

'Yes. Not difficult to access.'

'But they're locked up, of course?'

'Yes,' and then after a short pause, 'but I could get you the key.'

She didn't ask why and he didn't ask how, but Guillermo could tick off stage one of his slowly emerging strategy, and it was all thanks to Christina.

As she was leaving that evening, Christina put the key on his desk and told him, without emphasis, that if he left it in the one drawer in her desk that wasn't locked, she would ensure it was returned when she got in, in the morning. 'And here's the key to my filing cabinet,' she added, 'in case you want to put anything in there. Leave it with the other key.'

Guillermo knew he was a lucky man to have such a treasure working for him. Christina might well have saved his life.

Later that evening, Guillermo hunched at Christina's desk methodically typing, one careful finger at a time, a short letter to Caridad. He tore up the top copy, put one of the flimsies in the vault and the other in the file marked 'Caridad Silva' which he found in Christina's filing cabinet with nothing inside. He put the keys in Christina's drawer, then went out and got drunk.

The next day, with a blinding headache but feeling slightly more confident, he made an appointment to see

Pilar's uncle. Guillermo was torn; he had no idea what, if anything, Caridad had done or who she associated with when he was not with her. What he did know was that he had to get her out of the clutches of the State.

* * *

The old field gun and the battle tank mounted on concrete plinths on the lawns in the front of the Libertador Headquarters looked strangely superfluous. In normal times they symbolised both a ceremonial guard and the long-range fire power of the gaunt, white, French renaissance-style building. Now the sandbagged fortifications by the main door and round the perimeter fencing underlined the vulnerability of the status quo, the frailty of freedom in the Republic.

Guillermo noticed none of this as he hurried up the steps. His mind was on the delicate task in hand: to plead for Caridad's life without endangering his own. He gave his name to the sentry who looked on a list and immediately let him pass. A young corporal was waiting for him inside the hall; the steel tips of his shoes tapped on the marble floor as he ushered Guillermo upstairs and along a broad corridor on the first floor, lined with identical doors on either side.

Guillermo had only a moment to wait in General Horloz's outer office, before the general himself came to the door to greet him. 'Come in, my boy. What a pleasure.'

'Thank you for seeing me. I know you must be busy. How's your arm?'

The older man shrugged. He was tall, slim, every inch a soldier. His boots and Sam Brown shone like burnished metal; his hair, silvered at the ends, was slicked down. He still carried his arm in a sling and might never have the full use of it again but, compared to what some had experienced, that was a small price to pay for a terrorist bomb. 'It's getting along fine, and I'm never too busy to see you, my boy. How's Pilar? And your mother? A wonderful woman.'

It was Guillermo's turn to shrug. 'They're both very well, General, thank you.' Then, uncomfortably: 'Er, they know nothing of my visit here this morning.'

Any fears he might have had were quickly dismissed; Guillermo was among men. Women here were worshipped, enjoyed, cast aside; mistresses might be told a secret, mothers and sisters might enjoy a confidence, but the business of men was for men only.

'Quite so, my boy, quite so.'

Guillermo heard a military band start to play outside. He could not see the group of fresh-faced recruits as they marched across the court yard inside the Edificio Libertador but he could imagine what they looked like: young boys of seventeen and eighteen, certain of their cause and of their future.

Guillermo and the general discussed the war by way of an opener to the discussion that was to come.

'There's no point in putting them in prison to serve a sentence and then letting them go,' the general stated. 'For what? So they can regroup and attack again? That's what Peron did. This time we have to do away with them for good!' There was a chilling finality to his words.

'But without trials, without appeals?' Guillermo argued and the general, although surprised at the younger man's argument, dismantled it patiently. Horloz had known and loved the boy since he had married Pilar, and now he was part of the family.

'Guillermo, my boy, I can speak to you like this because of your family, because of your background and because we know each other so well.' The general paused and drew breath. 'We know who we're looking for.'

'But are they all guilty?' Guillermo was conscious that he was getting into an uncomfortable argument with a man who regarded Pilar as his daughter and Guillermo himself almost as a son.

'Who is guilty? Just the ones who pull the trigger? I'm surprised at you.'

'But you haven't got all those people in jail,' Guillermo said, reddening.

'Not yet, but we will get them. The ones we have will tell us about the ones we are looking for. They always tell us.'

The real purpose of Guillermo's visit was not articulated in so many words: Caridad's name was never mentioned. As Guillermo got up to leave the general, canny as ever, asked him, 'Was all this,' and he waved his good hand vaguely at where they had been sitting for the last thirty minutes, 'because of some girl you've taken a fancy to?'

The cigarette smoke hung above the table, stabbed with shafts of sunlight from the Venetian blinds. Guillermo thought of the light reaching through prison bars. 'No

General,' he lied. 'It's a friend of mine who wanted to know... I said...'

'The innocents will always be safe. They are the ones we are trying to protect.'

At the door the general adopted a low, almost conspiratorial tone. 'We've thought this through for a long time, agonised over how we should deal with them. We now have a *policy* to stamp out the Monteneros, the ERP, every communist and everything they stand for. We are not executing people unnecessarily but we have to eradicate some miscreants. So they can never come back.'

'It's all a plan then?

'Of course it's a plan. We're not barbarians.' The drawbridge had come down; there was no room for argument, for doubters, and certainly not for opponents. The policy had been decided and now it was being carried out without question.

Outside the building Guillermo eschewed a taxi and walked back toward his office, sitting for a while on a park bench in La Valle Square. The great Central Court Building loomed over him. The Army were in charge now, the first among equals in the military junta. The president was an Army general; a secret passage linked his office in the Pink Palace with the military chiefs in the Edificio Libertador.

The court across the square, grand but silent, was excluded from the procedure; the law was circumvented. The very notion of *habeas corpus* was derided by the military, just as Caridad had argued, but if he, Guillermo, was a real lawyer, he should be able to do something about it. Even though he wasn't a criminal lawyer, much less one specialising in treason cases, he knew he should try to do *something* – and he knew he could not. He had no way of finding out what Caridad had done or who she had seen. The military and their surrogates in their Ford Falcons watched everything, knew everything and would sort out everything with no questions asked.

Guillermo put his head between his knees and retched.

* * *

Two days later, Pilar took Guillermo to a cocktail party at her mother's house. He would have avoided it but among the guests there was someone he was anxious to see.

'My God, Willie, I wish I could help but I can't do a thing. You know that.' Like most of the English, Peter Tomlinson always called Guillermo 'Willie'. Tomlinson was tall and lean, one of his government's brightest young diplomats. He and Guillermo played polo together, shared a number of mutual friends and interests, perhaps even a mistress or two, though their friendship did not stretch to talking about that. Tomlinson certainly lusted after Pilar and she was not above leading him on. Pilar and Peter's wife, Betina, had joined the rest of the party inside and the two men were alone on the terrace.

'I was only asking you to make a few enquiries, Peter. There's very little the law can do ... in these cases.' Guillermo's dress shirt felt stiff and uncomfortable. Peter on the other hand remained relaxed. He was thinking more of his hand on Pilar's bottom earlier that evening than of his friend's rather vague problem.

'What on earth could we do, Willie? She's not even British. Is she?'

'No, she's not,' said Guillermo quickly. 'But doesn't the British government have a wider interest?'

'HMG's policy is very much hands-off. Give the new junta a chance.'

It was uncharacteristic of Willie to discuss business like this, Peter thought. It was also beginning to get sticky and he wanted to end the conversation and get back inside. Personally, he felt repugnance at some of the junta's excesses, but he had been a diplomat long enough to know when to keep his feelings to himself. Besides, he was looking forward to inspecting Elana's famous azaleas and perhaps a flirtatious walk with Pilar.

'Take it from an older man,' he said, looking around for some more champagne. 'Write it off to experience and forget about her.'

'For Christ's sake, Peter, she's a client. Or she was.' Guillermo was angry at his friend's insensitivity but even more at his own impotence. He knew this was a last chance. He had already tried the Americans the day before. It was an embarrassing meeting from the start because he knew – and didn't like – the US counsellor whose help he had sought and whom he had almost begged for a meeting. The animosity was mutual and went back a long way but Guillermo was desperate.

'Without a complainant there's very little I can do,' the counsellor had told him. 'Hell! There's damn all I can do anyway.' Marshall Ingrams was a small man and

Guillermo towered over him. Maybe that was why the cause of Ingrams' antipathy. Guillermo dismissed the thought; he knew that he had been uncharitable in the past, rude even, both to and about this hard-working American from a humble background, partly because of the work Ingrams had done for those who had fallen foul of the junta. Now Guillermo needed him.

'I know you've often been able to help, where others have failed.'

'Yeah, well I need a husband or a mother or someone's name as the inquirer. Unless we make every goddamn case a diplomatic stare-out!'

'I've already approached ... senior military people,' Guillermo confided. 'They've told me to leave well alone. I'd be putting my ... my family in a dangerous position.'

'The whole goddamn country's in a dangerous position.' Sometimes Ingrams wondered how he stood the job. 'The actions of the junta have been condoned by so many that it's now completely out of hand.' It was an easy jibe but it gave Ingrams some satisfaction. This smooth-talking bastard in front of him was one of those apologists for the military: arrogant, idle, Ivy League. And now he had the gall to come to the US embassy to ask for help. 'Jumping my queue won't help your lady friend! You've got to stick your neck out, far enough to get it chopped off!'

Maybe Guillermo had feet of clay or he was too wretched to rise to the jibes. He hunched like the boxer too numbed or too weary to protect himself from the blows raining down on his face and body. 'I'd appreciate your help, anyway. I really would. Anything you could do. Anything.'

Ingrams suddenly felt sorry for this Argentinean peacock who had become a chicken and almost regretted his own hostility. 'I know the dangers you lawyers are into. I'll put her name on the list. Without a complainant. It might get you something.'

'Thank you.'

Guillermo believed the American would do what he could but that it would very likely bring no result. The British were perhaps a better hope but now they, in the person of Tomlinson, would not give him a hearing. The irony made him shudder. Caridad's impassioned arguments flooded back to him, and they came out of his mouth. 'She won't have a trial,' he said deliberately. 'And she'll never be seen again.'

Peter Tomlinson did not reply except with the faintest shrug of his shoulders. The evening air was pungent with frangipani blossom. To Guillermo, it could have been myrrh for betrayal. And whatever his friend did or did not do, he, Guillermo Leopold Fortunato Haynes, was the betrayer.

Peter suggested they join the others and Guillermo waved him inside. Turning, he went down the steps towards the sunken fountains where, alone on a stone seat, he broke down and cried. He had never admitted it before but he knew now that there was no hope. The Argentines, those in authority to whom he had gone for help, had listened politely, even warmly, and then warned him in icy tones to leave well alone. The Americans, begrudgingly, had offered help but no hope. The British, to whom he felt closest by birth, by history, forsook him before he had made a proper case; they would not even try.

Guillermo knew he had lost Caridad forever but, above all, he was scared for his own life. The thought made him cringe. He sat in his office or at home, waiting for the knock on the door from the police that he knew must come soon. Or maybe she had not told them anything? No, they would have tortured her until she revealed those who were guilty as well as those who were innocent.

* * *

It took the police less than a week to contact him, to knock on his office door as he knew they would.

'Captain Raul Martinez and Lieutenant Fabio Crans,' Christina announced as she showed them into his office.

The two men sat down and starred at Guillermo, without speaking.

'What can I do for you?' Guillermo asked eventually.

'It's more what we can do for you,' Martinez said. He looked sullen and cast his eyes around Guillermo's office without saying more. Guillermo waited.

'Nice place,' Martinez ventured, then lapsed into silence again. Finally he spoke again: 'Which university students do you represent, Señor Haynes?'

Guillermo was surprised at the directness of the question. 'University students don't normally come to this kind of practice.'

'You're sure about that, are you, Señor Haynes?' Captain Martinez repeated Guillermo's name after every question; each time it became more threatening.

'I remember one girl about six months ago but I can't remember her name.' Guillermo started to leaf through his diary as the two men continued to stare at him. Eventually he suggested that he should ask his secretary to look up the name and they nodded. Guillermo flipped down the intercom on his desk and ordered Christina to come in. When she arrived he asked her if she could find the name of the student who had come to see him about six months ago and bring him the client file.

'*Sí*, Señor,' was the only response from Christina.

The two militiamen said nothing as they waited for Christina to return with a file. She handed it to Guillermo, who looked at it briefly. 'Yes, this is the one. I think this is the only one.'

'You'd best be sure, Señor Haynes.'

'Yes, I'm sure.' He read through the file and the copy of the letter he had written only a week before. 'This is the one. 178 Quilmes, Capital. I remember it now. A property dispute: her parent's house, I think. I wrote her a letter but I've not heard any more.'

'Did she pay her bill?'

The question alarmed him. 'I think we waived the fee,' Guillermo stumbled. 'I remember now. I had met her once before, socially, and she came in for a chat about her parents' house. I simply wrote that letter.'

'That was very generous of you.'

Guillermo handed the file and the letter to Raul who

scarcely glanced at it.

'Where is she now?' Guillermo asked.

'I don't know. How would we know?'

'I thought… I thought you knew…'

'Why should we know?'

The question hung in the air long after the two policemen had gone. Alice in Wonderland had come to Buenos Aires: Guillermo was playing the confused Alice and the two policemen were the King and Queen of Hearts. Did they know that he was lying? Guillermo played the question back and forth. They must do and they would be back – but he did not know how long it would take.

What Guillermo was certain of was that he had lost Caridad. She had been trapped, stuffed in a sack and taken to a place of execution, a vile, dark place the like of which he could not imagine. She had been taken by men working for Guillermo's kinsmen, men that he had supported, succoured, and benefited from. She had screamed for mercy but there had been none. Now there would be none for him.

CHAPTER 15

1983 – six years later

Guillermo knew that the Malvinas War had changed everything. In March 1982, when Constantino Davidoff first went to the old whaling station on South Georgia to look for scrap metal, the Army had sensed they could use him to start something. They included some of their own men with the demolition team and they hoisted the Argentine flag over the island, proudly flying it in the roaring wind. For a week or so it looked as though they might simply take over the island, and thereafter the Malvinas, without a shot being fired.

The muted rumblings of rage from the Palace of Westminster in London could scarcely be heard in South America, let alone in South Georgia. But the military, so long out of touch with reality, had misjudged the British and their lady Prime Minister. Mrs Thatcher, perhaps seeing a confrontation with Argentina over a forgotten group of islands as a distraction from problems at home, quickly amassed a huge naval task force and despatched it half way round the world. The result was a thrilling victory for the British and an almost immediate change of government in Argentina.

It was too late now to think about how easily it might have ended differently. If only the Air Force and the Navy's Super Etendard jets from France had had a bit more luck and sunk an aircraft carrier instead of a supply ship. If the Argentine cruiser, the *General Belgrano* had not been sunk so early in the conflict, with the loss of nearly everyone on board, including Horacio. And if the Navy had not then turned tail, run for port and stayed there. If the troops sent to Port Stanley had not been almost entirely young conscripts unused to war. If the general commanding the troops on Malvinas had not been such—

The junta was forced to resign and those searching for the Disappeared were given a massive shot in the arm. The Army was thoroughly disgraced by the war and lost its place in the upper echelons of society. The Navy's mechanical school in Buenos Aires was singled out as the epicentre of torture for the innocent and guilty alike. Only the Air Force escaped the opprobrium which welled up inside most Argentines, for whom the beloved Malvinas Islands were now even further out of reach.

Guillermo felt easier in the company of people who, before the war, he would not have considered of his class. If he met Caridad now, he told himself, things would be very different. He had stayed with Pilar because he was a coward but he still thought of Caridad and imagined himself in a better place with her. Life was easy and he wanted for little, except the love of a woman he had lost so carelessly.

Guillermo had not had Caridad to talk to when his brother Horacio died. Then it was a phone call from Admiral Anaya's office and a call from a Navy commander. He felt Mama would have preferred him to have been killed, rather than Horacio. Guillermo had always been the favoured son until he had forsworn the military, then Horacio took on the hero's mantle. He died too soon in an uneven contest between an ancient Argentine battle cruiser and a British nuclear submarine, among the first of the fatalities in that ghastly and futile war.

It was too late, much too late, but a plan was forming in Guillermo's mind: perhaps he could at last do something about it. Could he atone for his failure to find Caridad? No. Could he help bring to justice those who had committed those terrible crimes? Yes. Yes, he could, and he was determined to do so, whatever the cost.

Caridad was in his mind so much and yet so far from his reach. What would he tell her mother when he met her; what would he tell the world about Caridad and their child? He put all that firmly to the back of his mind, but he knew what he had to do. That walk through the square last Thursday, that news broadcast on the television, that chance glimpse of Caridad's features on a poster held up by her mother; all that, and perhaps the Malvinas War, had given him the impetus that he needed.

Guillermo was confidant, clever, rich, handsome. He had been dealt all the best cards; now, for the first time in his life, he had to play them in order to do some good. Suddenly he had a passion, a purpose.

The following Thursday he almost ran down to the Plaza de Mayo to find Clara. He knew he was offering help to the Grandmothers to salve his conscience but he also felt genuine remorse for what he had done – or rather, what he had not done.

He had not dared telephone the Grandmothers' offices, thinking they would believe him only if they saw him in person. They might recognise him as a decent man who was offering his legal expertise to help them.

'I saw you on the television last week.' Guillermo looked as closely at Clara as he dared without alarming her as he marched alongside her in the demonstration. He recognised Caridad in her: the same strength in the small mouth, the dimples and the wide cheek bones. There was no mistaking the lips, too, thinner and paler here and with lines at the edges, but pursed in the same way when speaking. Clara's thick, dark hair was heavily streaked with grey; her skin had lost its bloom but not its softness. Above all, she had the same dark, dancing eyes as her daughter, full of compassion, but sadder.

'Have you lost a relative?' Clara asked the tall man who was walking with her round the square.

'No. As I say, I'm a lawyer and I thought I might be able to help y...your group.' Guillermo was getting into his stride but he was a better lawyer than he was a liar, at least in the company of this woman. 'Whether the adoptions were illegal or not is something the courts will have to decide on evidence which, by and large, is going to be years out of date. You'll need good lawyers.'

'I've no doubt of that...' she paused to look at his

business card '...Señor Haynes. But we have very limited means. I don't think they will run to such a prestigious firm as yours.'

He laughed. This woman was smarter than she looked. He dared not appear too eager but, equally, he dared not let her go. 'We will be no more expensive than...' He waved his hand, as if teams of lawyers from every practice in Buenos Aires were marching with them. 'In fact, as a large firm, we can offset many of the costs, and our fees will be *pro bono*.'

Guillermo had already made up his mind to help the Grandmothers in any way he could without discussing the matter with the other senior partners at Berruti, Pasquale and Haynes. He figured that times were changing and he should be in the vanguard of that change, leading the company towards a new range of clients and redressing the emphasis on the military.

'Why should you do that?' asked Clara. She said it without suspicion but he was glad he was looking round the square. Had she seen through him already, or was she simply intrigued? There was a second's pause, a very long second, long enough, it seemed, for Guillermo to sing the entire national anthem.

'We are all culpable, Señora,' Guillermo said at last.

* * *

'We are all culpable,' Caridad had told him that day in Tigre, during one of their many political discussions. 'It's our country which is doing this and we are all culpable.

139

Everyone is doing it on one side or the other.'

She had a way with words and a way of delivering them. She spoke with a controlled passion which said, 'I'm right; just believe it.'

But Guillermo did not believe it, at least not then. 'Don't be ridiculous. I haven't done anything, nor have you. These people are terrorists, murderers.' Guillermo was always gentle with his arguments, always worried that she would suddenly fly off like a frightened coscoraba swan, just as she had that first time in his office.

Caridad, by contrast, never minced her words. 'They're fighting for what they believe to be right. For justice! For the right to have a voice.'

'You wouldn't say that if your father had been killed by them.'

That had shut her up. She had reacted as though it had been her own father, and he remembered how comforted he had felt by her concern. Guillermo knew who to blame; it was not him, or his family or the Army. The blame lay firmly with those who had planted the bomb which had snuffed out innocent lives with a flash and a thud. You never forget the sound of an explosion that close. It rocks your ears; you wake up in the night and hear it again and again. You taste the fear in your throat and feel the warm blood before life goes cold, so quickly cold.

Caridad had answers; she always had answers, even for the terrorists. But they were never excuses. She had guessed how his mother had blamed him for not being in the Navy when his father was killed, as if that would have made any difference. And she could find answers for that too. Everyone came within her sphere of understanding.

* * *

'Have you any particular cases in mind, Señor Haynes?' Clara was sitting with him at a table underneath a *ceibo* tree, its broad, bulbous leaves shutting out the sun.

Guillermo sipped his tea. 'No, I just want to help.' Lying would not be that difficult but now, six years later and sitting with Caridad's mother, Caridad's accusation rang in his ears. Was he trying to be a real lawyer now?

'All of us in the Grandmothers' Collective,' Clara said, 'are looking for our own grandchildren as well as the grandchildren of others.' She was drinking strong black coffee, just like Caridad used to do. She was smaller than Caridad, shorter and a little heavier. She had the same neck, long and arched; the head of a lion on the neck of a swan. 'We've rescued nine children so far; we've identified thirteen more who we know were illegally adopted. We're searching for thirty-six more children by name, or their parents' names. Families are knocking on our door every day.'

Guillermo hesitated to interrupt her. In full flow, she was magnificent: determined, invincible, compassionate. Alexander's armies would have shivered at the sight of this diminutive woman.

'We will trace every stolen child and reunite them with their families. At the very least we will put the real families in touch with the new families. We don't want retribution, we want justice.'

141

'Do you know the whereabouts of your own grandchild?' Guillermo asked when Clara paused momentarily for breath.

'Not yet.' She slowed but did not stop. 'I know I'm looking for a child who is nearly six years old.' Her voice was softer now, almost a whisper. 'I shall find him, or her. We shall find them all.'

No one in the city who heard her words could have doubted them; Guillermo certainly did not. The week before, when he first saw Clara on the television, he had already decided that he needed to help the Grandmothers in their quest for justice. But he had also decided not to tell Clara why he wanted to put the legal might of his company behind an organisation that was founded in opposition to everything he had grown up with, every privilege he had been given. That would be much more difficult.

'Do you know who the father was?' he asked.

'Caridad never spoke about him,' Clara said. 'But I know she loved him. The child was conceived out of wedlock but very much from love.'

Guillermo felt a lump rise in his throat and tears welled in his eyes. Fortunately, Clara's gaze was fixed elsewhere.

'Everyone one who works for our organisation does so for nothing,' Clara told him. 'We have to rent our offices and pay for some professional help, printing and the telephone and so on, but we are working for nothing because it's the only way we will ever find our children. For us, it's the right thing to do. But you, you have to make a living.'

'I'm sure there will be court costs and other things which we will have to pay for and those will be very high,' Guillermo said. 'But I offer you my services for free. I want to help.'

Clara seemed to be convinced. 'You're very generous,' she told him. 'I look forward to working with you. We have a lot to do to blot out this stain on our past.'

The Mothers of the Plaza de Mayo had existed throughout the Dirty War, bravely seeking their children and often risking their own lives. Despite this, they had escaped the gaze of the majority of Argentines almost completely. If they had registered on Guillermo's radar it was as troublemakers and impotent adversaries in a war which had to be won for the sake of decency, order and the survival of the State.

Guillermo had wavered in the middle of the Dirty War but the years passed and he had come to accept the correct order of things. He had not agreed with all of the junta's methods but he had lined up four-square behind the status quo. Now the Malvinas War had been lost, everything had changed. Guillermo, and many other Argentines, welcomed the transformation even if they couldn't claim the Malvinas as their own. Inflation was running out of control and he was still putting his spare cash into American dollars, but he was born an Argentine and he would die one. The new government promised a lot and delivered little but they had instituted the Presidential Commission for the Disappeared.

Guillermo was elated when he left the coffee house. Later that afternoon, in the stillness of his office, he turned over how and when he could tell Clara his real reason for helping. She's bound to find out eventually, one half of him said; she'll never find out, the other half countered. How could she? Your name is safe. But one half of him wanted to find something of Caridad to cling onto; he wanted to atone for his sins.

His meeting with Clara brought to the forefront something which he had never stopped thinking about: why had Caridad been taken? Why had she, a young, innocent student, a radical but certainly not a revolutionary, why had she been targeted? It was a question he'd often asked but never been able to answer.

He couldn't concentrate on any of the papers on his desk so he left early, driving fast to Hurlingham where he thought practising his polo swing would set him right. There were a dozen tennis courts at the Polo Club as well, and there was always someone to play against to help vent his frustration. Failing everything, he could swim. If he could not work out a solution to his problem, he could simply drown!

CHAPTER 16

Four elderly women, their faces lined with age and fatigue, sat round the large table which took up most of the living room-cum-hallway. The table was heavy with files, photographs, newspapers and books. The atmosphere was charged with quiet energy. These ladies had been looking a long time and sudden breakthroughs were rarely in the Almighty's scheme of things.

The sun shone in through the windows on Montevideo Street and traffic noise punctuated the pen scratching, paper cutting and the restrained voices. The muted telephone rang frequently. 'The Grandmothers' Collective,' said whoever answered, and there usually followed a long period of listening and meticulous note taking.

Across the wall by the door was a large pin board covered in family snapshots: young men and women at graduation ceremonies, on the beach, in restaurants, having fun. Some were wedding photos, or pictures cut from newspapers with a story: Eugenie, aged twenty-two, awarded first prize, or Peter, nineteen, joining IBM as a management trainee. Pinned to some of the photos were others of babies or toddlers. Like pages from a giant photograph album, they told the story of an extended family, of individual hopes and joys returned as tragedy.

In the two small bedrooms, the kitchen and even the bathroom of what was previously an ordinary apartment, more elderly women worked at tables heavy with files. Only the lavatory was left for its original use.

'You know very well what he told me.' Clara was hunched over a table in the main room. 'He said he wanted to help.'

Estela Mackay and Miranda Orloz were with her; two small, squat towers carved from the same block of womankind: gentle, generous and implacable.

'It's not very prestigious work for him,' Estela said. She was the smallest and the oldest of the group. In a few years she would be wizened but for the present she wore her age like a coat that was becoming increasingly threadbare. 'But he seems a good man,' she added, slowly, weighing the words like the leathery, learnt judge she increasingly resembled. 'With a social conscience.'

'His father was very high up in the Navy?' It was both a statement and a question from Miranda. Her own son would have been about Guillermo's age; his daughter, the granddaughter she now sought, was less than a week old when she was kidnapped with her father and mother. Miranda had seen the child once in hospital. Her son, his pretty wife and their darling daughter all disappeared before they arrived home. Miranda was already predisposed

146

towards Guillermo but his presence made her own scars hurt more.

'And his grandfather, for all I know,' said Clara. 'But he is offering to help.'

The three women continued with their chores. Clara worked simultaneously, as they all did, on the cases in hand and the children they themselves most wanted to find. Clara only knew the approximate date of birth of her grandchild, but she had a date fixed in her mind from that one visit to the doctor with her pregnant daughter. Only today she had learnt of the whereabouts of another child who might have followed the same route out of the prison. Tomorrow, or the next day, or the next, she would learn more.

The elevator was broken, as it was frequently, so Guillermo had to trudge up to the sixth floor. He had only been here a couple of times but he had already spent considerable time on the Grandmothers' cases. It was a joy to get his teeth into something substantial. The professional advice the women had received so far had been patchy, to say the least, and for a couple of weeks he seemed to do nothing but pick holes in the cases, demand additional documentation to prove a point and gently introduce a smoother procedure to facilitate future research and analysis.

Guillermo kept to himself the terrible irony of his now expert knowledge of family law; in the last half dozen years he had developed it as a branch of the practice and made considerable money from it. Most of his clients were rich families willingly or unwillingly dividing their estates because of death, divorce or sibling rivalry.

Guillermo did not like to dwell on his first 'client', a young woman whose ghost now appeared before him at the Grandmothers' offices. He remembered that ridiculous letter he had typed with one finger and stuffed in the appropriate file; it might have saved him but it did not liberate Caridad from the clutches of the State.

'Whatever the president says, the courts are against you,' he told the Grandmothers at their first formal meeting. 'You will need to provide them with an incontrovertible case.'

He had already caught a change in atmosphere from some of his colleagues at court. 'Not your regular kind of client, old boy?' He had expected questions from friends and colleagues, even their exaggerated concern, but the animosity and the warnings that often greeted the news that he was now acting for the Grandmothers shocked and hurt him. He was sure he had nothing to be afraid of politically but socially he had badly miscalculated, and the dry feeling of fear sometimes touched his throat. It hung there, ready to throttle him, like the memory of Caridad's cruellest jibe: 'If you were a real lawyer, you wouldn't be so worried about your position; you might start thinking for yourself!'

* * *

Tiny beads of sweat were dripping down Guillermo's back as he reached the sixth floor. He planted his footsteps mechanically as he might on a treadwheel, his legs feeling no strain but his heart rate beginning to rise. He wondered how the old women did it every day; he never heard any of them complain.

He rang the buzzer and, shortly afterwards, he heard the footsteps and felt the eye spying on him through the lens in the door.

'Can I help you?' The grey-haired figure who opened the door, one of an apparently inexhaustible supply of women anxious to help the organisation, did not recognise him.

An hour later, Clara, Estela and Guillermo walked up the steps of a long-disused office block in the centre of town. A drab, concrete monolith, it had once been the headquarters of an ordnance company. Now it had changed sides and the ground floor had been hurriedly pressed into service to provide a home for the Presidential Commission for the Disappeared.

Almost from the moment the two great stainless-steel doors creaked open for business, there was a queue of people waiting to tell their tales. Makeshift partitions along one side of the building provided booths in which people could confide terrible accusations, suspicions and even confessions to someone of their own sex. The queue waited patiently on the other side for a woman who sat at a desk in the middle to beckon them forward. She talked quietly to them individually before detailing an usher to escort them to one of the booths, or sometimes to a line of offices at the far end, where men and women with maps, files and index cards sifted and sorted and sighed.

There was an unmistakable air of reverence and

humility, the distant incantation of evidence like plainsong. If incense had burned on a table, or a chorister had sung the Nunc Dimittis, it might have been a cathedral. Not, to be sure, the richly accoutred church opposite the Pink Palace where the State worshipped; not even the restrained Navy chapel where a remembrance service was held for Horacio and the others who went down in the *General Belgrano* at the start of hostilities in the Malvinas war. This was more like a plain mission church in a dirt-poor, up-country village, offering only space and shelter for the needy. But, like the great temple at Angkor Wat or the ruins at Karnac, there was no doubt that this was a house for a God believed in.

In Guillermo's mind it was a God who had forsaken a great swathe of the people. Some of those had been driven to arms to overthrow the State; thousands of others merely disagreed with their rulers and wanted the freedom to object. And then there were those who were only *thought* to have disagreed, or who might disagree at some point in the future; they were, according to the State, safer disappeared. For Guillermo, expecting not a church but a courtroom, it was a culture shock. Perhaps, he thought, this God was simply The Truth and it had been a long time coming.

The stories he overheard were more shocking than any he had dealt with in court. As he walked along a corridor created by Hessian screens behind the booths, he heard an old man weeping. 'Everyone was raped. The Jewish women got even worse. I could see them ... with Lela. But I had nothing else to tell them.'

Guillermo glimpsed the man; his head was bowed and he was pulling at an imaginary thread on his jacket, his tears dropping to the floor. It was a portrait of a broken man, tossed and kneaded by the State and then thrown into the gutter. He was one of the lucky ones who escaped with his life but what did he have left to live for?

During the past week, Guillermo had read testimonies from the Commission and from the human rights groups that had opened some of their files to the Grandmothers, but nothing could have prepared him for the sound of a human voice telling of inhuman acts. The screaming had ceased, replaced now by bleak, interminable cries, desperate pleas not for help, not for justice, but for... Guillermo could not determine what these tragic figures were searching for, but the sound of their voices grew louder and louder in his ears and made him retch.

'When they took me to the torture room,' a woman was saying, 'I was dragged naked, through their dining room. Only my eyes were covered so I could not see them. The soldiers always laughed. Many times I was raped, right there, by five, ten – who knows how many.'

'The *picana*?' This time it was the soft, searching voice of the official in the next booth. 'The *picana*?' and a voice said, 'The electric cattle prod?'

There was silence but Guillermo could see through a crack in the Hessian screen. Another old man was nodding, slumped in a chair, his hands clenched together, his back bent and his spirit broken. Eventually he said: 'I told them everything. Truth, lies, anything to stop the pain.'

The official tried to reassure him. 'Everyone talked. *Everyone*! It is nothing to be ashamed of.'

The old man was not convinced. 'I gave away my son. They let me go but they killed him.'

This man's tears rolled silently down his cheeks, an Amazon River of tears as part of the nation cried and the rest of the nation ignored them. Guillermo's eyes were moist too. What he heard brought back terrible, terrifying memories. He had not cried since that night, alone in his office after the police had paid him a visit, when he realised what a fool and a failure he had been. His eyes were moist today because he realised he still was.

The nightmares had lessened over the years; the soldiers who tore him limb from limb and carved his body into pieces until only his head was left to scream did not come as regularly as before. Now they were coming again. Men without faces dragging Caridad away in the night; he was running behind them but the faster he ran, the faster Caridad was dragged away, screaming for him, pleading for him.

Clara tapped his arm. 'Listening to the testimony gives you the emotion but it doesn't give you all the details. Come on. We need to continue with the files.'

She had quickly fallen into his lawyers' jargon. She was learning about course, argument, plotting, research, position. He doubted Clara had her daughter's intellect but she had the same animal savvy. She had already begun to take control of the arguments, or at least plot their direction.

Two of the Grandmothers were laboriously taking

details from the card indexes. Every reference to a name – prisoner, policeman, soldier, doctor, town, prison, road – was copied from the testimonies so it could be cross-referenced. These were women who had probably never worked in an office and Guillermo marvelled at their application. They had not been trained to research a subject or write a brief but they attacked their task like the brightest intern. In time they hoped they would build a complete paper record of every prison, detention centre or place of torture: who served there; who suffered there; who was born there; what happened to them.

The Commission officials were mostly young. Some were graduates who had come back to Argentina after the fall of the junta; others were idealists who had given up their jobs to work here for a pittance. They contrasted sharply with the Grandmothers who came to work alongside them. It was slow and arduous travail, which the elderly women approached with a special kind of zeal. They had already lived for five or more years without hope; with hope, they could last however long it might take.

Guillermo was reminded uncomfortably of the week he had first come into brutal contact with The Disappeared. The diagrammatic plans of innumerable prison buildings had a theatrical quality, becoming sets for another production of *Fidelio*. Beethoven's brilliant but chilling cadences rang in his ears and brought to mind the horrible pictures of the skulls retrieved from shallow graves and the first time he had seen them on television.

Clara drew Guillermo's attention to the testimony of a twelve-year-old boy which had turned up as a result of two cross-references. Two women had described a similar child; one of them had placed the events at San Juan prison and yet another testimony had linked that to Caridad, though not conclusively. Now the child himself had come to the Commission and told his story. He was six years old when his mother was arrested and he had been taken along with her to the prison. For some time, he did not know how long, he had not seen her. Then one day he had been taken to say goodbye.

'She asked the soldiers to take the hood off her head,' the boy said, 'so she could see me to say goodbye. But they wouldn't! They wouldn't. I couldn't kiss her goodbye.'

The testimony described how the boy had broken down in tears at this point and the interview took some minutes to resume. But further questioning was pointless, as the child refused to say another word. The official had asked the boy whether he had ever seen his mother again. The boy remained transfixed, immobile. Finally, slowly, he shook his head.

The numbing cruelty took a moment to sink in.

'These are the kind of people we are dealing with,' Clara told Guillermo as he stared in disbelief at the boy's testimony.

At least this story had a happier ending. Clara described how the boy was sent to an orphanage nearly two hundred miles away. A year later, on a day out, his mother's sister recognised him. She fought for the boy's release with considerable courage and was now bringing him up as her own. It was she who had brought him to the Commission.

'Can you imagine how that boy must feel, coming here?' asked Clara. But Guillermo was already reeling. In that one story was all the ghastliness and cruelty of the whole world, and yet there was also the good fortune, chance, bravery and the incredible luck which had plucked the boy to safety in the arms of a relative who loved him.

* * *

Guillermo nosed the car back into the traffic outside the station. It had been a traumatic afternoon and he was glad to drop Estela off and have Clara to himself.

'You don't have to take me home,' she told him.

'I'd like to,' he said. 'I need you to help me unwind a bit after all that.' His left hand gripped the gear stick; he clung onto to it for fear of falling.

'That boy was lucky, you know,' Clara said as they crossed Libertador and turned down to the Avenue of the 9th of July.

'In finding his aunt?'

Clara nodded. 'Yes, but also long before that,' she said. 'He had a club foot. Many children who were considered unsuitable for adoption were simply killed. Babies born deformed, children "contaminated" by their parents' politics, Jewish babies, or babies not "white" enough.'

'There was no policy to kill children.' Guillermo was insistent. 'The idea was to protect the innocents.'

'What makes you think that? Did you know what the

policy was?'

Guillermo drove on in silence, gripping the steering wheel ever tighter. Why was he being so defensive? Because he did know what the policy was? Because it had been cruelly spelt out to him, first by his brother-in-law and then by an Army general. He could not tell Clara that, but he could remember. Jesus Christ, he could remember; he would never forget.

'Did Caridad never speak about the father of her child?' Guillermo asked. They were nearly home now and he was eager to find a way of telling Clara at least some of the things he knew. The better he got to know her, the harder it was to explain why he had not yet been completely honest with her.

'Caridad and I had no secrets until she met the man who made her pregnant. She loved him, I am sure of that. She thought he loved her but I don't think he knew she was pregnant.'

Guillermo turned away to look at some imaginary traffic hazard. He closed his eyes but a screech of brakes snapped the tension and anyway, they had arrived outside Clara's apartment.

'Thank you,' she said before getting out. 'You are a real strength.'

'I only wish I could do more, and more quickly.'

'Patience is a virtue of the old.' Clara touched his arm and kissed him as she got out of the car. 'I wanted Caridad to study law. Her father wanted her to be an engineer. When she decided on economics, he decided she would run the Corn Exchange and then the government. A new

Eva! It finished him when Caridad disappeared.' And then she added: 'He never recovered.'

Guillermo did not know what to say. Death was final and he did not have the words to put people at ease when they were discussing it. He was uncomfortable in death's company in a way that Clara was not.

'I wish you had known Caridad,' she continued. 'She would have liked you. But then women do, don't they?' There was an impishness in her that he had not seen before; she was able to joke after all that they had been through today. She gave Guillermo one last glimpse of her smile, Caridad's smile, and a flash of her dark eyes, Caridad's eyes, before turning to go inside.

Guillermo waited until she had disappeared. He felt his tears welling again. The sun was setting behind a thin layer of cloud and he felt the end of the world was approaching.

CHAPTER 17

The squeals and shouts of a small child having a good time filled the room and flowed out of the window and down the street for everyone to hear. Balloons were tied in batches to door handles and pictures; a large, cardboard '6' hung from one balloon, and 'Happy Birthday Paulo' in large letters was strung along one wall.

'Bravo, Paulo, bravo!'

'Can I have a wish now, Papa?'

'You must have a wish now.'

Paulo shrieked with delight. Surrounded by boxes, cards, candles and candies, every day should be like this. For once the little apartment was a mess, with toys on the floor, wrapping paper and even clothes and shoes strewn everywhere. But Mama did not mind today.

'You mustn't tell anyone what you're wishing, otherwise it won't come true,' she said, and Paulo put his hand to his mouth. He was about to wish for birthdays every day.

Mama was Madonna: round-faced, angelic, with a mop

of dark hair and a permanent smile. She was soft, cuddly and almost never said no to a small boy. Over the years Eva Bollini had learnt well how to manage the money they had; even though it was not very much, particularly now, her family lacked for little. What they did not have by way of shiny new things, she made up for with careful repairing and recycling, and masses of attention for Paulo and Franco. She skimped on clothes for herself, so sometimes she did not look as pretty as she might. But today she was wearing her Sunday best: a green wool skirt with a matching jacket and a cool printed blouse, which she had bought in the sales last year.

The apartment was neat and comfortable, usually spotless but always homely. She and Franco struggled to ensure that Paulo had presents at Christmas and birthdays, new shoes for school and lots of books, just like Papa's.

And Papa? He was a giant, just like Paulo was going to be when he grew up. Papa was the best friend a boy could ever have. No ball was lost forever, no toy broken beyond repair, no story told so often that if could not be told again.

Franco held his son with one arm, almost losing the child within his shoulders. He stretched out his other hand for Eva's. 'Come on, wish,' he said.

Eva reached behind her, took another package from the shelf and handed it to her husband. While Paulo's eyes were closed, Franco put it down in front of him. With more wrapping paper on the floor, Paulo was soon playing his first tune on a new mouth organ.

'It's like yours, Papa.'

'Just like mine,' said Franco as he joined the boy in an elaborate accompaniment. 'Now that you're six,' Franco said when they had finished, 'you're getting heavy.' He threw the boy up in the air with a whoop and then lowered him gently to the ground. 'Besides, I have to go to work in a moment.'

'Papa, no! Who is taking me to school?' Paulo clung to Franco, but to no avail. His father swung him upside down, then deposited him firmly in his mother's arms.

'I am taking you to school this morning,' Eva said. 'And I will read you a story tonight, if you're a good boy.'

Mama always read him a story. Papa always kissed him goodnight, sometimes telling him another story, sometimes playing him a tune on the mouth organ or singing him a song in a mellifluous, bass voice that made every scratch better and dried every tear.

Franco was already wearing his uniform. The short-sleeved white shirt just covered the dagger and scroll tattoos on his upper arms. Eva had cried when she first saw them when he had come home on leave. Now he was ashamed of them but resigned to their presence. Nevertheless, he eschewed the cut-off sleeves that men were wearing now. He did not need to accentuate his muscles. He was a powerfully built man, almost fearsomely so, with hands like hams. He was confident of his own strength and rarely needed to exercise it and he had a surprising lightness when he held a book, played the piano or held Paulo.

Soon he would have to clip the security insignia onto his epaulettes and leave for his shift. It wasn't a bad job really and he had plenty of time on his own. Sometimes he played chess with a colleague or read. The pay did not leave much for luxuries, but Eva was a good manager and the shifts meant he could spend a lot of time with his son.

Franco Bollini threaded his epaulettes into his shirt and fixed the great badge to his front pocket. 'I will make you breakfast and then I must go,' he told Paulo as he gave him one last kiss.

* * *

It did not take long for the practised lawyer Guillermo Haynes to hang a case on Franco Bollini, though it was nothing that would yet stand up in court. He had only told Clara the evening before and now, on a Saturday morning, they were driving to a small children's playground on the south side of the city.

'I'm proud of you,' said Clara. 'I hope that's not being too familiar.'

'No, of course not. Anyway I haven't done anything yet.'

Guillermo was embarrassed; he had been working with them for only a couple of months but was increasingly fêted by the Grandmothers. Everything he did for them was received as a gift from heaven.

Clara sounded just like her daughter; even her touch on his arm, though older and less urgent, had the same sensual quality. 'Of course you've done something. You've found...'

'I've located a child who fits the jigsaw,' he interrupted

firmly. 'I haven't begun to find the proof.'

'I am sure.'

'This could be a false errand; you mustn't get your hopes up, even though it all fits.'

'Stop speaking to me as a lawyer and tell me how you found him,' Clara said impatiently as the car drew out into the traffic opposite the Grandmothers' Collective.

'A bit of luck and a lot of hard work. The St Juan detention centre was situated across the street from a police station. It turns out the commandant of the police station, who might have been an Army officer, had a child about the same time as Caridad's child was born. It may be nothing more than a coincidence.'

It was a very thin case but Guillermo was confident. He had a nose for these things and the circumstances were too much of a coincidence for the family not to bear examination.

They drove on in silence for a while, before Clara demanded, 'What do mean, "he had a child"?'

'Well, everything suggests he, or rather his wife, had a child. But there's something slightly strange about the birth records. Wait and see.'

The hours of reading and cross-checking, of following up leads which then petered out, of turning up children who were too old or too young, was forgotten as they prepared to check out this particular family.

Clara and Guillermo positioned themselves on a park bench on a path which led to the children's playground. Every Saturday, it seemed, the family came to this park, to this children's playground. This Saturday was no exception; a man in his forties, accompanied by a small boy, perhaps five or six, walked along the path towards the swings. Clara and Guillermo appeared intent on conversation, barely giving the man a glance, but Clara's eyes were fixed on the boy.

'Franco Bollini,' said Guillermo, softly. 'Aged forty-one, now a security guard, but he was once in charge of the sub-police station opposite San Juan. He has no known connections with the Dirty War but his wife suddenly appears with a child in 1977, a boy they've called Paulo.'

The playground was shabby. The swing needed a coat of paint; next to it a roundabout was jammed into the ground at one side like a beached boat. Despite this, the man and his child were having the time of their lives.

'Not yet, Papa. I don't want to go home.'

'We are late. Mama will be waiting.'

'One more minute.' The boy held up one finger. It was obviously a family joke. They both laughed.

'One more minute.'

'Look at the way he walks, just like Caridad,' said Clara. 'I am certain.'

'It would be easy, and understandable, to make a mistake.'

'I am certain,' Clara repeated. 'He is my grandson.'

Guillermo could not see the likeness and felt nothing for the boy. There was no biological impulse clutching at him across the park; in fact, he was beginning to feel deeply troubled. If that was Caridad's son, it was his son too. Sometime soon he would have to admit that to Clara, to his wife, to everyone. And if it *was* his son, he had no idea what should happen next.

Clara, however, was certain, who the child was and what action to take. 'We must take him away, now,' she said. She rose from the bench and went towards the boy playing on the swings with the man he called Papa.

'Wait! For God's sake, wait Clara. You can't just take the child.'

Guillermo leapt up and grabbed Clara before she had moved a metre. He looked around him in case anyone had seen him. The boy and his papa continued their game, oblivious to Guillermo's frenzied actions as he hauled Clara back to the bench. Clara sat back down.

* * *

Later, as they drove back into the city, she was as pensive as he had ever seen her. She did not notice the mimosa blossoms like gold dust on the verges when they got into Palermo. When they passed the university she said: 'Caridad and I had no secrets, until she met this man Leo.'

Guillermo dared not take his eyes from the road but he wished he could see her face. There was an agonising pause as he tried to speak, to admit his affair, to beg forgiveness for deceiving Clara and for failing Caridad. But he remained mute; the motor signals from his brain refused to open his mouth.

'I thought it was odd that she only told me his first name,' Clara said, unaware of the silent century that had passed. 'Leo.'

The name hung in the air. Guillermo Leopoldo

Fortunato Haynes, named after his father and both his grandfathers, was silent. He'd heard the name before from Clara, of course. The first time they had met Clara had told him of the mysterious man called Leo to whom she had never been introduced and who was probably dead as well. Guillermo knew better.

CHAPTER 18

In the six months it had been in office, the new government had gone a long way towards dismantling the apparatus of the military state but nevertheless the innermost workings of the military establishment retained their dark secrets. There were one or two casualties, like Captain Astiz, who had been charged with killing two French nuns, but for the most part the sinners remained invisible although their sins were uncovered daily.

Long lists of people who had been tortured appeared every day; even longer lists were compiled of those who had disappeared, together with a growing number of children thought to have been kidnapped by the State and passed on to so-called respectable families. There were tales of aircraft flights over the River Plate where the living and the dead were heaved out into the sea below; details of students and trade unionists being strapped to metal bed frames and tortured; of the innocent and the guilty being clubbed to death or strangled or shot in the head at close range; of rape and carnage committed against people who, once captured, were considered less than human; all this was common parlance. People were still careful about who they spoke to – and how loudly – when they repeated the horror stories; the police still drove around in their Ford Falcons.

Guillermo came back from the court seething with anger. 'With all this going on,' he bellowed at the first person he saw at the Grandmothers' office, 'how can the fucking judges be so blind?'

Then he saw Clara and her calm face reset his mood instantly. 'I'm sorry,' he said. 'I'm just very annoyed.'

'Come and tell me what happened.' Clara walked with him towards the little kitchen. 'I'll make you a cup of tea.'

Guillermo had tried to get the courts to release some police records and had been refused. Franco Bollini had been easy to find but his past was difficult to track, which made his guilt seem even more certain. Guillermo needed proof and the courts were refusing to give him the wherewithal to find that proof.

'It's as though the judges don't recognise there was ever a Dirty War. Yet now it is supposed to be over. How does that make sense?'

Clara was more sanguine about the pace of change. 'These things take time, Guillermo,' she said as she cleared away some files from the only chair in the kitchen and made him sit down.

That was the thing about Clara: she seemed to have all the time in the world, even though every day away from her grandson was like a lifetime. She had honed patience into a life-saving coverall, which surrounded her in everything she did and protected her when things took longer than expected.

Except with his horses, when he could show a saint-like patience, Guillermo was used to getting his own way immediately and he had real problems when he did not. His office was beginning to question the amount of time he was devoting to his *pro bono* work. The other partners, particularly Kingston Berruti, recognised the need to move with the times, to stay in touch with the new government and to distance themselves from the old ways, but time was money and Berruti, Pasquale and Haynes were used to making money every day. Guillermo, as the newest partner, could be allowed a bit of slack but there were limits.

It was nearly a fortnight since Clara and Guillermo had first spied Bollini and the child in the park. With every day's delay, Guillermo was more certain that the boy was his and Caridad's. He would soon have to confess but he couldn't simply jettison all his legal training; he had to have proof before he spoke.

When he arrived at his office, Christina brought in the post. 'Good morning, sir,' she said.

'Good morning to you,' said Guillermo. 'You're looking particularly fetching this morning.'

Christina laughed and left the office. Guillermo was always kind to her and she enjoyed the flattery. But this morning she was anxious to hear what Guillermo would make of one missive, which she had placed at the bottom of the pile of usual letters and bills.

Guillermo quickly worked his way through the letters then came to the neatly pinned sheaf of cyclostyled paper. Christina had left the envelope in which it had arrived clipped to the front. He searched for an accompanying note but there was none. The contents, however, were gold. The name Franco was clear on the file, but the surname had been redacted on every page that it appeared. 'My God,' Guillermo exclaimed when he looked at it. 'This looks like Bollini's police file.'

Included in the papers was a copy of a letter Bollini had written to resign his post as the commandant of the police station and San Juan detention centre. It was dated 10 May, 1977 and addressed to the chief of police. In the middle of the two-paragraph letter were the words: 'We now have our baby and we want to make a life for us all in the country...'

'If we needed any more proof that the guy was guilty,' Guillermo said to himself, 'then this is it.' Except, of course, that the file, and everything in it, was nameless.

Why did Bollini resign? Maybe he was just waiting for a child and then he was off. What did he do for the rest of the Dirty War? And when did he get his present job? The papers raised almost as many questions as they answered. Bollini obviously never went to the country or, if he did, he had come back to the capital to find work. But the dates meshed. If Caridad was pregnant the last time Guillermo saw her at the end of November 1976, she had been carrying his child for about three months. She would have been delivered of the child by May the following year, when Bollini was in charge of the camp.

Then he took the baby and resigned.

Guillermo could scarcely contain himself when he told Clara. 'I'll go to the court first thing tomorrow. They'll have to grant us a subpoena for Bollini to answer – although I'll have to find a way of proving to a judge that the file is Bollini's.'

Guillermo deposited the papers at the court the following morning. It would take at least a week – probably a month – before a writ was produced but it was a start.

As he was leaving, Guillermo ran into a friend. 'Still battling on for those Grandmothers?' It was said in jest, but with a slight sneer.

Guillermo, almost used to it by now, waved and passed on his way. He went back to his office and put in a credible day's work but his mind was elsewhere. He chaired two meetings, wrote some letters, saw two clients about ongoing cases, took a few telephone calls, had a sandwich for lunch.

Late in the afternoon, he went home via the Grandmothers' offices. He stared for a long time at the large map of the capital on the wall of what was once the sitting room. San Juan was indicated with a pin and a piece of red paper. Other pins, with pieces of white paper with a number on them, showed the location of every child found in the Buenos Aires district; on other maps around the walls, there was the location of every child found across the country. Each child had a number; Clara's missing grandson was number four. He had recently been upgraded from 'child' to 'male child' and now he had a name. The Grandmothers referred to him as Paulo.

In the top drawer of the old fireproof steel filing cabinet, the files related to those numbers held every scrap of information about the children. In the second and third drawers, there were lists of children who had not yet been found, filed by the name of their parent or parents if their own names were not known. So far the Grandmothers knew of the existence of 42 children. Some were memories of grandchildren that were known and loved and had disappeared along with their mothers or fathers; most had never been seen outside the prison camps where their mothers had died. The Grandmothers were confident that they could rescue them all, however long it took, and bring the perpetrators of these terrible crimes to justice.

In the bottom drawer was the apotheosis of that belief: the names of the nine children who had been reunited with their birth families. Every night, one of the Grandmothers solemnly locked up the filing cabinet and hid the key. Another key was deposited at their bank and a third was with their lawyers. Every morning when they came into work, the women feared that they would have been robbed overnight until they opened the cabinet. It was not paranoia that governed their feelings; the secret police had targeted the Mothers of the Plaza de Mayo before now and once, in the early days, someone had ransacked the Grandmothers' offices.

As the number of children they found grew, so the amount of information in that cabinet expanded. But the Grandmothers prided themselves on having another failsafe: each time a new child was located, one of them committed all the details to memory. Between them they could remember every detail of every child.

* * *

It was pitch dark by the time Guillermo arrived at his house. He took his dinner from the oven and retired to his study to eat it. As he ate, he thought about his son.

Guillermo stared at the small oil painting on the wall at the side of his desk. The rest of the study was decorated with photographs of Guillermo playing polo, racing, and one from a hunt near New York, with Guillermo clearing a tiger trap on a hireling. This painting though, by Nazareno Orlandi, was one of his favourites; he had bought it at a sale years ago and it was the only art work in his study.

Orlandi was one of the so-called Argentine School of painters, even though he was Italian by birth. This picture showed a small boy, aged about five, astride a large horse. The boy's legs did not reach the stirrups; he looked as though he were just sitting, posing in the sunshine. Even with the impressionistic daubs of paint that made up his face, you could tell that he was laughing. It reminded Guillermo of himself as a boy, sitting on one of his father's horses, and how much he had always wanted a son he could imbue with all his horse sense. He had long given up on that idea; Pilar could not, or would not, have any children. Now he had a son whom he had only just discovered but who he could not yet claim. He went to bed with a troubled mind long before Pilar came home.

* * *

After dinner the following night, Guillermo and Pilar adjourned to the drawing room to watch the television news. Pilar was leafing through a magazine as the headlines rolled. President Alfonsin's speech to Congress … the World Bank loan in jeopardy … a train crash in Tucuman Province killed four people … another secret burial site discovered in the grounds of San Juan prison.

Before the newsreader launched into the top story, the telephone rang; it was Clara. 'Are you watching the news?'

'Yes. Did you know?'

'No, not a thing.'

Guillermo swore under his breath. How did the journalists find out these things? Why didn't the authorities tell the people who were looking for their relatives? The questions raced through his mind as the news rumbled on in the background.

'Let's watch the story and talk afterwards,' he said to Clara. When he put the phone down he turned to Pilar. 'Do you hear that? If they had to execute people, why couldn't they do it legally? Why couldn't they return the bodies to their families? Why…'

Pilar did not let him finish. 'We were fighting a war!' she shouted. 'It was a long time ago and, frankly, I'm not interested.' She flung down the magazine on the sofa and stormed out of the room.

Guillermo was interested. In recent weeks he had read of a professor in England called Jefferies, who was working with DNA, matching samples taken from hair or skin and even bones. With Clara still alive, maybe they could identify Caridad's body from those discovered at

173

the graveyard. Maybe, Guillermo pondered, if they could get a DNA sample – a hair or something – from little Paulo, they could prove beyond doubt that Clara was his grandmother and Caridad was his mother. And that he, Guillermo, was Paulo's father.

Guillermo watched the news about the human remains found at San Juan with mounting irritation. A dog walker had uncovered a bone and the police were called in. Initially they thought they had found just one body; after more digging it was obvious that there were two bodies, and then many more. What started off as a possible murder investigation became a hunt for a serial killer and then, in the space of less than an hour, something more sinister.

A tip-off to a journalist at Channel 7 brought out a television crew who linked the site to the San Juan detention centre. The now-derelict prison buildings were less than less than a quarter of a mile away from the site and between the two were the remains of dog kennels and an old barn. The perimeter fence was broken in several places and the waste ground was increasingly used by dog walkers or courting couples, a sure sign that the terror of the past regime was slowly lifting.

The police had stopped digging and were now standing guard over four indents in the soft earth, screened by banks of trees and about fifty yards from an earth track. Over the last two or three months, they had become more circumspect about digging up the remains of the Dirty War; there was evidence to collect and that took time. It was getting dark, a spokesman said, and a forensic expert from the Presidential Commission for the Disappeared would visit in the morning.

On the telephone afterwards, Guillermo and Clara plotted their day. 'There's no point in going first thing in the morning,' Clara said. 'But I will phone the Commission and find out who will be there.'

Clara already knew about Professor Jefferies in England, and about Dr Clyde Snow in Oklahoma and Dr Mary-Claire King in California, all doing important research work with DNA. But then Clara knew pretty much everything there was to know about tracing children. She had been involved with the Grandmothers since they set themselves up a few months after Caridad disappeared. She had battled through the whole of the murderous time during the Dirty War, the Malvinas War and its aftermath. Now she was safe, but her quarries certainly were not. Clara Silva would bring the whole weight of the law down upon the people who had committed, sanctioned or covered up these terrible crimes.

CHAPTER 19

It took Clara two days to get permission from the Commission and the police for her and Guillermo to visit the burial ground. Given the precision and thoroughness with which the digging team were going about their work, they would not have seen much earlier. A research scientist from America had attached herself to the Commission and taken charge of the work, recruiting a team of doctoral students from the university to help her. Dr Ana Collaris was in her late thirties and had been working with Mary-Claire King at Berkeley when this job had come up. The Commission had previously found burial sites at the ESMA, the Navy's mechanical school in Buenos Aires, and at a site in a market garden. These sites had been partly dug up by bulldozers and much of the evidence ruined. The Commission had realised they needed outside help.

Clara and Guillermo arrived at about ten o'clock and surveyed the scene for some minutes before speaking to anyone. They could see four people excavating the ground and there were probably another three or four hidden from view. The diggers worked in pairs, shielded from the sun by white tarpaulins stretched over four poles pegged to the ground. It looked like back-breaking work as they hunched on their knees, lifting clods of earth carefully, examining each one before placing it on the ground beside the grave.

Clara and Guillermo moved along the orange plastic perimeter fence and asked the nearest young man where they might find Dr Collaris. They followed his directions.

Ana Collaris was expecting them and greeted them warmly. 'We've found six almost complete skeletons so far,' she said matter-of-factly, 'three of which are women. They will have to be examined properly later. But this place should fill in lots of details which we are unclear about.'

They chatted for a few minutes about the Commission's work and how long Dr Collaris intended to stay in Argentina. That would depend, she said, on how much work there was. What nobody could guess was how many bodies they would find on this one site.

Clara asked how difficult it would to work out which of the women might have been pregnant or had recently given birth, and how soon before DNA might be used to establish who the victims were, but she already knew the answers. Some of the women would have recently given birth but it would probably be months before that information could be verified; it would be much longer before the DNA process could be used successfully in

Buenos Aires. And everything would cost money neither the State nor the Grandmothers had available.

Even from the first cursory digging, before Dr Collaris and her team started excavating, it was obvious that there were a lot of bodies buried here. Guillermo went back to the barn and stood on a wall to get a sense of the scale of the place. From his elevated position, he could see very slight differences in the colour of the ground. It looked as though someone had dug long trenches to take the bodies; when one trench was full, they had started another a few feet away. Every body dumped in the trench was covered with earth and presumably a bulldozer had spread earth over the bodies. Some Army engineer had worked out exactly how to dispose of multiple bodies, one or two every day, with the minimum of effort.

Clara, meanwhile, was watching Ana Collaris extract a skull and then a collar bone from a grave. It seemed that two bodies had been flung in here; Clara could already see a second skull protruding from between the leg and foot of another skeleton. Collaris used what looked like an ordinary paintbrush to dislodge the dirt from a skull.

'First inspection: assassination with a bullet,' she told Clara. 'This looks like a bullet hole, shot at close range.' She put the end of her little finger into the hole at the side of the skull then turned it over looking for the exit wound but could not immediately find it. 'The bullet might have emerged below the jaw or even from the neck,' she said quietly. She placed the skull in a cardboard box beside her and reached carefully for the collar bone protruding from the grave. 'All the other skulls we have retrieved don't show that as a method of killing. The skeletons will have to be examined further before we can establish how the people were killed.'

'I think we can be sure they were murdered,' Guillermo said.

'Skeletons are great witnesses,' Ana Collaris told them, before she resumed her careful search. 'They speak softly but they never forget and they never lie.'

'You can tell which are men and which are women but can you tell if the women were pregnant, or had been pregnant?' Guillermo asked.

'Sometimes we can, but not here,' Collaris said. 'That requires work back in the lab. But we can find out everything we need to know from the skeleton: age, sex, when they died, how they died. You'll get a full report, I promise.'

'We should allow the scientists time to be certain,' Clara said to Guillermo, as they thanked Dr Collaris and moved away.

Clara and Guillermo shared a coffee with the diggers and then watched them until lunchtime, chatting sometimes but mostly observing the careful, painstaking work. In those three hours, the excavators had located but not yet unearthed three more skulls. There was clearly much work still to be done at San Juan, much sifting of the evidence and much more evaluation and research. It was a process that could go on for months, years even. Clara, though, never had any doubts: they would get her grandchild back and punish those responsible for abducting him and for murdering his mother. And they would do the same for every child that had gone missing.

On the way back to Clara's apartment, Guillermo again tried to tell her that he was the man Caridad had never spoken about, the father of her child, but the words failed him. He played over in his mind the conversation he had had with Caridad; did she deny that she was pregnant because she was not sure? Or was she not sure of him, of his reaction? He remembered how their rows about politics always got in the way. How right she had been and how wrong he had been, and probably still was. He could not accept all the changes Caridad had wanted but he saw now, clearer than ever, that what she believed in was what any decent person should expect from life. And she had given her life for those beliefs.

'Are you OK?' Clara asked him when they arrived at her apartment. 'It was so horrible.'

'I'm fine,' he replied. 'Maybe a bit shaken by the magnitude of it all.'

They sat for a moment in the car. Guillermo fiddled with the books in the door and then wiped the windscreen. 'Just suppose,' he said at last, without looking at Clara, 'that Bollini and his wife are completely innocent of kidnap. Suppose he didn't do anything illegal in the Dirty War but he was given Paulo as a baby.'

'I know what you are going to say,' Clara said.

'No, hear me out. You saw the relationship between Bollini and the child in the park: the man is besotted with Paulo. After five or ten years of a happy life, what right do we have to take a child away and give him to elderly grandparents? To people he has never known, to...'

Clara put her hand on Guillermo's arm. 'If,' she said slowly, 'if Señor and Señora Bollini are completely innocent, they might be allowed to keep the child although they would have to share him with his real grandparents. The child must know about his past; he must know that his mother and father were killed and that he has blood relatives. And they must be allowed to see the child and to nurture and love him. But if the Bollinis connived in the adoption they must be punished.'

Guillermo had often asked himself the questions he was now putting to Clara, and had never come up with satisfactory answers but now he was getting into his stride. 'Whose rights are we protecting? The child's or the grandparents'?'

'Always the child's. Always. But listen to me. Suppose *you* have a child in the future, and suppose in a year or two the child discovers that he or she was adopted and that you and your wife hid them from their true parents. What would the child think? How damaging would that be?'

'But you still wouldn't take the child from me?'

'If the adoption was completely legal, we could not. But if the adoption was *illegal*, if their real parents or grandparents had no knowledge of it, if the children were *stolen*, if their parents were *murdered*, that is another thing altogether.'

Guillermo was not entirely convinced. 'How could you be sure the child, the children, would be happier in their new homes than they are with the parents they have known all their lives? Surely that is important too?'

'Of course it is important. But it is equally important

that the children know the truth. Otherwise, when they are fifteen or twenty and they find out, they will reject their adoptive parents.'

Clara never raised her voice, never wanted to win for the sake of winning, but she was absolutely convinced by her argument, just as she was convinced of the legitimacy of her case against the Bollinis. Soon, she thought, she would be with her grandson and, through him, reunited with her daughter, Caridad.

Guillermo drove slowly back to his office, worrying about his son and the consequences of finding him. He immersed himself in work for the afternoon, increasingly conscious of the time he was putting into the Grandmother's cause and the questions this was raising at the firm.

CHAPTER 20

It took ten days for the court to grant the paperwork to deliver to the Bollinis. It would take much longer for the bodies uncovered at San Juan to be identified and the causes of death established.

Guillermo was both elated and deeply worried as he and Clara drove out to the suburbs to confront the Bollinis. The day of reckoning with Clara, and with Pilar, was drawing ever closer. He thought about Caridad's child; how could he bring him into his family? One of Guillermo's tennis partners had adopted his illegitimate son and brought him up with his son and daughter. The marriage had stumbled along for a couple of years before it exploded and the man was left with none of his children. The wife had, rather valiantly, Guillermo thought, taken on the boy and kept him, but the whole family had completely rejected Guillermo's friend. The boy was now twelve years old and he despised his father. The wife, meanwhile, now with her adopted son and her own two children, had married again and moved to Chile.

Guillermo knew that was only one case. There were probably hundreds of examples where everything turned out right in the end, where the wrongs of the past were quietly forgotten, where the husband confessed his sins and said 'I'm sorry' and the wife pulled him and his bastard child to her bosom and they all lived happily ever after. He did not think things would end up that way with Pilar.

Guillermo and Clara drew up outside Bollini's house soon after six o'clock. They watched for a moment before Guillermo said: 'Right, let's get it over with.'

They walked up the path to the front door and rang the bell. A few moments later, Eva Bollini answered the door. She didn't say anything but her wide eyes asked the question. It was Clara who answered her. 'Señora Bollini? My name is Clara Silva and this is Guillermo Haynes. He's a lawyer. We've come to ask you some questions. Is your husband here, please?'

'Questions? What about?' Then Eva called to Franco. She turned from the door, making sure she did not open it any wider, and called again, shouting this time.

Franco appeared holding Paulo's hand, and the little boy pushed forward in front of his mother. 'Hello,' he said. 'What is your name?'

The sight of the child made both Clara and Guillermo step back. They were somehow surprised to see him, addressing them as though he were already their friend. Eva Bollini grabbed the boy and pushed him behind her, telling him to go to the kitchen. The moment, if there was a moment, for Clara to talk directly to her grandson, was gone.

'We believe your son is adopted,' Guillermo said firmly. 'He is one of the so-called stolen children, illegally adopted by military or police families during the Dirty War.'

'We believe he is my daughter's son.' Clara took a picture of Caridad out of her bag and pressed it towards Bollini.

Bollini, surprised, took hold of the picture as he moved back into the doorway. 'What do you mean … stolen children … adopted? Is this a joke?'

Guillermo could see that he was flustered. 'I'm serving you with this writ which requires your presence in court.' He flung down the envelope on the mat inside the door. 'We'll see you in court.'

Guillermo and Clara backed off. Bollini raised his arm to threaten them, then looked at the picture and dropped it onto the mat. He clenched his fists and shouted, 'Get out, get out!' then slammed the door hard as he retreated inside.

Bollini's wife was crying. 'Paulo is our son! They can't take him away,' she wailed as Bollini put his arm around her.

'They won't, they can't.' Bollini was already thinking about how he could stop this pesky lawyer in his tracks but for the moment he felt impotent. Since he had left the police force, he had tried to put the Dirty War and everything about it in the background. He'd forced himself to forget the horrors…

After Paulo had gone to bed, he and Eva sat in their small living room and Bollini fretted about the possibilities. Lots of women went through the camp, he thought, but how many were pregnant? He studied the picture that Clara and Guillermo had given him. The name, Caridad Silva, did not register with him; the picture of the dark, attractive young women only told him that she was obviously the daughter of the elderly woman who had ranted at his door.

Bollini was angry with himself for not being able to remember the people who had passed through the camp. Those details had sickened him then, had nearly cost him his marriage and his life. He had struggled to put as much distance as he could between his life then as a cop and his life now, as a low-level security guard at a factory, a husband to Eva and father to Paulo.

'The Grandmothers are picking on me, on us, because they found out I was a policeman,' Bollini muttered to himself. 'I was only doing my job.'

* * *

In the beginning being a policeman was the best job anyone could have. Driving around in a car in a smart uniform, helping to find lost children, rounding up stray animals, bringing villains to justice impressed Eva. Eva, and everyone else, looked up to him; he had a duty to perform and a purpose to his life. He was happy.

Initially he had wanted any job that could save him from working in the leather factory where both his father and mother worked. Their blackened hands and smell were ingrained from his childhood; he remembered them coming home dead tired at the end of the week with little to show for their efforts? He had hated leather ever since; though he still wore shoes, he always wore a fabric belt and never wore a leather jacket.

Bollini was big for his age and handy with his fists; he had thought of becoming a professional boxer but, after a couple of fights in the gym in the town, he looked elsewhere. He drifted into the police by accident after seeing a recruitment poster on his way home one evening and joining up there and then. It took him away from the village, away from the leather factory and into a new life in the city. He could clean his hands of the black tannin that had permanently stained them; he could breathe, without his parents watching. And he could marry Eva because he would have a reasonable salary to keep her and the children they both hoped to have.

Eva was the girl next door in Regaza, two years younger than Franco; they had grown up together. Her parents also worked in the leather factory; Eva herself worked there briefly after she left school. She was so proud when Franco turned up in his police uniform and asked her father if he could marry her. They were young but already lovers, and she followed him first to Cordoba and then on to the capital almost at once. They were married within a month, at the little church at Lujan not far from where they had both grown up.

At first Franco was happy in his job and his advancement was rapid but then politics became more and more divisive and policeman were increasingly used as the hired heavies to protect the government. Then the Dirty War started in earnest; policemen were killed and the hired heavies became hired killers. Franco Bollini could sympathise with the extreme left and yet he despised them.

Eva was scared stiff and wanted him to leave but he had progressed quickly up the chain of command because he could read and write properly and was good at maths. His superiors could see that he was a patriot and an intelligent one, too.

'What price a patriot now?' Bollini thought to himself, when Eva complained about his job.

'We're fighting a war, for Christ's sake,' he would say angrily, and then add up the cost to him and his beloved family of a war over which he had no control.

Unlike some of the men under his command, he did not enjoy torturing or killing people. He thought that most of his prisoners would say anything to stop the pain of the *picana*; they would name another innocent person who would suffer the same as they were doing. Whenever possible, he left the extraction of information to others and did the minimum required to keep his superiors happy. He made it a cardinal rule never to speak of his work at home.

In the end he began to doubt the wisdom of his government and to sympathise with the ideals of some of those who were dying in his jail. What would it hurt, he reasoned, if the rich were taxed a bit more, or vast estates were broken up and given to impoverished peasants? He imagined what would happen to him, and to his wife and parents and cousins and friends, if anyone suspected that he was thinking that way.

The people who arrived at his jail were tortured horribly and most were killed, and for what? To provide a few more names for his henchmen to arrest and bring back for more of the treatment and the same end? Anything would be better than this, Bollini thought. As soon as they were blessed with Paulo, he delivered his resignation letter.

He expected a summons from headquarters, perhaps a dressing-down for evading his duty and a period in semi-disgrace as he saw out his notice. In the event, he was summarily dismissed, not by the commandant who he never met but by a junior aide who spat out his name with contempt as he handed Bollini an envelope with a cheque inside for two thirds of the month that he had already worked. Bollini was sure that was illegal but he did not have the courage to question it.

He handed in his side arm and was marched out of the office, seething with rage but content that he was rid of the job he had grown to hate.

* * *

'I think we should go to bed.' Eva's statement pulled Bollini out of his reverie but did not change his mood. He was racking his brains to remember the women that the people on the doorstep had been talking about.

'No, I'll stay up for a bit. I need to clear my head.'

After a while, when Eva had finished moving around in the bedroom upstairs and silence fell on the little house, Bollini got up and made some *mate*, the traditional Argentine drink made from *yerba,* and sucked through a silver straw. Normally *mate* was a communal drink; many times Bollini and his wife had shared it with friends, handing round the tin cup, pausing only to refill it with hot water. But tonight Bollini sat on his own, sipping and refilling the cup, striving to get some strength from the grassy *yerba* weed. If he could only remember the woman, he might be able to form a plan. He kept looking at the photograph that Clara had forced into his hand.

Since he had left the police force six years before, he had not kept up with his old colleagues. One or two counted as acquaintances; most he had tried to excise from his memory, along with every day he had served at San Juan. But as the night wore on, and the circumstances of the death of the woman and the birth of her son continued to evade him, Bollini resolved to contact the one man who would remember: his deputy Raul Martinez. Bollini had not heard from Martinez, had no idea whether he was alive or dead, but figured it would not be too difficult to find out.

Eva Bollini found her husband slumped in the chair the next morning. She'd slept fitfully, worrying about little Paulo. No one will take him away from me, she thought, then spilt more tears onto the bedclothes.

'You must take Paulo and stay with your sister. You must go to Ushuaia,' Bollini told her when she woke him. Eva's sister had married a fitter in the Navy, who was based in Ushuaia; they could guard her and Paulo until all of this blew over. Franco had that part clear in his mind, even if the main elements of his master plan had still to evolve.

'What about school? What about...' But Eva was

as worried as her husband and couldn't argue with him. In the end, she thought, she would leave Buenos Aires, maybe even Argentina, if that was the only way to keep Paulo.

'When Paulo's at school today you can arrange everything. You must go immediately. They are trying to get at us because I was a policeman.'

'You did nothing wrong, Franco.' Eva was being more brave than truthful but Franco would have none of it.

'You know damn well what I did.'

Bollini had intended to keep the bitterness, the resentment, to himself, but it leached out and attacked the one person he did not want to hurt. The couple were silent for the rest of breakfast, with Eva scarcely able to look at her husband. She did not know the details of what he'd done at San Juan, but she knew that people were taken there and most of them did not come out. She had not liked it, but she had put it all behind her. Now they had a son and could live the life they had dreamed of that day in Lujan when they married. But now the past was alive again, stabbing her in the heart with razor-tipped memories. Those memories had long been confined in dark, never-to-be-revisited depths; last night they had reared up and danced in front of her eyes in Technicolor.

When Eva Bollini took Paulo to school, they walked down the street to the cross roads and then turned right to the bus stop. Along the route, pasted to street lamps and garden fences, were copies of the same poster. The posters showed a small girl looking lost; underneath was written: *My grandma is looking for me. Please help her find me.'* Under that were the names of the Grandmother's Collective and the Commission for the Disappeared, together with the legend: *'Help find the Children of the Disappeared'*

Eva Bollini was certain that the posters had not been there the previous day. She tried to ignore them but Paulo was fascinated and pulled his mother to a halt after they had past the third one. He was a bright boy and was practising his reading. 'Is that girl lost, Mama?'

'No, I don't think she's lost, darling. Come on.'

'Why is her grandma looking for her then?'

'I don't know.' For the first time in her life she was upset that she had taught Paulo to read before he went to school.

* * *

As he made his way to work a short time later, Franco Bollini also noticed the posters outside his house and along the road to the bus stop. That lawyer must have put them up. He cursed violently: the lawyers, the Grandmothers' Collective, the police, the Dirty War, anyone he could think of.

As soon as he could slip away to a phone, he called Alfonso Diaz, the only person he had remained friendly with after he left the police. Alfonso told him he had not seen Martinez for years but thought he was alive and could probably locate him. Bollini arranged to meet Diaz at the football on the Saturday.

Franco Bollini took little Paulo to watch Boca Juniors

play football whenever he could, and particularly when they were playing at La Bombonera Stadium, their home ground. The sound of their cheers rocked the whole neighbourhood as the brilliant Diego Maradona wove his magic on the pitch; deafening roars rose up and the fans jumped in unison whenever Diego scored a goal. That Saturday Boca were playing their long-standing rivals, All Boys, but Paulo would already be on a flight to Ushuaia. At least he would be safe, thought Bollini. The fucking lawyers wouldn't find him there.

'You found Martinez?' Bollini demanded when he met Alfonso at half time.

'Yeah, I found him but I didn't learn much. He pretty much flipped when I asked him anything. I think he's cracking up.'

'He deserves a bit of pressure. He put enough on other people.'

'I don't think you'll get anything.'

'We'll see about that.'

CHAPTER 21

Raul Martinez did not look fit when Bollini and Alfonso Diaz showed up at his apartment later that afternoon.

Bollini did not want Martinez wriggling away now that they had located him. He told Alfonso as much at the football game. 'We'll go today. We'll go past my house and collect my car,' he announced using the full authority of his previous rank. Alfonso didn't really mind. What he had planned for that Saturday night could easily wait. He went back with Bollini and waited by the car for him to get the keys.

'Get in,' Bollini ordered. The two men drove in silence for about ten minutes heading for the Aeroparque. 'What's the address?'

All the horrors of Bollini's time in the police, particularly during the Dirty War, were coming to the surface. He could direct a lot of the hate towards Raul Martinez, his nominal deputy and a man who had certainly not helped him in his fight with his bosses. Bollini felt a new authority cloaking him; he sat taller in the seat of the old Buick as he trundled down towards Avenue Almirante Brown and then across to Azopardo.

The two men rang the doorbell. As soon as Martinez unhooked the latch, they burst into the small, scruffy apartment. Martinez took a moment to realise who they were, then sneered when he recognised Bollini. 'Well, well, Il Commandante. What do you want?'

The words were still coming out of his mouth when Bollini struck him hard in the gut and then slapped him across the mouth, figuring it was better to get his attack in first. Martinez staggered backwards, spluttering and spitting; he looked up for a moment and then sat down on the ground and kept his head down.

It was Bollini's turn to sneer. His ring had cut Martinez's lip and a trickle of blood ran down his chin. It was true what they said about boxers: if you really believe you can win, you can win. He barked at Martinez. 'Get up.' Then, much more softly, he added, 'I want some information and you're going to get it for me.'

'All the records have…'

Bollini kicked Martinez hard in the gut. He could not remember when he had felt this empowered. 'I want everything there is to know about this woman, Caridad Silva.' Bollini had Caridad's photograph and he held it up as he banged Martinez's head against the wall. 'You got that? Caridad S-I-L-V-A.'

Martinez looked blank. 'I got it, but there'll be nothing...'

Bollini did not let Martinez finish. He grabbed him

by the throat and banged his head against the wall again, once, twice, three times. 'You'll know where to find it. I'll be back on Monday. Make sure you get everything there is otherwise I'll cut your ears off and jam a *picana* so far up your arse you'll wish you were dead.'

With Martinez still hanging his head, Bollini gave him one more vicious kick to the jaw. As Martinez fell to the floor, Bollini turned and strode out of the door. Alfonso Diaz ran after him.

It was dark and quite warm as they walked along the road to the car and there was the aroma of jasmine blossom in the air. The single street light cast a glow along the wall and across the road, and they could see a cat walking languidly through a gate on the other side. A dog barked a bit further down the street but the cat did not alter its stride.

'Do you think he will find anything?' Diaz asked as they got into the car. 'I'm not sure there are any records.'

'He'll find them,' Bollini said confidently. 'Or I'll put some more pressure on him.' He spat out the word 'pressure'. Martinez had put enough pressure on other people in the past; it was nothing that he didn't deserve.

Bollini could not remember the dark, good-looking girl who'd been brought in for questioning long before her pregnancy showed. They must have kept her for five or six months or even longer, but a number of pregnant women had passed through the camp. But he could remember being sickened by Raul Martinez's casual brutality. Martinez was brutal to everyone who came in.

On the Monday Bollini drove to Martinez's house

straight from work. He figured that Martinez was now scared of him and would not try anything funny; nevertheless he packed his old Bersa pistol, which he had bought from the police department about a year before he left them. He had not used the gun since; it sat in a drawer by his bed. Now it was in his pocket though he was sure he would not need it.

Bollini drew up at the house, which was in complete darkness. He banged on the door but received no reply. He did not want to waste time so he shouldered it open and marched in, holding the gun. He could see enough in the gloom without putting the lights on. He wandered first into the sitting room and kitchen and then into the bedroom. As he pushed open the door he saw Martinez's legs dangling, his body suspended from the ceiling by a length of lighting flex.

He cursed himself as he felt Martinez's thighs; they were cold and the man had probably been dead for some hours. On the dressing table were some papers and two manila folders. He flicked through the papers: a few bills, a holiday brochure for Cordoba, nothing of interest.

In the first folder Bollini found a copy of Martinez's birth certificate, a letter of commendation from a Commandant Roberto dated 2 June 1980 and various papers relating to a child that Martinez had obviously fathered. There was also a passport, a marriage certificate, a couple of bank statements, three photographs of someone Bollini didn't recognise and a rent book.

In the second folder were photostat copies of two police files, one for Caridad Ernestina Silva, arrested

1 December 1976, and the other for Mercedes Flora Gilluime, arrested 18 February 1977. At first Bollini did not recognise the second name, but on reading the file he certainly did. Mercedes Gilluime, whose mother lived close enough to President Videla to be on friendly enough terms to write to him, had died under interrogation.

'Too much electricity,' Martinez had told him at the time, almost gleefully. The instruction that Bollini had was to send her body back to her family so they might bury her, and he passed that instruction on to Martinez. Martinez had called him down to the room where the body was laid out. Her outstretched legs faced the door. Bollini was almost sick when he saw the body, bruised but otherwise unmarked except for blood around her vagina and the top of her legs. Now he remembered the practical joke that Martinez had played on him.

'She died before she told us anything,' Martinez said. 'So we cut her open and shoved a live rat up her cunt, and then we sewed her up. That will be a surprise for the family!' Bollini had visibly blanched. 'Don't put your hand in there now, Commandante,' Martinez jested. Then he added with relish: 'How much will the rat eat before she gets home?'

What had made Martinez think of Mercedes Gilluime and then kill himself? All Bollini knew was that he would have killed Martinez there and then if he were not already dead. He covered his face with his hands and swore quietly, before attending to the other file.

He was familiar with these innocent-looking clusters of papers and quickly scanned down the first page to the 'Completed…' line. There was just a date in his own handwriting '10 April 1977'. He knew instantly that just having the date meant that the subject had been eliminated, *murdered* by whatever means were convenient at the time after a long period of torture. Bollini had filled in dozens of forms like that; if they didn't say 'Released' or 'Sent to' it meant only one thing.

The printing was faint, the blue of the carbon copy fading now, but the date was clear, as was the fact that Caridad Silva was delivered of a baby on the same day at the prison hospital. He could not make out the child's sex. The attached forms were records of interviews connected with the girl, almost always with people named under torture.

The first related to Lisabet Melissa Orlandi, who was arrested on 2 December 1976. She 'eventually cooperated', the form said. There was half a page of notes about what she had said including: '…says father of Silva's child can only be Guillermo Haynes, lawyer…' Bollini almost fell off the chair as he read that.

The next form was the transcript of an interview with Guillermo Leopoldo Fortunato Haynes and the date 6 December 1976. Raul Martinez and – Bollini could not read the name of the other officer involved – had gone to his office to ask about the circumstances of his association with Caridad Silva. 'Interviewee not very helpful,' Bollini read. He scanned the notes to see if there was any mention of Haynes fathering the child but there was none. At the bottom of the page there was a handwritten note: 'No further action at this time'. Bollini could not decipher signature but the rubber stamp beneath it said 'Capital Police Department'. Underneath, in the same hand as the signature, the remark: 'Ref 22/4/77 618723 Ministry of Defence'.

Bollini understood what that meant: Haynes had been interviewed but not been picked up. 'No further action at this time' meant that, in those days, Haynes had powerful friends in the military. He probably still had.

Bollini gathered up the papers related to Caridad Silva, threw the rest of the folder's contents in the fire grate and reduced them to ashes with his cigarette lighter. There were things he did not want to be reminded of, things he had put to the back of his mind years ago. As the smoke wound its way up the chimney, he thought about the information he had but he was not sure how he could use it without it rebounding on him.

He watched the paper crumble; the fire would be cold by the time anyone else ventured into this bolthole of an apartment. Before he left, he wiped everything he could remember touching with a handkerchief in case the police looked for fingerprints, although Martinez's death certainly looked like suicide.

Bollini wondered why Martinez had ended his life. Perhaps the events of the Dirty War had finally overcome him, or he remembered what he had done to a young woman who was probably completely innocent. And to dozens like her. Bollini shivered when he thought of the things he had done himself, had had to do.

Martinez's flat suggested a pretty impoverished existence: the crumpled, dirty bed linen; the chipped coffee-stained mugs, some still half-full of cold black coffee; a tattered and stained sofa, and a broken kitchen chair. Below the body was another kitchen chair that had obviously been kicked away. There were a few papers and two books, a number of empty bottles, a clock and some dirty washing strewn about, a half-empty carton of milk on the sideboard. It did not amount to much.

Bollini realised he had been lucky to have got out of the police before the senseless killing numbed him forever.

As the ashes still smouldered in the grate Bollini backed out of the door. He had to think about his own future and how he should best deal with Guillermo Leopoldo Fortunato Haynes.

CHAPTER 22

The sun was already hot as Bollini arrived at the private estate; as he drove through imposing iron gates the sky was cloudless and there was not a breath of wind. It had rained heavily during the night and there were still puddles by the roadside; the trees were well into leaf and the shrubs in full colour. On any other occasion, Bollini would have welcomed the weather. Summer had finally arrived and people were out enjoying themselves. Today, though, he was tetchy and a little nervous. He was not sure where his quarry would be, though when he had rung Haynes' office the previous day, pretending to be an old friend, he had been led to believe that Haynes would be here.

Bollini parked in the shade of a larch tree and sauntered down to the pitch. A game was already underway. This was inter-club polo, played every Saturday in the season, and often during the week as well.

To his left, Bollini could see a row of parked horse boxes and a number of horses tied up or being walked about. He walked over and spoke to a female groom. 'Excuse me,' he asked as casually as he could. 'Do you know if Guillermo Haynes is here today?'

The girl looked up and smiled. 'You've just missed him playing. I think you'll find him over there.' She pointed to a horse box about thirty yards away. 'His ponies are tied up behind that box. He'll be there or up at the bar.'

Bollini knew from past experience that the polo set was tight-knit and pretty much everyone knew everyone else. 'Thanks a lot,' he said, secretly congratulating himself as he walked off.

He could hear horses galloping to his right and the cheers from the crowd, some standing, some sitting on the grass with a glass of wine. He could smell the *asado*s and the beef grilling, and he could feel the heat of the sun burning down on him, but he was oblivious to it all. He had his eyes firmly fixed on a pale green horse box. As he rounded the back of it, he saw his quarry. Haynes had not long dismounted and was talking to a groom, his back half turned towards Bollini.

'Señor Haynes.'

Haynes turned and stared at Bollini for what seemed an age. 'Señor Bollini, I didn't expect…'

'You didn't expect me here.'

Haynes recovered his poise and steered Bollini away from the horse box so they could talk with more privacy.

Bollini scarcely missed a beat. 'Perhaps I should have warned you,' he continued. 'But you came to see me, so it seemed only reasonable—'

'What do you want?' Haynes snapped.

'I found out some interesting facts about the Silva case,' Bollini said slowly. It pained Guillermo that Bollini could refer to Caridad in such a way. He was silent, his throat paralysed. Finally he said, rather lamely, 'What are you talking about? If you think some cock and bull story about…'

Bollini raised his hand slowly to silence Haynes. 'I was a constable in the police when I first came here. I came to arrest a man, just like you, who had stolen some gem stones. He said it was a "cock and bull story" too. When his friends found out, they completely disowned him. His behaviour wasn't cricket, or polo or something. "Mine honour is my life…" I'm sure you know your Shakespeare.'

'What are you talking about?' Haynes blustered, walking further away from the crowd.

'I have proof about your relationships with Caridad Silva, Señor Haynes. If it were to fall into the wrong hands…'

'If you're trying to blackmail me, you must be desperate.'

'Señor Haynes, let's not play games. You and I both know what proof there is.' Then he added slowly: 'I don't think your wife would like the details of your affair to go public. Nor would your friends in the Ministry of Defence.'

Haynes, first cowed, then cocky, then cowed again, was now angry. 'If you have proof, you'll need nothing from me. Though I didn't think there was anything illegal about two adults screwing! Even the military allowed that.'

It sounded crude and he had not meant it like that. His relationship with Caridad was different from his other affairs, and never just about sex. Moreover, as he entrenched himself deeper with the Grandmothers, he knew that he should leave Pilar and give up whatever it was that she could contribute to his life. It would never match what he could have had with Caridad, he knew that. But it was as though he could fly a flag for Caridad and somehow be truer to her memory if he were alone.

He attempted a bluff response but Bollini cut him short. 'Hear me out, Señor Haynes. This is the girl whose child you accuse me of stealing. Your work for the Grandmothers' Collective is laudable but to concentrate on this case, which involves a former lover, may be considered...'

'What are you suggesting?'

'Not me, Señor Haynes. But other people might think that, in view of your connections with the military, you could have done more to get her released.'

'That's preposterous.'

'Or maybe you didn't want her released because the child she was carrying was yours.'

Haynes stopped him in mid-stream with a punch which Bollini, surprisingly agile for someone of his size, managed to avoid. 'Did I did say something to alarm you, Señor Haynes? Are you feeling guilty?'

Bollini had had reservations about going to see Haynes; he was worried about his role at St Juan and the memories it might uncover. The sudden realisation that Haynes was the father of the child had dealt him a completely new hand of cards and had to play them. Now it was Haynes who risked discovery and shame. Bollini could leave the polo ground feeling very satisfied with the afternoon's progress.

Guillermo left the ground like a dead man walking. The time was coming much faster than he had anticipated. It would be like the Day of Judgement, when all truths were told, all memories laid bare, all feelings discovered. Guillermo was not sure if he could stand the beacon of light which would illuminate all the shadows in his life and uncover every last secret.

* * *

It was past ten by the time he arrived home. Pilar was awake and furious as he came in the door. 'Where have you been?' she demanded as he walked across the kitchen.

He had been in a bar, trying to decide how to tell Pilar. He had drawn a complete blank and did not wish to be drawn into a lengthy argument now. He muttered, 'I was having a drink after the polo.'

'Don't fucking lie to me.' Pilar didn't normally swear but she was livid. 'It's bad enough having my husband chase every woman under twenty and having their fathers or husbands breathing down the phone at me,' she shrieked. And then, as an afterthought, she grabbed the nearest thing and flung it in his direction. The silver picture frame caught Guillermo under the chin and dropped to the ground, its glass shattering on the marble floor.

He could feel the blood running from the wound in his chin. 'For Christ's sake, Pilar…'

'So what if it's broken. It's mine! Everything in this

apartment is mine,' Pilar shouted, warming to her theme. 'And the company is mine too, and don't you forget it.'

'Who phoned you?'

'I don't know who phoned but I know what he said. You bastard!' She threw another picture frame at him but this time he ducked.

'I'm sorry you had to find out about this … in this way. I really did not want you to. It was a long time ago.'

'So what are you trying to do now – atone?'

'I'm just trying to make sure that those who committed crimes are punished for them, and—'

'The only person who is being punished is me, and I don't like it.' Pilar picked up another picture frame but Guillermo grabbed her hand.

'For Christ's sake, Pilar, I'm only doing my job.'

'Your job?' Pilar screamed. 'Your job?'

'Look, I meant… My work with the Grandmothers, it's what we need to do if we're to stay in business.' He was trying to appeal to Pilar's link with the company, her love of money, anything. He was desperate. But then he misjudged her. 'Don't tell me you've never—'

'You know damn well I haven't, in spite of plenty of offers – half of them from your friends. You disgust me.' She turned and strode into the drawing room.

Guillermo shouted after her, 'It was all a long time ago. I'm sorry.'

Pilar was breathing heavily, regretting her loss of temper. She sniffed and straightened her back, as though she were about to return to Guillermo. Then she smiled and said quietly, 'Has it ever occurred to you who shopped your little girlfriend all those years ago.'

She regretted saying it immediately the words were out of her mouth. She had known for a while that her marriage with Guillermo was faltering, that they were growing apart. His involvement with the Grandmothers was part of that.

All those years ago she had never intended to have Caridad killed. Had her brother not been in such a powerful position in the Army, things might have been different. She remembered voicing her fears about Guillermo's affair and her brother telling her: 'Don't worry about it. Consider it done.' And it *was* done. And now she had told Guillermo.

It took a moment for Guillermo to understand what she had said. His Caridad, his baby, consigned to death by a deliberate act by his wife. It was too horrible to contemplate. 'You did that. Why?'

'Why do you think? I wanted to save our marriage!'

He caught his breath, leaned on the table, spat out the words. 'You bitch, you utter *bitch*.'

She laughed. 'I didn't know she was pregnant, by the way. What are you going to say when you find your precious son? Will you tell him that your wife killed his mother?'

He was already moving towards her. He grabbed her by the arms and pushed her against the wall. He raised his hand to slap her before the dreadful realisation of what he was doing caught up with him. He let her go and stepped away, hanging his head. 'I'm sorry,' he said. 'I'm so sorry. I really didn't want you to find out this way.'

Pilar snorted. 'If you think I give a damn about that woman, you're wrong. You're very wrong. Now get out!' She picked up another picture frame to throw at him.

Guillermo was angry with himself but even angrier with Pilar. He collected his car keys and drove off into the night. He needed to think about his future. He could never live with Pilar now, not after what she had done. But he knew that if he had confessed to Pilar immediately Caridad had disappeared, he might have saved her. Sobbing, he drove furiously, tyres squealing round corners.

Later that evening he drove back to the house. Pilar had gone out; at least, her car was not in the garage. He made no noise going in, just in case she was there, but the house was dark and empty. He packed a small suitcase of clothes and wrote a short note, telling her that he could not possibly stay with her knowing what she had done. He would check into a hotel temporarily and arrange to collect his belongings at a later date. His problems, however, were far from over.

'Don't reproach yourself,' Clara said next morning, when Guillermo told her the story of his meeting at the polo ground. He had mentioned nothing of his clash at home. Now Pilar knew he had fathered Caridad's child and Clara did not. He had been searching since the beginning for a time to tell Clara, but this was definitely not it.

'Bollini must be scared to have threatened you, which means we're on the right track,' Clara continued. She looked at his chin and the ugly welt that Pilar's picture frame had caused. 'He certainly caught you a blow,' she said sympathetically.

Guillermo bit his tongue. How could he say it was Pilar rather than Bollini who had drawn his blood? He also omitted to say that he, Guillermo, had tried to floor Bollini and that Bollini had simply walked away. He wanted to tell Clara why Bollini had threatened him but somehow the words would not form. He could not, at that moment, explain anything to Clara.

'Are you frightened?' she asked him.

'Not of Bollini.'

'He must be scared, to threaten you and to strike you.'

'He seemed so cocky. He did say he'd been to the club before, when he was a police constable.'

'So how did he end up at San Juan?'

'The police station and the prison, across the road from each other, were obviously one place.'

'But we've been down that road before.' Now Clara sounded despondent. 'We've scoured the whole area and there's still nothing to tie him in.'

'Exactly. Everything we have on Bollini is circumstantial; nothing that would convict him in court.' Guillermo grew slightly pompous. 'For a lawyer that is not sufficient.'

'For a grandmother, it is not necessary to have proof that will stand up in court. We know our own blood.'

Clara hugged him as he left, holding him close and kissing him on both cheeks. 'Don't worry. It will come.'

Guillermo knew he should have confessed to Clara but, as so many times before, he chickened out. Tomorrow, he thought, as he left Clara's apartment.

CHAPTER 23

The following morning rose bright and blue-skied, though rain was forecast for later in the day. Guillermo drove out to Hurlingham for a ride and a swim and some time in the gym. He wondered whether he should ring Clara when he got to work, or wait for another tomorrow.

When he arrived at his office, Clara had already rung him. There was a message on his desk saying simply: 'Ring me. It's urgent.'

Guillermo put off making the call for about twenty minutes as he desperately tried to think of something he could say to expiate his guilt. He should have told her about his affair with Caridad weeks ago but his cowardice had been too great.

Clara rang again and this time he took the call. She spoke quietly, and without emphasis. 'Can you come over?'

'I think I know what this is about and I can…..'

'Come over *now*,' Clara said again.

'Alright,' he replied meekly. 'I'm on my way.'

'I had a phone call, from a man,' Clara told him when he arrived at her door half an hour later. 'He didn't say who he was, but he did tell me some things about you.' She was calm but she had obviously been crying.

'I wanted to tell you. I did try to tell you many times,' Guillermo mumbled. His past triumphs with the Grandmothers seemed puny compared to his deception. But, true to form, he had been a coward before and he was a coward now. 'I did not actually lie to you. I swear I didn't know Caridad was pregnant until I saw you on the television news at the Plaza de Mayo. I swear that.'

'You didn't even tell me you knew her, that you had a relationship with her. You kept the last months of my daughter's life hidden from me,' Clara said bitterly. She started to cry again. 'There was so much you could have told me.'

Guillermo's eyes were wet; he bent forward, his hands on his knees, his shoulders hunched. 'I was going to ask her to marry me. We went out to a restaurant and a man was arrested. We argued and I never saw her again. We spoke on the phone and we made up. But I never saw her again.'

The clatter of traffic outside filtered up to the fourth floor and the harsh midday sun streamed through the gaps in the curtains. The apartment was, as always, immaculately polished and neat. For once, though, Clara was not in control; she sat low in her chair, her back stooped and her hair flopping over her face.

Guillermo's almost legendary capacity to argue, to defuse a situation with a sane interjection or timely comment, had completely deserted him. He respected Clara, had grown to love her, and he hated himself now for the trouble he was causing. It would have been better, he thought, if they had never met.

If the television had not been on in his office that evening, he might never have known of Clara's existence. If the cameras had not alighted on Caridad's picture, held aloft by one of hundreds of white head-scarfed women marching round the square, he might have remained unaware of the terrifying progress of the Dirty War. He might have grown old thinking that the junta was right all along. But he had seen the picture and he had seen Clara and he had met her.

What could he have done to save Caridad? He had never found the answer but today he was certain he could have done something, *should* have done something. It was not because he did not love her enough; it was because he could not muster the courage.

'I think you had better go now.' Clara spoke firmly. As she got up, she straightened her skirt and pulled down her cardigan. 'I need a little time to grieve on my own.'

Guillermo stumbled to his feet and made for the door. At the door she announced: 'Perhaps we will speak tomorrow.' She turned away before he could say any more. He walked slowly down the corridor to the stairwell, then down the stairs.

Guillermo was unclear where he stood. He fretted about it all the way back to the hotel, all that night and all the next morning. He mulled over Clara's last words to him; they gave him hope and despair in equal measure.

Several times he went to call her but each time he stopped with his hand on the phone, or put the receiver down half way through dialling the number.

That lunchtime, he walked out of his office and drove across town to the offices of the Grandmothers. As he parked the car and mounted the steps to the fifth floor, he was determined to see her but, as the office grew nearer, his pace slowed. He was shaking when he rang the bell. He heard footsteps and the bolts and chains being unlocked; he nearly fled but then the door opened, and Clara was there.

For an instant she didn't move and then, as usual, she kissed him on both cheeks. She held him a little tighter than had been her habit until now. 'I know a tiny bit more about Caridad now,' she said quietly. 'I know the name of her lover, the father of my grandchild. Come, we have much work to do.'

Guillermo told Clara that he had left Pilar and had moved into the Intercontinental Hotel. She would have found out the minute she had phoned him at home and he had nothing else to hide now.

That night, long after he had left the Grandmothers' offices, Guillermo sat in his car watching the moon rise over the Palermo lakes. He had driven out to Palermo instead of going back to his hotel because he needed to think. He felt as though he had achieved something even though, realistically, all he had done was escape the consequences of lying to Clara. Deep in his heart, he knew that this was not a time to congratulate himself.

He felt like a cat that was rapidly losing its nine lives.

He had lost a life when Caridad went missing and another when the police came to his office. He had probably lost a life when the bomb exploded and wrecked General Horloz's arm, and another when his father was killed. Did he have enough lives left to put Bollini in jail and to find his son?

CHAPTER 24

In the week that followed, Guillermo realised how few people he knew in the police force. He was determined to mine them for any information they had; pretty soon he learnt that that wasn't very much. He also discovered how few of his friends he could really trust.

Guillermo was past caring about himself. He would find out about Bollini's past and he would nail him for everything he could. He felt empowered, ruthless, unforgiving. He used the full force of his legal practice to persuade reluctant military personnel to cooperate and he even persuaded his fellow partners at Berruti, Pasquale and Haynes to bear with him.

'It's good for business,' he argued with his fellow partners at their weekly meetings. 'We have to move with the times. We've got a new president and we need to keep in with him and the new government, otherwise they'll chop us off at the knees. It will be good for our business generally to have a clients from all shades of the political spectrum.'

It was not an argument his colleagues embraced but even they could see the advantages of sucking up to the new regime. Business was business after all, and times were hard. Inflation was rocketing and the firm was not exactly booming. On the other hand, their military and ex-military clients still sought their services now that they needed defending, and the partners did not want to do anything to alienate them. The arguments between the partners became increasingly heated but, for the moment, Guillermo had his way.

Guillermo was playing a clever game. He actively sought clients who had fallen foul of the *ancien régime* but whose patriotism could not be doubted, and he spread these out among the other lawyers. He lunched with the heads of various charities and the NGOs which had sprung up in the benevolent climate of the new democracy, but he never neglected the families of his existing clients whose affairs he had dealt with for years. He used every ounce of his charm to placate the elderly widows of ex-military officers who still yearned for the old days. 'This government is what the people wanted, and we should give it a chance,' he said. 'We need to sort out the economy first and by the time of the next election we can vote for a government which we want.'

It sounded convincing to the lonely old women who had lost their husbands and whose world had now suddenly changed, or to the old soldiers who had been overtaken by events but who clung to the belief that everything in the past had been right and eventually would be returned to them. Meanwhile, Guillermo feverishly searched for anything which would link Bollini to the Dirty War.

He was in court one day, sitting in the public gallery listening to the testimony of a minor official at the San Juan prison. The judge was being especially lenient and allowed the questioning to go on, often in purposeless directions, whilst the advocates on both sides sought to tie up the case. Guillermo had come to hear the evidence of the defendant; eventually the defence counsel called the man to the stand.

The prisoner, Lieutenant Jorge Amrico, lumbered up, swore his oath on the Bible, and then stood passively waiting for the questions. He was a swarthy man, aged about forty; his past had now caught up with him but so far he had only been charged with holding prisoners illegally.

The court room was stuffy and Amrico was sweating.

'You witnessed a number of incidents of torture but you didn't take part yourself?' his counsel asked.

'Yes, sir.'

'Even under orders?'

'Yes, sir, I mean no, sir.'

The case droned on, clearly going nowhere. When the judge called the proceedings to a halt for the day, Guillermo was glad to get outside. A plan was already forming in his mind, a plan that would surely nail Bollini firmly to the cross.

In the lobby Guillermo came face to face with a woman he could not place. He was about to walk past her when she put out her hand to stop him. 'Advocate Haynes.'

'Yes? I'm sorry, do I know you?'

'I'm Lisabet Orlandi.'

Six or seven years had etched lines on her face and bags under her eyes. She walked with a slight stoop, which made her appear older than she was. Her hair was tied back and she carried her glasses in her hand. Guillermo looked blankly at her.

'I was a friend of Caridad's.'

And then he remembered. He felt a crushing blow to his ribs and he spluttered and coughed; he was panic stricken. He had never met Lisabet but she had spoken to him; he could hear her voice on the telephone on that terrible, rain-soaked morning, pleading with him when she told him that Caridad had disappeared. He could trace all his troubles to that very moment.

'Of course,' he muttered when he could finally speak. 'I'm sorry I didn't…'

'We never met when…' Lisabet couldn't finish, but Guillermo knew what she was going to say.

'Yes... I mean no…'

'I knew you were helping the Grandmothers,' she said and they looked at each other in silence.

Guillermo remembered the day they had talked on the telephone. He remembered his panic and hers. He remembered telling Lisabet to go back to the university and not to tell anyone that she had talked to him. Leave it to him, he had said, and he would sort everything out. He thought about that day often, wondering how Caridad would have reacted if their positions had been reversed. And now he was facing Lisabet for the first time.

Eventually Guillermo said slowly, 'Did you know Caridad was pregnant? She didn't tell me. I asked her but she denied it, she—'

Lisabet interrupted him. 'She was going to have an abortion, but she couldn't go through with it. She wanted to have your baby.'

Guillermo ushered her outside and across the road to a tea shop. 'I don't understand why she couldn't tell me,' he said when they were sitting down. 'We never lied to each other, or at least I never lied to her.'

'She loved you, that was all.'

There was another long silence, broken eventually by Lisabet. 'I was lucky. I got out.'

'What do you mean?'

'They let me go.'

It took Guillermo a moment to understand what she meant. 'You mean you were arrested? They let you go?'

Lisabet started to cry. 'Yes,' she mumbled.

'I've not seen your testimony. I've read every line of everyone who—'

'I've been too ashamed to go to the Commission. I failed Caridad too.'

'Were you tortured? No, I'm sorry, I shouldn't ask...'

'Yes, I was. Look at me.' She opened her arms as if she were revealing something to Guillermo. 'But I told them everything I knew straight away. After about a week they let me go, just threw me out on the street outside the prison. I could hardly walk but I was alive.' She paused. 'I told them about you too. I'm sorry.'

'What could you tell them? The police came to see me

and I said that Caridad had visited my office with some legal query after I met her in a restaurant. I think they were just fishing.'

Guillermo had not told them how he was ready to change his life for Caridad, of their shared passion and laughter, of the arguments they had and the joy of making up. He had not told them any of that, and he did not tell Lisabet either.

CHAPTER 25

Rank, status, social position, call it what you will, still carried weight in Argentina, at least among the functionaries, and Guillermo counted the minions in the police and the justice department, those who kept the wheels turning, as functionaries. A couple of phone calls, some flattery, some threats and a liberal sprinkling of the name Berruti, Pasquale and Haynes usually got him what he wanted.

It was soon after eight, pitch black, and the building looked every inch a prison even though it was an ordinary office block with cells below. Guillermo walked across the road from the high court and down a street to the left, and then into the side entrance. He went down a flight of stairs and came to the night reception desk. He rang the bell for service; eventually a man unbolted the door and emerged. Seeing Guillermo, he paused then stretched out his hand for the cash. In the end that was all that was needed. Guillermo was escorted down another flight of stairs and through a reinforced door to the cells.

'Here we are,' said the man. 'Don't be all night. I'm off at eight o'clock.' He unbolted the cell door on his left, ushered Guillermo inside, and then re-bolted it.

The corridor down which they had walked was gloomy but it was bright inside the cell; the fluorescent light shone unmercifully and illuminated every corner. In the corner there was a chamber pot and a bucket of water; to the left a bed, and on the right-hand wall a small table and a chair where the prisoner was sitting. He was quite small and had a long scar on his forehead, as though someone had tried to cut him open and take out his brain. He was balding, his remaining hair silver-grey, and he had a grey moustache which looked as though it would trap soup. He wore a grey shirt and blue jeans which had not been washed for a while. He looked up in surprise as Guillermo entered.

'You don't know me,' Guillermo said quickly, silencing the man's unasked question. 'But you soon will if you don't cooperate.'

Jorge Amrico looked fearful; there was something about this man he did not like and it worried him.

Guillermo sat down on the bed and lifted his briefcase onto his knee. 'My name is Guillermo Haynes and I'm a lawyer. I might be able to help you.' He paused and took some papers out of the case. 'Or I might leave you in very serious trouble.' He accentuated the word 'very'. 'It's up to you.'

'I don't know what you're talking about, b—'

'I want some information.' Guillermo interrupted. He didn't want any discussion with this man, only answers.

'If you provide that information, I will help you. If you don't…'

'What information can I possibly have for you?' Amrico asked. 'I am on trial for doing my duty and I can only tell the truth.'

Guillermo removed some papers from his briefcase and placed it on the floor, next to his feet. He didn't once look up. 'Let's see, shall we? Who ran the adoptions at San Juan detention centre?'

'What adoptions?'

Guillermo smiled then flicked through the pages in his hand. 'This is the testimony of Elenore Micheala. She was one of the rare ones freed from San Juan after being severely tortured. She describes and, where she can, she names her torturers – or at least gives their Christian names. You are not among them. Yet.' He paused. 'Though your face is quite easy to describe.' He smiled and turned the page towards Amrico so that he could read it. Then he continued. 'I have nine testimonies from former prisoners at San Juan and I can get your name on each on them as a torturer. You understand what that would mean?'

The half-smile of confusion on Amrico's face froze then slowly disappeared. His eyes narrowed; suddenly he wanted to negotiate. 'Look, if anybody finds out I've been talking to you, even now, I could be—'

'Your name on these testimonies will do you far more damage than anyone you're protecting. For a start, it'll put you away for ten years.'

'Look, Señor, I really don't know anything. I was a driver at San Juan.'

'And you'll become a torturer at the stroke of my pen.' Guillermo pulled out his pen as though to write on one of the forms.

'Please, Señor...'

'Just tell me who ran the adoptions at San Juan.'

'As far as I know it was the commandant.'

'Name?'

Amrico paused, then he looked straight at Guillermo. 'Duarte,' he said firmly. 'Franco Duarte.'

Guillermo was dumbfounded. 'Duarte,' he repeated. 'Are you sure?'

'Yes, I'm sure.'

Guillermo thought for a moment and searched in his briefcase for the photograph he had of Bollini. 'Is this him?'

Amrico studied the photograph. 'I'm sorry, I can't tell. But the commandant was called Duarte.'

Guillermo was struggling to retain his temper. He looked around the room. Finally he said, 'Describe him to me.'

'It was a long time ago.'

Guillermo wanted to strike the man but he swallowed his temper and simply repeated the command. '*Describe* him to me.'

'One metre eighty. Heavily built, big man. Short thin hair, brown. Big nose. Left handed.'

Guillermo smiled slowly. His mind flashed back to that afternoon at the polo ground when he had thrown a punch at Bollini. Bollini had squared up to the attack and then backed off, dropping into a classic boxer's position, with his right hand raised and his left poised for the big jab. Guillermo had not realised it before but Bollini must be left handed.

'Left handed,' he murmured as he put the photograph away.

It was hardly evidence that would stand up in court: a driver at San Juan didn't recognise the picture of the supposed commandant, remembered his name as something different, and said he was left handed. But Guillermo had a spring in his step and was smiling as he left the police station. Bollini must have changed his name; how stupid that Guillermo hadn't thought of it before. That was obviously why those painstaking searches had not turned up a shred of evidence to put Bollini in the police force, let alone be the commandant of a prison unit and the torturer of hundreds, perhaps thousands, of victims. It was why Bollini's name had been excised from the records which Guillermo had found in Martinez's apartment.

The following morning, Guillermo was in his office early, rifling through papers, barking orders down the telephone and despatching his clerk to trawl through the Army and police records for a man called Duarte. Possibly, probably, Franco Duarte. By 11.30 the clerk was on the telephone saying he had found nothing.

'For Christ's sake!' Guillermo yelled. 'There must be another copy of the Army list or the police list somewhere that has his name in it. He was in the fucking Army or the police!'

The clerk went back to his searches, a little put out

by Guillermo's reaction. Guillermo himself, despite his frustration at the delay, was ecstatic; he was getting nearer to his quarry and he had to relay the news to Clara.

'I've got some good news and some not so good news, but it's going to get better,' he blurted out as soon as she came on the line.

CHAPTER 26

It was soon obvious to Franco Bollini that his idea of outing Guillermo had not had the desired effect.

The dark clouds rolling in from the South Atlantic, up the River Plate basin and over Buenos Aires, were nothing compared to the storm that was raging in Bollini's head. Two days ago he had received a letter at his home addressed to Franco Duarte, from Haynes' firm, asking him to confirm his change of name. The day after a summons from the court was delivered, addressed to Franco Bollini, but the name mattered little. Just as he had decided, when little Paulo was born, that it was time to leave the police, to change careers for the sake of Eva, Paulo and himself, now it was time to stop Guillermo Haynes once and for all. If it meant he had to murder Haynes with his bare hands, he would, for Eva and for Paulo, and… His thoughts stumbled. He had some letters to write.

The next day Pilar saw Bollini's letter on the hall table,

a long brown envelope with a typewritten address: Señora Pilar Pasquale-Haynes, 20 Marcello T. Alvear Street. A similar envelope had been addressed to Berruti, Pasquale and Haynes, and been hand-delivered that morning. Bollini was not sure if Pilar knew about Caridad, but he was sure the company did not. Inside both envelopes was a short typed note explaining the circumstances of Guillermo's relationship with Caridad Silva plus copies of her police file.

It certainly caused an explosion when Guillermo breezed into the office that morning. 'Señor Haynes.' Christina's face was flushed when she burst into his office a moment after he arrived. 'The partners would like to see you in Señor Berruti's office. Now.' She did not know the reason for the call from Kingston Berruti's office, but there was no doubt of its urgency. When Guillermo seemed unmoved she said again, 'Now, if you please, sir. I think it's urgent. I *know* it's urgent.'

Five of the eight-man board of Berruti, Pasquale and Haynes were gathered around the table in Señor Berruti's room, with Kingston Berruti at the head of the table. The air was thick with cigar smoke, the atmosphere pungent with hypocrisy. All their pent-up anger and emotion over the Dirty War and its failings, the anger about lost patronage and lost business, focused on Guillermo. They had been forced to recognise that a turning point in Argentina's political history had been reached and that Guillermo's arguments for a more egalitarian approach had substance and they hated him for it.

Almost every man in the room had a mistress, some

of them installed in apartments on Avenida Sante Fe or Marcel T. Alvear Street, others residing with their husbands who themselves probably had mistresses. Even though they did not utter a word and left the talking to Kingston Berruti, the board members condemned Guillermo for dragging the company into an unseemly struggle with the past for the sake of a woman.

Their terms were simple. One: he must leave immediately and not use the firm's name in any of his future dealings. Two: he must offer his shares in the company to the other board members who would give him a good price. Three: he must sever all relations with the firm. Three was unstated, since his relationship with Pilar remained, but the future governance of the company was removed from his shoulders. The company name would revert to Berruti and Pasquale, even though there were no Pasquales working at the moment; the name Haynes would be excised from the company and its collective memory as quickly as possible.

A document for Guillermo's signature had already been prepared, detailing the terms and his pay-out. Kingston Berruti left him in no doubt that the latter would be in jeopardy if he refused to sign immediately. So Guillermo signed, using the black Mont Blanc fountain pen which Caridad had given him and which he had kept in his office ever since, keeping it safe to remind him constantly of her.

I really thought that I could hang onto the firm, even though I was going to separate from Pilar, Guillermo thought, although that seemed entirely academic now.

'I signed. What else could I do?' Guillermo explained

to Clara on the phone, as he cleared the personal items from his office under the watchful eye of Alberto, the faithful old security man he had always liked.

As soon as he put the phone down, it rang again. This time it was Pilar, asking him to come to the house immediately. He drove home; the car was the only thing that belonged to the office that he could keep, until the lease ran out.

He had not spoken to Pilar since she had told him what she had done. For the first time since he was fired, he choked and fought back tears. He still could not believe that Pilar had sent Caridad to her death.

Guillermo was about to open the door with his key when it was opened for him. Pilar was not alone; she was flanked by her brother, Felix, and Alphonso Spengetti, one of the lawyers from the office. Guillermo had always regarded Spengetti he as a friend but clearly now he was acting for the other side.

Pilar was icy cold and controlled. She walked into the drawing room and sat down, motioning to the others to do the same. Guillermo was about to speak but she silenced him by raising her hand slightly and holding her eyes on him.

'You have already left this house but this makes it official. If you go now, having signed this document, we will make it easy for you. If you do not…' She waved her hand at Spengetti who opened his briefcase and produced a three-page letter. He handed it to Pilar who passed it to Guillermo without a word.

Spengetti broke the silence. 'I think you should read

this and then sign. There will be no discussion.'

It was obvious that Pilar had been to the office. Old man Berruti had had the morning to work out what to do and he had used the time sensibly, as one would expect a wily lawyer to do. He had determined the company's response and been generous, but he could not dictate Pilar's response in the same way, even though he'd known her since she was born and her late father was his former partner and his oldest friend. Berruti could only advise and did so, then left it to Spengetti, an earnest and able partner in the firm, to hone the details.

Guillermo saw that Pilar and Spengetti had also been generous with their terms, but there was no doubt that they wanted him out without a fuss. He put his head in his hands and reflected on the mess he was now in. Like a firefighter watching a building burn, he saw the rafters of his soft and easy life crashing down, one by one. He could envisage his whole life ending as a pile of smouldering rubble.

'I would like a moment to read this through again and consider my position. I won't be long.'

He stood and walked to his study. By the time he got there, his head was clearer. His thoughts of heading straight to the gun safe in the study and blasting his brains out had been dismissed.

A wind was blowing and he smelled mimosa wafting in from the garden. It was not the Zonda wind that blew across the Andes in the west of the country, which he remembered vividly from his childhood, but it felt like it. He could taste the breeze as he stood at the open window and it cleared his mind. He had to address his predicament as a lawyer would.

He read Pilar's terms again, and then a second time. Just like the company, she was making a once and final offer. Pilar and he would formally separate and Pilar would seek to have the marriage annulled, something that he would not fight. *In extremis*, they would divorce.

The proposed financial settlement would pay for the upkeep of his polo ponies for a while, but clearly he would have to start earning some proper money if he was to maintain anything approaching his present lifestyle. He was thankful now for his pay off from the company and for the sale of his company shares; for a year or two he could live well. And he could keep the house at Tigre. That clause made him smile ruefully; the house at Tigre was his anyway, though he would not bother to point that out to Pilar and her team of lawyers. It had never belonged to Pilar or her family, and he knew she hated it. Guillermo had inherited it from his father and shared it with his brother until Horacio was killed in the war; the house had been a refuge to both brothers since they were children. But Guillermo was not in the mood for arguing and he accepted the settlement gratefully. He signed with Caridad's pen, and that was that.

CHAPTER 27

There was no food in the house in Tigre, and no telephone. Guillermo had lit a fire but he was still cold. Dawn was creeping in, grey and overcast, affording no respite from the long, dark night.

He had come to Tigre the night before, hastily checking out of his hotel in town and arriving on the last boat. He had flopped down on the sofa and sat looking at the wall, the blank television, the Indian rug, the woollen blanket, the empty room. He pulled the rug around him when it grew colder and eventually lit the fire which still flickered in the grate but did not emit much heat. Every hour or so he put some more wood on it and for a while it blazed before subsiding again. He dozed, fitfully. He could see Caridad here, feel her skin, hear her laughter, smell her body, inhale her breath. In this house she had always been close to him. But now she was far away. Gone. Dead. Now the house seemed empty, forlorn, unloved.

He would have to go back into town to get some food

if he was going to stay. He knew he would not stay for long. The little house at Tigre was for weekends and fun, for parties, surprise visits, a little of what the British still called 'how's your father'. Much as he loved it, it would not suit him to stay out here even for a week. He had come here the previous night to consider his future, to plan his next move, and he had been completely unsuccessful.

He thought of going down to the *estancia* and staying with his mother for a while but he knew that would not work out. He had to go back to town and get on with his life.

Guillermo was off the ferry and driving back into Buenos Aires before he worked out exactly what he would do. He thought of checking back in to the Intercontinental Hotel but decided against it. He ran through his friends and decided against each one. Either their politics or their wives would prevent him staying with his married male friends long term; even a day or two would be embarrassing. Some friends were unmarried or divorced but he couldn't envisage sharing his woes with any of them. He realised that he didn't know any of his female friends well enough to ask to stay even for a few nights; anyway, most of them were also Pilar's friends. He thought of Lisabet and hatched a hare-brained scheme to camp out with her, the one other person in the world who felt guilty about what she had not done for Caridad. But he knew that was hopeless and he did not even try to look up her number.

He drove aimlessly up one avenue and down another until he turned into Tucuman and checked into the

Claridge Hotel. The grand pillars at the entrance spoke of its former grandeur and the rooms were large and comfortable. It was not the kind of hotel where he would bump into friends unless, like him on one previous occasion, they had booked a room with a girl for the night.

His friends would soon know about his fall from grace but at the moment he did not relish the thought of explaining the situation to anyone. It felt worse to be thrown out of his house and job rather than leave of his own volition and the real reason for his downfall, his relationship with Caridad, would soon set tongues tittle-tattling all over town.

He told the clerk he was not sure how long he would be staying. He still had only the suitcase he had packed at home the night Pilar told him she had reported Caridad to the authorities. He would have to make an appointment with Pilar to collect some more of his belongings from the house. He marvelled at his wife's self-control and then cursed her for her haughtiness; he cursed her more for sending Caridad to her death.

His life had unravelled at a furious pace. Yesterday he was a partner in one of the capital's most prestigious law firms, with a house and family and friends, a solid position in society and a full social calendar. Today he had nothing. He thought of going to Europe for a couple of months, or to America or Brazil, but no destination beckoned. Besides, going away would delay him putting Franco Bollini on trial for Caridad's murder and for kidnapping his child.

Guillermo resolved to press on with this work; his next

appointment had to be with Clara and the Grandmothers. A little while later, he walked up to the fifth floor of the Grandmothers' building and rang the bell.

Clara opened the door, looking fresh and composed and quite unlike the wretched figure he had last seen in her apartment two days before. 'I thought you had abandoned us,' she said as she embraced him. 'I rang your office yesterday and Christina told me what had happened. What are you going to do?'

'I am going to find my son, your grandson.'

'Good. You have achieved so much for us already, but this will be your finest achievement.'

That evening, Guillermo had dinner with Clara. It was early and there was hardly anyone else in the restaurant. They were tucked away at the back, with no other diners within earshot. Guillermo explained Pilar's terms to Clara, and that he had checked into the Claridge for a short period.

She was clearly upset for him. 'You men,' she said, shaking her head, as they plotted their next move. She put her hand on his. 'I feel sorry for you and for your wife, but I'm sure it will all work out for you in the end.'

'Thanks,' he said, and a moment later: 'I don't deserve you.'

'Because I am not angry? I am angry; very, very angry.'

'Then why?'

'I wasn't married to you when you had an affair with Caridad. And it was a long time ago.'

'I did love Caridad. You do believe that?'

'Yes, I think you did love her, in your way.'

'And you do believe that I wanted to marry her? I was about to ask her. You believe that, don't you?'

Clara paused and looked away, then turned back to him. 'I believe that. But did you do everything you could to free her after she was taken?'

Now it was Guillermo's turn to look away. The Grand Canyon opened up between them. 'I thought I did but I didn't, did I?'

'I don't know.'

They were silent for a while then Clara said: 'I know that if you help locate your son, and others imprisoned by that ghastly regime, that will make some amends.'

Guillermo realised that Clara thought better of him than he did himself.

* * *

The next morning, Guillermo Haynes was back in business on his own. He was determined to create an even bigger company than Berruti, Pasquale and whoever. Within a few hours he had found a two-room office in a building not far from the station, put down a deposit and moved in. It was almost empty except for a telephone, which did not work although it was connected to a telephone line. Even with a hefty bribe, it was almost impossible to get a telephone line to a building which did not have one; as it was, though still with a bribe, he had the number connected before the end of the day.

It was not in the most salubrious part of town but the office would do for the moment. Guillermo looked at the other contents of the room: a desk and an old metal filing cabinet. Without hesitation he threw them out and ordered new furniture. If he wanted to get any clients, his office had to make an impression.

By the following day Guillermo had installed two desks and two chairs, a filing cabinet, a sofa and two side tables. He was 'on the list' for an extra phone line, which hopefully would come in a few days. He had instructed a firm of office cleaners, ordered some office stationery and business cards, and had knocked on the doors of three of the adjoining offices to say hello.

The next task was to call Christina and offer her a job. He had been in her care for too long; he could not manage without her. He had always been kind to her, partly because she was so loyal to him. When her father died, he had nearly gone out of his mind because he had given her leave of absence, but she came back after a couple of weeks. She had leant on his arm at the old man's funeral and introduced him to her invalid mother. The poor girl certainly had a lot to contend with. No wonder she did not get married.

Guillermo offered her the same money as she was earning at Berruti, Pasquale and Haynes, and she jumped at the chance to join him. He wondered whether they would make it difficult for her to work for him but the next afternoon she arrived with a taxi driver in tow carrying a box of files she had secretly copied, and a box of photographs and bits and pieces from Guillermo's old office. She was also carrying a large bunch of flowers in a vase. 'I thought we could do with these,' she said as she put them down and surveyed the office. 'They'll brighten the place up a bit.'

'I couldn't cope without you,' Guillermo said, as he hugged her. 'Welcome to the offices of Guillermo Haynes and Partners.'

The driver put down the boxes. Guillermo dug his hand in his pocket to pay him Christina stopped him. 'It's all paid for by the company.'

Guillermo whistled. 'How very kind of them,' he said.

'It was,' she said. 'They were very kind. I think old man Berruti was glad you didn't put up a fight. For all his bluster he is very fond of you. Anyway, what's the price of a cab to them?'

'And they didn't mind you going so quickly?'

'No, I think it suited them. I gave in my notice, and whoosh, it all happened. And they paid me a month's salary, plus my leave entitlement.'

'You deserved it,' said Guillermo, hugging her again.

Christina opened a box and pulled out a large framed certificate that had always hung on Guillermo's wall. 'Here you are, so everyone knows you're a proper lawyer.

'Thank you.'

'Señor Berruti said I should take everything from your office that belonged to you. He was very nice, and he asked me to wish you the best of luck for the future.'

'That was kind,' Guillermo said. He remembered arriving at the firm after he had finished *summa cum laude* at Harvard, returned to Buenos Aires and married Pilar. Enrico Pasquale, Pilar's father, had been alive then and it was obvious that Guillermo would work for his company.

Guillermo had a filial affection for old man Pasquale but he always felt more relaxed with Kingston Berruti. Two years later, Pilar's father died and Berruti had started leaning more and more heavily on Guillermo.

As Christina unpacked the treasures from the boxes, he went to his desk. 'There's a lot to do,' he said, but he was heartened by Christina's presence; at last he could see a way out of the mess he was in.

Christina ordered a brand new IBM electric golfball typewriter and one or two other office essentials. By the following day, she had sorted out the office, and she provided Guillermo with his breakfast, much as she had every morning for the past ten years or so. She bought another rug, a kettle and a coffee pot, and she hung most of Guillermo's pictures on the walls. She also ordered a sign for the door and some proper business cards and stationery.

'These simply won't do,' she said, disgusted when she saw what Guillermo had ordered. 'We need to drum up some business, and you've got a position in this town.'

Guillermo smiled. He had never had to bother with such things before and he was more than grateful that Christina was here to relieve him of these domestic trials.

Before very long, Christina had increased her role to become a researcher. She was no longer his secretary; she could style herself as his assistant and she made full use of her new position. Guillermo dispatched her to Army and police bases across the capital, to libraries and clubs, indeed anywhere where they might turn up the name of Duarte. At every one of them, she drew a blank. Duarte had disappeared as surely as the parents of the children they were currently seeking.

CHAPTER 28

The retired officers' club in the centre of Buenos Aires was formerly a palace, built in Louis XVI style in the late nineteenth century, like so many of the major buildings in the city. In the vaulted central hallway, the tall marble columns reached effortlessly to the sky; the light from the midday sun was filtered through small windows at the top and heavy brocade drapes hid most of the sun that shone through the long windows that overlooked a beautiful garden.

Not two weeks after Christina had joined him in his new office, Guillermo had had her make an appointment here, with his full, new title, Guillermo Haynes, Attorney at Law, from Guillermo Haynes and Partners. An usher led him into a large room on one side of the hall and asked him to wait. The walls were hung with portraits of old soldiers and sailors; on the table in the middle of the room was a huge display of fresh flowers as well as newspapers and magazines. Old club chairs and sofas, with coffee tables nearby, were arranged around the walls. Guillermo waited.

A few minutes passed before the usher reappeared and beckoned Guillermo to follow him down the corridor. They passed four identical doors; the usher opened the fifth door and ushered Guillermo inside before closing it behind him.

It was almost dark inside the room. The curtains were drawn and a single shaft of sunlight fell across the floor. In an armchair in the corner sat General Horloz, Pilar's uncle. He was now retired from active service and looking rather frail.

'Good afternoon, General,' said Guillermo. 'It is kind of you to see me.'

'It's always good to see you, my boy. How are you?' Horloz raised his hand to take Guillermo's. 'How is your mother? Do pass on my best wishes.'

'She is very well, thank you. And I will, I certainly will.'

The general motioned Guillermo to sit in the chair opposite and they sat silently for a moment. The Guillermo outlined why he had come.

'I'm surprised at your interest, frankly,' Horloz said when Guillermo had finished. 'A lot of damage has been done by dragging up the past.'

Guillermo was not sure if this was a reference to his marriage with Pilar or to his investigations into the Disappeared. 'I'm only trying to do my job, sir. As a lawyer.'

'The Army did what it had to do and it's no use crying about it now.'

'Sir, I only...'

'We served,' the general boomed. 'As we will serve again.'

'But, General, times have moved on. We have to take account of that.'

'Nothing has changed, my boy. We had a policy, as we have always had, and it worked. We crushed the Monteneros, and you and your generation are the beneficiaries. We eradicated them. Should they re-form, we will crush them again.'

'But, General, we now have a democratic government.'

'Perhaps our one failure was to allow that to happen.' The General paused. 'I'm sorry, there is nothing more I can help you with, Guillermo. You and your colleagues will have to deal with the present situation.

'But all I want to know, sir, is the...'

The General put up his hand to silence Guillermo and outstared him. 'You should concentrate on getting back with your wife.'

After a moment, Guillermo got up. 'Thank you, General,' he said, 'but I don't think that is going to happen.' He made his way back along the corridor and down the steps to the front door.

Outside, Guillermo wandered aimlessly. He thought of his own political leanings and how they had changed, firstly because of Caridad and then, rather latterly he knew, because he thought the situation in his country was wrong.

He remembered what one of his English university friends had told him at Harvard: 'I'm a socialist now, but I suppose that when I'm forty I'll be voting Conservative like my Dad. It's what we end up doing.' If anything, Guillermo was moving the other way. He thought about Caridad; she would not have lost her ideals, the beliefs that made her the person she was. He went back to the small apartment he now rented and thought about his son. What chance did *he* have of becoming a socialist?

CHAPTER 29

The telephone was ringing when Christina unlocked the office. 'Guillermo Haynes and Partners,' she said.

'Christina, it's Clara. Is Guillermo there?'

'He's not here at the moment. Can I take a message?'

Just then the door opened and Guillermo came in. Clara handed the receiver to him. 'Guillermo, is that you?' Clara said impatiently. 'Where have you been? I've just got the testimony from the Commission from a woman who was at San Juan jail. She says she knew the commandant before she was jailed!'

'And…'

'His name, she says, was Franco Yirogin-Duarte. Maybe if we looked that up, we might find him.'

For days Guillermo had employed people to comb the Army lists, the register of voters, the telephone directory in every city, and every other list of names he could think of to try and locate a man named Duarte.

'No wonder we couldn't find him under Duarte,' said Guillermo, suddenly as excited as Clara. 'I'll get onto it right away.'

It was no longer a state secret to know who had been in the Army or the police; the Alfonsin government had declassified the Army list in one of a number of Acts which, at the stroke of a pen, made the armed forces more accountable to the newly elected government. It was the same for the police. Maybe, thought Guillermo, Mr Franco Yirogin-Duarte/Bollini had not managed to excise his records. You just had to look in the right place.

Guillermo sent Christina out to search the records and within an hour she was on the phone. 'I've found him,' she said triumphantly. 'Franco Yirogin-Duarte. He was dishonourably dismissed from the service in 1977 from his post as commandant of the San Juan prison and police station. He was married and there is no record of any children.'

'Brilliant,' Guillermo nearly shouted down the phone. 'Get back here as soon as you can.'

His excitement was hard to control. 'We've got him, we've got him!' he muttered and then went back to the desk to phone Clara. He had no sooner put the phone down when he heard the outer door open and footsteps in the next room. Christina could not be back that quickly, he thought…

Two burly men, with stockings over their faces, were advancing on him. 'What the…' It was all he managed to say. The first man grabbed him by the neck and pushed him to the ground. The second kicked him in the side and the head, then the first picked him up and threw him across the room. One held him while the other rained blows onto his face, his head and his body. They might have done more but suddenly there was a scream from the doorway. A woman from the neighbouring office stood there with her hand over her mouth. When the men turned and saw her, she ran down the hall.

The men looked at each other and decided it was time to leave. They let Guillermo go and he crumpled in a heap on the floor. The next thing he knew, he was lying on a trolley in a hospital. Two nurses were leaning over him and there was a doctor nearby. He tried to speak but could not. Neither could he see properly; one eye was closed completely and the other only slightly open. He blacked out again.

He came to some hours later. Now he was in a bed in a darkened room and there were two more nurses and a doctor talking to someone. Guillermo couldn't raise his arm and he realised he still couldn't speak. He grunted and the doctor looked over at him.

Clara came forward, lightly touched his hand and then leant over and kissed his bandaged forehead. 'My poor, dear Guillermo,' she said.

When he tried to speak, no words came from his mouth. He was vaguely aware of the doctor coming forward, leaning over him. 'You are in hospital and you're quite safe but don't try to speak. We've wired up your jaw which is broken and you've got a few other injuries too. Just rest and you'll be fine.'

Guillermo still couldn't see clearly but he could hear

beeping and buzzing. He was aware of Clara near him. He felt very tired; moments later he was unconscious again.

It was fully twenty-four hours later before Guillermo was awake enough to focus on what had happened. He could now speak, though only with difficulty. He could not see his face but he knew it was very swollen. He was told he had a ruptured spleen, four broken ribs, damage to his kidneys and liver, which the doctors had not been able to fully assess, a detached retina in one eye and possible bleeding on the brain. His two assailants had been professionals: they knew exactly what to do to inflict the greatest punishment in the shortest time. The police were still looking for them but it was extremely lucky that that the *señora* from down the hall had interrupted them when she did because it was unclear whether they meant to frighten him or kill him.

'Could you describe the men?' a policeman asked him the next day. Not in a million years, Guillermo thought, and shook his head. He had not seen their faces and now he could not even remember whether they had brown jackets or black trousers; they were a complete blur. He wondered whether one of the men was Franco Bollini, or Franco Yirogin-Duarte as he should start calling him, but he could not be sure. He reckoned they were both big men but he was sitting down when they came in.

It was nine days before Guillermo was allowed home from the hospital and even then he was unsteady on his feet. The doctors were still worried about any brain damage that he might have sustained. He lied when they asked him if he had anyone at home who would look after him but he checked back into the Claridge rather than returning to the apartment. At least in the hotel there were people he could call if he needed anything.

His face still looked as though he had been kicked by one of his horses, and his stomach and chest felt as though he had been too. His jaw was still wired, which made speaking difficult, but he was alive and undeterred. He vowed that he would make Bollini pay for his own injuries as well as the suffering he'd inflicted on everyone who passed through the St Juan detention centre.

Christina arranged for the hotel to supply his meals in his room; they were liquidised so he could suck them through a straw. She came to the office every morning even though Guillermo was in no state to work. He suffered from constant headaches, he could not concentrate and he was better resting or asleep. At the end of the week, Christina suggested he fly down to his mother's *estancia* and, with very little argument, he agreed. Christina accompanied him in an air taxi to ensure that he arrived safely and then left him in his mother's care.

At the farmhouse, Guillermo sat in an easy chair with an alpaca rug over his knees and watched the world go by. Gina, his mother's maid, kept him supplied with tasty morsels, all carefully mulched. Sometimes he walked down to the old mares that were contentedly munching grass in happy retirement in the field below the house, or he wandered a bit further to a field of young stock, which the farm manager kept down there. He had a couple of horses shipped down from the farm and started to ride gently. He had to be helped in and out of the saddle at first but once there, he was as comfortable as he was sitting by the fire.

The weeks went by and Guillermo recovered. Three months after the attack, he flew back to the capital to have his jaw unwired and to get back to work. He was not completely fit, far from it; he still had headaches and his memory sometimes failed him. After visiting the hospital he walked, with only a slight limp, into his office with a large bunch of flowers for Christina and a new resolution to get Bollini. This was the end run.

CHAPTER 30

The phone on Guillermo's desk rang and he picked it up. It was almost two months since he had gone back to work. He was walking normally now and the cuts and swellings on his face had completely gone. His stomach was still tender when he stretched but he swam every morning in the pool at a new club he had joined, where he had made new friends. He had started riding seriously again; the polo season was coming up and he really wanted to play again.

Angelika, the pretty groom who looked after his horses at the Hurlingham stables, rode out with him; he could now spend two hours in the saddle and still walk afterwards. In different times, he might have tried something with Angelika but he was not ready for that yet. One of the most serious injuries he had endured during the attack came from the vicious kicks to his testicles. They had swollen to the size of tennis balls and his penis had been bruised and mangled; he was still tender down there.

On Sundays he took Clara out to Tigre, and they sat in the sunshine and devoured the steaks he cooked on the *asado*. They read the papers and slept until it was time to come back. Guillermo thought a lot about Caridad on Sundays, what life might have been like if he had abandoned his wife when he first fell in love with Caridad and whisked her away to the United States or to England.

Sometimes Guillermo felt like a time-traveller because Clara was just an older version of Caridad.

'What are you thinking about?' Clara asked him.

'I was thinking about Caridad. I was thinking I could have taken her away from all this.'

'It's too late to think that now,' Clara said. 'We are so close to finding Caridad's child and yet you are becoming more and more depressed.'

'Maybe.' It was all that he could say. He desperately wanted to have his son with him but even more he wished he still had Caridad. She was like an illness that he could not shake off; she became more real to him every day, and every day she seemed further away.

One Monday, Guillermo struck lucky and got a small reward for the hours of hard work that followed every lead, every scintilla of evidence. Christina put the call through to him. 'It's Señor Silvenson from the detective agency.'

Guillermo was immediately attentive. 'Put him on,' he said, and when the line clicked: 'Señor Silvenson, what have you got?'

'We've found out where Señora Bollini, Señora Yirogin-Duarte, is living.'

'Well done, well done.' Two months of Silvenson's time

had finally paid off. He noted that there was no mention of Señor Yirogin-Duarte but surely her husband would not be far away.

This was not a time to sit back and pat himself on the back; there was too much to do. A series of phone calls took most of the afternoon.

After flying down to Bahia Blanca the following day, Guillermo, Clara and Rigas Finero, a large man hired mainly for his bulk, were speeding out of town through the countryside. Rigas was employed by Guillermo as a bodyguard but the two men had become friends in the last couple of months. He was personable and his interest in American rock music and in keeping his body fit struck a chord with Guillermo; his knowledge of American artists like Rockwell and Warhol also gave them plenty to talk about. He and Guillermo had been out running together and now they played squash whenever they could. Guillermo had not put Rigas on a horse yet but no doubt that would come. For now, Rigas sat at the wheel, concentrating on the driving and flexing his biceps and thigh muscles but, in Clara's presence, not saying much.

The tension rose with every passing minute. Clara and Guillermo talked animatedly in the back of the car. The road snaked through a range of hills and then straightened for the long run south; soon they would turn off and head for the town of Villa Romano, where Señora Bollini was now apparently living. Almost an hour after they had started driving, they pulled up in a small street.

'We'll wait here,' Guillermo said, rehearsing the arrangements that had been agreed hours before they started.

'That will be best,' Clara said as she climbed out of the car. She held her right hand half upraised, with two fingers crossed over.

'We'll be right outside if you need us.'

'Relax,' said Clara. 'I'll call you if I need you.'

With that she was gone, disappearing through a garden gate in the hedge. The house in front of her was silent and the curtains in the front windows were drawn. Clara listened at the door for any sounds but heard none. The garden looked well cared for, with neat bushes on one side still waiting to flower and a large walnut tree in the middle of a small lawn,. There was an Angel's Trumpet tree on one side, its large, white, bell-like flowers waving silently. She stood for a moment and then knocked on the door.

There was a scurrying noise and the door opened. A small boy looked out. 'Hello,' he said. Clara had time only to smile before more footsteps came to the door and Eva Bollini appeared. She looked startled, grabbing little Paulo with one hand and forcing the door closed with the other.

Clara put her foot inside the door frame. 'Señora Bollini, I am here on my own. I just want to talk to you. Woman to woman, mother to mother.'

There was a long pause before Eva Bollini released the pressure on the door, and it inched open a little more. 'Go and play, Paulo. Mummy needs to talk a moment.'

Paulo looked up at her and back to Clara, then he sped off to the back of the house, apparently without a care in the world.

'How did you find me?'

'Señora Bollini,' said Clara. 'Or should I say Señora Yirogin-Duarte? It doesn't matter. I'm here and I'm alone.'

Eva blanched at the name. She looked up and down the road beyond the confines of her hedge. Then she said: 'You'd better come in.' She led Clara into the front room, neatly if sparsely furnished, and motioned her to a chair.

'I have much sympathy for you, Señora. You clearly love your little boy,' Clara said.

'He is my son. You can't take him away from me. I will never give him up.'

'Señora, isn't it better that we decide Paulo's future amongst ourselves, rather than through the courts? That way you could at least continue to see Paulo. We already have the proof of who he is.'

Eva Bollini was not listening, she was crying, 'Paulo is my son, my SON!'

Clara moved uncomfortably in her chair but remained determined. 'But he is my grandson and I want him back.'

'No, NO!' Suddenly Eva Bollini leapt up and ran from the room, as if to check that Paulo was still in the house. She returned a moment later and Clara, who had got up to follow her, was almost knocked over.

It was Clara who spoke first. 'Señora, please be calm....'

But Eva Bollini was not listening. She rummaged through a drawer in the small sideboard, then wheeled round. In her hand was her husband's Bersa pistol, the weight of which almost overbalanced her. She struggled and steadied the gun. 'Get out of my house. Get out!'

Clara got up from her chair slowly and backed towards

the door. She wanted to say something to calm Eva Bollini but the words would not come. With her hand behind her, she eased up the latch and stepped outside. Eva Bollini rushed to the door and slammed it shut.

Inside, Eva leant back on the door, the gun still in her hand. She noticed it almost absently and flung it to the floor. There was suddenly a deafening report as it went off. Eva Bollini screamed and tears flooded down her cheeks.

Outside, Clara was barely down the path when she heard the explosion. Rigas and Guillermo heard it too and were out of the car in an instant. Clara was already pushing at the door, against the latch and Eva's inert body slumped beyond it. As the two men came round the hedge towards her, she put up her hand to stop them. 'Go back to the car, I'm OK.'

It was an order. The two men stopped in their tracks then slowly returned to the car.

Clara turned back to the door, knocking on it gently and calling Eva's name. There was no reply; Clara could hear the sobs from inside but she couldn't get in. She heard little Paulo saying, 'It's alright, Mama, it's alright.' After a few minutes, listening intently and knocking gently on the door, she heard Eva telling her to go away.

Reluctantly Clara returned to the car where the two men were anxious for news. She said nothing as she got into the car, just ordered Finero to drive on. For a long time they journeyed in silence until she finally said: 'She didn't offer any explanation. She was adamant that the little boy is her son and then she waved this enormous gun at me and told me to leave. It must have gone off as she put it down, or dropped it or something.'

* * *

That evening, when Franco Bollini arrived at the house, Eva was still cuddling Paulo, fearful of letting him out of her sight. Together they prepared some supper and put Paulo to bed. Bollini tried to offer Eva assurances, comfort, sympathy, but she would have none of it. 'I will not gamble with my son,' she said, almost spitting out the words.

When Franco approached her, she shied away. When he tried to take her arm, she pushed him savagely. 'They know everything about you.'

'Eva, they are bluffing.'

'Why do they need to bluff? They *know*. They told me, and she told me again today. They know.' Eva started to cry again, and her husband was unable to hold her gaze. 'How could you have done those things?' she said at last. 'How could you?'

'Eva, you know, I didn't.'

'In my condition. How could you?'

'Don't torture yourself, Eva.'

By now, Eva's tears were in full flood again. They poured from her, soaking the tissues that she grabbed to dry them. 'How many were there?' she asked at last. 'Dozens? Hundreds?' This last was shouted.

'Eva, stop it, you'll go mad. I was doing my job, you knew that. I hated it and you knew that too.'

'Are you sure you hated it. Why didn't you quit sooner?

Why?'

'For the love of God, Eva, why are you doing this?'

'You don't seem to realise what you've done. How many people did you murder? Women… How many did you just watch?'

'*Eva*!' Bollini was angry now. He thumped the table and a vase tumbled to the floor and broke. Eva jumped. For a moment there was complete silence then Eva was aware of a sound from the door and suddenly Paulo was standing there, rubbing his eyes and crying. 'What is happening, Mummy?'

Eva immediately scooped him up in her arms, burying his head between her breasts as though to prevent him hearing more. She could not be sure how much he had heard. She rushed to Paulo's bedroom, almost suffocating him.

Bollini was left alone and close to tears.

CHAPTER 31

It was exactly a week since Clara visited Eva Bollini. She had been busy with other cases but kept coming back to the Bollinis. If the Bollinis continued to deny everything, she and Guillermo needed more than the circumstantial evidence that they had uncovered so far.

They had been in touch by fax with Dr Ana Collaris, the DNA expert, to find out how far that process had advanced. She told them that perhaps a hair from Paulo's head would be sufficient, but at this stage it would probably not be accepted by the Buenos Aires courts.

Clara prayed a lot but she seemed to get no nearer than before and she saw that Guillermo was becoming ever more morose. Her thoughts were interrupted by the door bell and she got up to answer the intercom. 'Who is it?'

The voice from the intercom sounded timid. 'This is Eva Bollini speaking. May I see you, please?'

For an instant Clara was worried for her own safety

but then she thought no more of it. 'Just a moment,' she said, as she gathered her thoughts.

Later Clara asked herself how long she remained in a state of mindlessness before she pressed the buzzer and allowed Eva Bollini to enter. Was it a single second or ten seconds? A full minute? It was never clear to her, but she knew that it was a moment which changed her life.

Eva Bollini looked stressed, emotionally drained, and she had been crying a lot. She hesitated at the door and for a moment it looked as if she might flee, but then she accepted Clara's outstretched arm and crossed the threshold.

Clara followed her through the narrow hall to the living room and beckoned to her to sit down. 'Would you like some coffee, or a glass of wine?'

'No, thank you. Maybe a glass of water.'

Clara went to the kitchen to fetch the water and Eva said nothing until she returned. She sat, nervously looking round the room and at the floor; even when she took the glass from Clara's hand, she could not look her in the eye.

The silence continued until Clara spoke. 'Señora Bollini, may I call you Eva? Please tell me what you want? I do want to help you because I want my grandson back, and….'

Eva Bollini screamed, 'No, you don't understand. Paulo is mine. *Mine.*' She leapt up from the chair, spilling some of the water on the floor. Clara put up her hands defensively then backed away and sat down. Eventually Eva sat down again and attempted to mop the split water with a tear-drenched handkerchief from her bag.

'No, no, don't worry about that,' Clara said, getting up again and fetching a cloth from the kitchen. 'It is only water, no harm done. Please, be calm and talk to me.'

Eva stifled her tears; she seemed to force them back into her eyes with her handkerchief. 'I have come a long way to tell you this. You have to understand,' she said finally. 'Paulo is my baby, my son.' And then her tears began again.

Clara was hesitant but eventually she said: 'Eva, we know your husband was in charge of San Juan detention centre. We know you changed your name when he left. You are really Señora Yirogin-Duarte are you not?' Eva nodded. 'Some terrible things happened at San Juan, which you may not be aware of…'

'I am aware.' Eva was almost shouting. 'But Paulo is my son. I only went to the hospital because it was an emergency. I would never have gone there, I wish I had *never* gone there.'

Clara was confused. 'I am not sure what you are saying. What you are telling me, Eva? Please take your time.'

Eva struggled to contain herself. 'I'm sorry I don't know what happened to your daughter's baby but I know that Paulo is my baby. He came from my body. It was an emergency and the prison doctor had to do a Caesarean very quickly. There wasn't time to go to the Mater Dei or any other hospital. There wasn't time, it was an emergency.'

Clara took a moment to collect her thoughts. 'Are you saying that Paulo was born by Caesarean?'

'Yes, yes, of course he was! He was born at San Juan; he should have been born elsewhere. But he is *my* baby!'

Now the reams of testimony from San Juan and elsewhere rattled through Clara's head like machine-gun fire. To be honest, Clara was not certain that her grandchild was a boy; all she was certain of was that Caridad had been delivered of a child. She did not know whether it was a natural birth or a Caesarean. No one had seen the child; Clara had not tracked down any witnesses so far.

Suddenly Eva jumped up again and pulled at her slacks. 'I have the scar here,' she said triumphantly, as she pulled down her trousers and her knickers. 'Look!' Sure enough there was a scar, a long, perpendicular scar rather crudely sewn up, incised into the fat on Eva's lower abdomen. 'Do you see?' Eva asked plaintively. 'Do you see?'

Clara did see, all too plainly, but she decided that Eva's scar proved nothing on its own except that Eva Bollini had had a Caesarean which may or may not have been successful. Given that she had gone to the prison hospital, she could have been given a prisoner's baby as she came round from the operation. No, Clara reasoned, all the scar did was to add another layer of fog to the fate of her daughter and her grandchild.

Neither of them spoke while Eva rearranged her clothes. Clara motioned Eva to sit down again. 'Can you tell me the name of the doctor who did this?'

'I can't,' said Eva desperately. Then a look of triumph appeared on her face. 'But I do know who the midwife was. Señora Mendez. She took me to the hospital.'

CHAPTER 32

Clara badly needed a drink after Eva left that night. Eva had constantly refused Clara's offer of wine or coffee or even *mate* but, when she left, Clara opened a bottle of red wine from Mendoza and downed one glass immediately. She took the second one more slowly. She was greatly troubled by Eva's apparent honesty and her scar. But what did it prove? Surely the research she and Guillermo and all the Grandmothers had done pointed to San Juan, to Bollini, to a day in April 1977 when Caridad's life was extinguished at the end of a terrible imprisonment? But not before she had endured the birth of a child which was still waiting to be claimed.

'We've got to find this wretched midwife,' Guillermo said when he spoke to Clara the following day. 'At the very least, she'll be able to tell us more about the Bollinis or, should I say, the Yirogin-Duartes. But we can discount the guff about the child. Why else would Bollini be so scared of us?'

'I'm not sure,' was all Clara would say. 'You're right. We have to find the midwife.'

For the next two weeks, Guillermo poured all his energies into locating the mysterious midwife. He went back over all his notes, searched through the card index system that the Grandmothers had set up and then went to the Commission to look at their card indexes. He searched under 'midwife', 'midwives', 'san juan', 'bollini', 'duarte', 'yirogin-duarte' and, of course, the supposed birth date and the days either side. He found absolutely nothing. Then he searched under every other prison or place of confinement and the nearby hospitals. Here he found plenty of midwives but none that fitted the picture. He telephoned every maternity section in every hospital or clinic within fifty miles of San Juan Prison asking for 'Señora Mendez'; when they all denied knowing such a woman, he went back to the hospitals and tried their personnel departments. Finally he exhausted every investigatory line he could think of; he was confident that there was no such midwife and that Señora Bollini's story was fantasy. But Guillermo had to be sure. If he was going to court, he needed to convince a judge that the midwife was a figment of Señora Bollini's imagination.

Then, one morning, he picked up the paper, *Clarin*. On page three was a picture of Silvania Mendez holding the one thousandth baby she had delivered. Señora Mendez, said the lines beneath a picture of a beaming resident at a nursing home in Mendoza, had been a midwife for over fifty years at the Mater Dei Hospital in Buenos Aires. She had delivered hundreds of babies and even assisted at the

San Juan Military Prison hospital, when circumstances demanded.

Guillermo immediately rang the hospital, demanding to speak to Señora Mendez. This time a different operator was on the line; she said that Señora Mendez had not worked at the hospital for at least three years. She thought the picture had been used simply to fill space, or perhaps someone at the hospital had just found it and thought the newspaper might be interested.

Guillermo went back to the hospital's personnel division; this time he had proof that Señora Mendez had worked there until a couple of years ago. They must have an address for her.

The hospital did have an address but they would not give it to him. After battling with the lady on the telephone for fifteen minutes, he flung the instrument down in a rage. Just then Christina looked in to say she was going home and Guillermo suddenly had a bright idea.

The following day, Christina appeared at the Mater Dei hospital pretending to be Señora Mendez's niece, recently returned from America. She had, she explained, been round to her dear aunt's house but found someone else living there, so she had come to the hospital where she knew her aunt had worked for many years. Could they please help her? There was a different woman in the records office; she must have taken pity on Christina because she eventually produced the last address that the hospital had for their long-serving midwife. It was a nursing home in the city. 'She's getting a bit frail,' the clerk said sadly.

Christina took the address and thanked the woman

profusely, promising she would pass on the regards of the whole hospital to her aunt. She left the building as fast as she could and telephoned Guillermo.

Guillermo looked at the address for a long time, wondering what he should make of it. Had he spent the last fortnight working himself into a lather simply to back up the Bollini's claim that Paulo was their own child? Or would the midwife's testimony, if he could get it, underline his own claim?

Guillermo was not entirely happy when he phoned Clara. 'I have an address,' he said simply. 'Can you come and see her now?'

He was silent as they drove to an old art deco mansion in the suburbs. It had once been a beautiful house but now a single-storey extension ran along one side, and something similar along the back. Bougainvillea was rioting against the front wall, its purple blossom spilling over the windows and covering the front lawn with flowers. A lone gardener was working in a large border as they drove in past a sign which said 'Our Lady of Mathilde Home for the Elderly'. Señora Mendez had retired well, thought Guillermo as he parked the car.

They rang the bell and, after a moment, a uniformed nurse answered and they went inside. It took them a while to explain their mission and convince Señora Mendez that they were not the police and were not trying to get her into trouble. Once she was satisfied, she was happy to chat in the garden at the back of the house under the shade of an old *ombu* tree, its umbrella-like canopy casting a huge shadow over the lawn. She listened intently to them, muttering to herself. Finally she asked them to excuse her for a moment.

When she returned, walking very upright despite her years, she was carrying two large leather-bound notebooks. 'I remember that child,' Señora Mendez said. 'I have the details in here.' She settled herself on a chair and opened one of the books. 'These were my diaries. He was breeched, I couldn't turn him.'

'So you sent the mother, Señora Duarte, to the prison hospital at San Juan?' Clara asked.

'Yes. It was the nearest. They had doctors there. I had been there before and her husband worked there.'

'So you knew her husband worked at San Juan, was in charge at San Juan,' Guillermo interrupted aggressively.

It was Clara who stilled him. 'Shh. We know that. Let Señora Mendez continue.'

'I called an ambulance and we took her there.'

'And you were there for the Caesarean?' Guillermo asked.

'No, no. That was for the doctors.'

'How soon did you see the baby?' said Clara.

'Oh, very quickly. I was just outside and I cleaned the baby and held him until Señora Duarte was wheeled out, and then she held him.'

'But you can't be absolutely certain that the baby you received was the baby that Señora Duarte gave birth to. It could have been another baby.'

'I don't think so. He was a darling child, not a blemish on him. He looked like a little angel.'

'But there were probably half a dozen babies born in

the hospital that day. You could have been given any one of them.' Guillermo sounded desperate.

'Young man, there were no other Caesarean births at that time, I am sure of that.'

'But if you didn't see the birth, how do you…'

Clara put her hand on Guillermo's knee to stop him saying any more. She had heard the confirmation she feared and it gave her great sadness but some relief too. 'Guillermo,' she said, 'the baby would look quite different after a Caesarean.'

'You've never seen a baby being born, have you, young man?' Señora Mendoza smiled as she spoke gently to Guillermo. 'It's a beautiful sight. During a natural birth, the baby has to struggle, really struggle to survive. During a Caesarean, the doctors just lift the baby out of the womb and he is as calm as he was inside it.'

Guillermo felt he was swimming underwater, through reeds. They swirled about his face and obstructed his view. The sunlight flashed and illuminated everything for a second, and then plunged him back into almost total darkness. Gradually his vision cleared. Señora Mendoza was still speaking to him. 'It is God's creation,' she was saying. 'Every birth is a miracle.'

Guillermo heard Clara thank the midwife for her time and say goodbye, then he was walking outside, back to the car and the real world. The two of them were silent until they neared the capital. 'So what does that mean?' he asked finally.

Clara put her hand on his knee and squeezed. 'I think,' she said, 'it means that we have to look again for Caridad's child. Everything pointed to little Paulo but it seems he really is … their child.' Clara had some trouble enunciating the word 'their'. She stumbled over it, not wanting to let go of the idea that that boy was her grandson. But he was not; he could not be. She would have to start looking afresh.

Guillermo could not come to terms with it. All the testimonies, the people he had talked to, the legal processes so diligently covered, the places he'd visited, the facts he'd uncovered, the newspaper reports he had pored over, the skeletons, the witnesses. He thought about the time he had spent as if it were on a lawyer's clock, ticking up the bill for a client. It was inestimable, since he had not kept count, but he knew he had devoted his life ever since he had met Clara to finding Caridad's child. Now it had come to nothing. He regretted, more than anything, that he had not devoted his life to it before.

'Do you believe her?' he said finally.

'Yes, I believe her.'

'But we will need to corroborate her story?'

'Of course, but I believe her. I'm afraid Paulo is not your son or my grandson.'

They drove on in silence, through the dusty streets of the capital, avoiding rubbish in the poorer areas and confronting traffic jams in the richer ones, past rows of glittering shops and then miles of small houses with neat and not so neat gardens. They drove past gardeners mowing lawns and street cleaners sweeping pavements, past people wandering aimlessly and stray dogs asleep on the verges, past children playing in the streets, past trees in leaf and in blossom, through sunlight and shade, until they reached the Grandmothers' Collective.

Clara got out of the car. She came round to the driver's side and kissed Guillermo on both cheeks. 'Let me adjust to this on my own for a while. I will see you tomorrow.'

Guillermo nodded and drove off. He also had to cope with this and already he felt that he could not do it. His world was unravelling like a ball of twine. If Paulo was not his son, what had he to live for? Maybe his son would never be found.

CHAPTER 33

Guillermo was drunk. He had been drunk pretty much all the time since the previous week, when he had left Clara at her flat and driven home, despondent and depressed. He had downed a bottle of wine almost without looking at it, then started on the Scotch, pouring tumblers of the stuff down his throat. He had fallen asleep in his clothes, woken the following morning at about eleven and started drinking again. When he ran out of alcohol he staggered out to a corner shop and bought a bottle of brandy; he polished that off before the sun went down. He did not eat or wash or shave and he was sick on the floor. He had never been overly tempted by alcohol before but suddenly it dawned on him that this was the answer to his problems.

The next morning he had fallen into the shower to try and sober up and wiped the dried vomit from the floor. His suit and shirt were stained with alcohol so he put on a pair of track-suit trousers, a clean shirt and trainers and stumbled to a nearby restaurant for some breakfast. The telephone was ringing as he left the apartment, but he ignored it. After all, who could it be? Certainly not his son!

One half of his befuddled mind accepted that Paulo could not be his son; the other half clung to the idea that it was all part of a plot by Franco Bollini to discredit him. Over breakfast he sobered up enough to realise that somehow he had to put Franco Bollini in jail.

On the way back to the apartment, Guillermo was sick again, vomiting his breakfast onto the grass by the side of the road. When he eventually arrived home, the telephone was ringing again. It was Clara. 'Where have you been?' she asked him impatiently.

Guillermo had not been drinking long enough to disguise the fact that he was still drunk; he did not have the guile of a confirmed alcoholic. And he was not very interested in what Clara was saying. He had believed that Paulo was Caridad's and his child; now that that hope had been taken away, his life had no meaning.

'I had a letter this morning from Señora Mendoza. You know, the midwife. I've been trying to reach you all morning.' Clara was in a state of high excitement. 'There was another baby born the following day at San Juan. Señora Mendoza saw the child when she went to collect Señora Bollini.'

The news floated over Guillermo. Finally he said, 'So?'

'What do you mean "so"?' For once Clara was irritated. The news from Señora Mendoza confirmed everything they had already discovered, except that it did not point directly to Caridad. But it was about Caridad's time and how many pregnant women could there have been in that ghastly jail? It was a start, something to grab hold of. If it was not Caridad's baby, it was another stolen child. It had to be.

'Stay where you are,' Clara said. 'I am coming round and you are going to start working again!'

'I'm not going anywhere,' Guillermo said weakly and put the phone down.

Within an hour, Clara and Christina were knocking on his door, almost beating it down. When Guillermo stumbled to it and pulled up the latch, they nearly knocked him over in their rush to get inside. Minutes later they were brewing black coffee and tidying up the apartment.

'You are angry because you have lost your son,' Clara told him. 'And I am sad because I have not yet found him.'

Guillermo swallowed hard, and tried to concentrate. 'OK,' he said. 'What do we have?'

'Well, surely we have enough evidence now to put Bollini, Duarte, Yirogin-Duarte or whatever he wants to call himself, in prison. We have an independent witness in Silvania Mendez.'

Guillermo struggled to concentrate. This was his last chance and he knew it. If he was not to throw his life away completely, he had to put the man responsible for murdering Caridad in jail. 'Yup, we do have that now,' he said. 'And he is going to go to jail. Let's have some coffee.'

Guillermo drank the strong black coffee and resolved to get back to work and finish the job he had started. Within an hour he was showered, shaved and dressed in a suit and tie, ready for a day at the office. Christina and

Clara waited for him and escorted him there, one of either side of him as he took deep breaths of air as he walked down the street.

He knuckled down as soon as he got inside the door, giving orders to Christina and Clara to get this or fetch that. By the middle of the afternoon, he had filed a writ with the court against Bollini stating that Bollini had been in charge of the prison at San Juan where tortures and murders were commonplace.

Surprisingly, the police acted almost immediately. Early one morning, before anyone was stirring from their beds, two squad cars and a Ford Falcon drew up at Bollini's house in Villa Romana. Three policemen banged on the door, while two more men stationed themselves at the back. They did not break the door down but waited for Bollini to appear at the door in a towelling gown, his eyes still weary from sleep.

'Where are you going, Papa?' said Paulo, but Franco Bollini could not give him an answer.

'Why did the policeman put handcuffs on Papa?' the little boy asked his mother, as Bollini was led out to one of the cars with a blanket over his head. Eva Bollini didn't answer as she wiped tears from her eyes.

The police flew Bollini back to Buenos Aries and for two days, he resided in a prison cell in the centre of the capital. Then he was released pending a full trial at some future date. Guillermo had thought the charges sufficiently serious, and the evidence sufficiently compelling, to keep Bollini in jail so his release and protestations of innocence affected the lawyer badly.

For a few days Guillermo operated almost normally; the effect on his mental state should have been obvious but he was becoming a master of deception. For years he had divided his life into different compartments, hiding his affairs from Pilar and from everyone else; sometimes he ran two or three mistresses at the same time and nobody knew. Now he only drank in the evening after he returned from work, away from the shrewd gaze of Christina or Clara. If he did down a bottle or two of wine and collapse on the bed in a drunken stupor, he was pretty sober the next morning and, after a shower, pretty respectable looking too.

One morning he drove out to Hurlingham to check on his horses but decided against riding. When Angelika asked him what was wrong, he said it was nothing, he had been very busy at the office. Angelika watched him drive away; she could still smell the alcohol on his breath.

CHAPTER 34

Guillermo retreated further and further into a black hole. As time passed, he drank more and worked less. Often he did not shower or shave. He stopped seeing his friends, gave up polo and didn't pay his livery bills until the stables sold his horses. The Piper Cherokee gathered dust in a hangar at the Aeroparque until the management there rang Guillermo's mother and she authorised them to sell it and pay off all the charges. She put the change into American dollars in a bank in Miami in her name, intending to pass it on to Guillermo should he ever come back to her.

Guillermo had only ever had a few clients at his new offices and he quickly lost them either by being rude or drunk or both. He refused to speak to anyone on the telephone; even Clara was *persona non grata*. Christina made excuses for him and claimed that he had just slipped out of the office or that he was seeing a client and would return her call directly. When Clara called in at the office on the rare occasions that Guillermo was in, he said he was just about to go out to see someone and disappeared. Clara and Christina would have a coffee and lament, then Clara would return to the Grandmothers' offices. Guillermo was slipping further and further away from both of them.

Occasionally Clara was able to reason with Guillermo and the two of them walked arm in arm down to the corner cafe to have coffee. Clara tried to ease the tension and strip away the guilt that was consuming him. 'Look how much you have achieved for us,' she said. 'We could never have achieved that on our own. And we are so close to finding your child. You can't possibly give up now.'

'You're right, you're right,' Guillermo said, as he did on every occasion when he was cornered. 'There are a couple of leads I am working on.'

Guillermo refused to see a doctor or go into rehab; when he was sober, he claimed there was nothing wrong with him and when he was drunk he just smiled.

'How can you give up on your life and your son? He is out there somewhere,' Clara shouted. He did not reply.

Sometimes Guillermo talked to Christina as they sat alone in the office. 'You're a good woman,' he said to her one day. 'You should get a proper job instead of wasting your time here.'

'I'm not wasting my time. And I'm always here if you need me.'

'I really fucked up,' he said. 'I should have left Pilar ages ago. Caridad and I might have been together now.'

'Why don't you concentrate on looking for your

child?' Christina implored him. 'You're so close.'

Often, when Guillermo turned up at the office drunk or suffering from the effects of alcohol, or worse after he'd been in a fight, Christina bathed his wounds or cooled his brow with a wet towel. He was not quite young enough to be her son but she certainly mothered him. She went in every day until Guillermo stopped paying her, and even then she went in for old times' sake.

One morning, Guillermo went into the office with a stash of cash in a plastic bag which he dumped on Christina's desk. 'Here you are,' he said. 'You may as well have it.' And then he was gone, oblivious to her protestations. The door slammed and Guillermo disappeared without looking back.

Eventually, Christina looked at the bundles of money; there was almost a year's salary. She looked at it and cried. She continued coming to the office for a while and started studying for a History of Art degree to while away the hours. One day she had to write an essay on Edvard Munch's paintings known collectively as *The Scream.* She did not read many of the accompanying notes but wrote furiously about the onset of madness brought on by loneliness, abandonment, self-loathing and guilt. And all the while she thought of her boss, Guillermo Haynes.

Christina knew that Guillermo was gone for good because there was not a shred of him left in the office. Over the past weeks and months, he had smashed the photographs and pictures and his framed certificate. The only thing he had not destroyed was a picture of Caridad and Caridad's pen, which he had told Christina about when she first came to work for him. She thought she would keep it as a memento of him. However, one day when she was having a coffee with Clara, she mentioned the pen. She thought Clara would like it.

'Thank you, thank you,' said Clara, visibly moved. 'One day I will give this to Guillermo and Caridad's child.' It was the first time that Christina could remember Clara referring to a child rather than to a son but she let the moment pass.

In due course the office telephone was cut off and one day, when Christina arrived, she found the doors bolted from the outside and a man waiting with a writ for non-payment of the rent. She had already been round to Guillermo's flat but found it had new locks and a sign outside saying 'For Rent'. She rang his mother, Pilar and all his old friends but no one had news of him. He just seemed to have disappeared.

Christina went back to her apartment that evening, hungry and cold despite the heat. She was sad beyond measure that Guillermo could abandon his whole life and that she and Clara were incapable of doing anything to stop it.

* * *

Guillermo's memory losses were more frequent now. Maybe it was because of the beating he had received, maybe it was the drink or the shock of losing his son, but he was not the man he used to be. He was sliding into the abyss. If only he could sleep, but the unfamiliar surroundings frightened him. He did not recognise the soiled bed linen, the smelly clothes, the battered suitcase unopened in the corner and the small, even more battered black Armani briefcase.

He thought that if he had real courage he would kill himself but each time he came to it he could not muster the courage. Had he always been a coward? Life had certainly crumbled over the last few … how long was it? Months, years? This garret was almost like a prison. But he knew it wasn't like *that* prison; nothing could be like that prison.

The dark, velvet night was still. The heat had gone out of the summer but in this small room it was still clammy. There had been a child, Guillermo was sure of that, and it left him a terrible guilt. His class and his country had stolen the child so it could never be tainted with evil and would grow up knowing only what was right. In a world of such certainty, there was no place for disbelievers and there was no room for questions. So the mother had to be killed and the father, too, unless he had very particular connections in the military. Guillermo wished that he had been killed; at least that would have put him out of his misery.

Sometimes he remembered Caridad vividly and then he felt calmer, but most of the time she was out of his reach. She was at the end of a long tunnel, behind bars or completely invisible. His feet were locked in mud and he could not reach her. Sometimes he heard her calling but could not see her. He could not focus on her, feel her, be calmed by her presence.

It was seven months before Bollini was brought to trial, but Guillermo was not there to see it. He simply abandoned everything and everyone in Buenos Aires, hid himself away and retreated into himself. He felt that he was going mad.

Bollini pleaded not guilty to all of the charges, claiming he was only following orders but eventually he was sent to prison for his crimes. The case ruined his family and made the newspapers. In the days that followed, several people appeared at the Commission to claim they remembered him at St Juan, although none could shed any light on Caridad Silva's baby.

For Clara, life continued pretty much as it had before. She redoubled her efforts for the Grandmothers, sorting and sifting and examining with the same precision and care, always looking for a clue that would take her towards her grandchild. She would find him one day, of that she was certain.

She scoured playgrounds and school gates, searching for a child who looked like her daughter, who might be her grandson or her granddaughter. At the same time, she kept her eyes open for Guillermo, thinking that perhaps that he would be doing the same thing.

As the days, weeks and months went by, she knew that the search was becoming more and more difficult. Alone in her little apartment at night, she knew she could never give up. She missed Guillermo, missed his warm, smiling face and the discussions they used to have; she had grown to love him like a son. Over the months she had known him, she had tried many times to bring him back into the fold, to keep him involved in the quest for the children of the disappeared. Each time he appeared to come closer and then retreat even further; now he had disappeared completely. She knew he was grief stricken and she had seen the signs that he was becoming increasingly unstable, but he had refused all assistance and Clara was powerless to help. That was probably the only task in her life that she failed.

CHAPTER 35

1995

Louisa Maria Elana Gandini tightened her seat belt as the Boeing 747 prepared to land at Buenos Aires' Ezeiza international airport. The thirteen-hour flight from Madrid was almost over and soon Louisa would see the country where she was born. She was now eighteen years old; she had left Argentina when she was three and had never been back. She was excited and a little scared, not knowing what she would find. Her mother, Isabella, held her hand as they began their descent. 'Nearly there,' she said.

Louisa and Isabella looked quite alike, even though they were not related. Isabella had never hidden the fact that she and her husband had adopted Louisa when she was eight months old from an orphanage in Bahia Blanca. Pedro Gandini was a naval officer at the base nearby. Eighteen months after they adopted Louisa, Pedro came to the end of his ten-year term in the Navy and decided not to sign on for another ten years. He and his wife, whose parents were Spanish, returned to Spain. A few months later, with Louisa added to Isabella's passport, they were gone, never to return until now.

Pedro and Isabella were wonderful parents and Louisa loved them dearly. She could remember nothing of her life in Argentina but she had always hankered to go there. In her last year at school she applied for a passport in preparation for a life of travelling Isabella had produced her birth certificate. From that, Louisa learnt that she had been born in Buenos Aires, the daughter of a Colonel Ignatio Speta. Curiously, only her father's name appeared on the certificate; Isabella often wondered about that but she assumed that was how things were done back then.

Towards the end her schooldays, Louisa read a lot about Argentina. Before the Second World War it was the world's fifth largest economy but now it had crippling debts and inflation. She read about how President Peron had kept his dead wife Evita in a cellar for years after her death; about Argentina's Dirty War and the Disappeared; about the Malvinas War and the new democratic government. She learnt of the glorious dark-red Malbec wine from Mendoza and Cordoba, and the millions of cattle roaming the vast pampas and supplying the best beef in the world. Louisa was an avid meat eater and longed to try the Argentine *asado*s; she constantly badgered her parents to take her to Argentina for a holiday. Then Pedro Gandini died suddenly of cancer in the middle of her final exams at school. It affected her badly because she was very close to her father but she struggled and completed her studies and was now waiting to go to university. Her mother decided that it would do both of them good to go to Argentina on holiday.

Isabella and Pedro had married in Spain when Pedro was studying at university there. He was born and brought up in Argentina and they lived there after Pedro joined the Navy. They tried to have children but nature had decided that they could not; they were searching for a child to adopt and chanced upon Louisa in an orphanage. They immediately fell in love with her and the adoption papers were signed within a week. Later, in Spain, they had wanted to adopt another child but that was not as easy as it was in Argentina. In the end, they were more than satisfied with lovely Louisa and she was brought up as an only child.

There was one question which Louisa dearly wanted to ask her mother, yet she felt embarrassed to do so and dreaded the reply. Before they left for Argentina she found the words. 'You and Papa never had anything to do with the Dirty War, did you? Papa was in the Navy…'

'No, darling, of course we didn't,' Isabella told her, shocked at the question, but understanding it too. 'It was a very difficult time.' She pushed Louisa's hair back from her face and then hugged her. 'You were quite safe with us,' she said at last. 'But it was a very difficult time. The Monteneros were bombing everywhere, civilians were being killed, but in Bahia Blanca it was easier than in Buenos Aires. And the Navy didn't have patrols out in the streets like the Army.'

'But what about ESMA, the Naval Mechanical School in Buenos Aires? That was one of the centres of torture and…' Louisa's words dried up.

'I couldn't say anything about ESMA,' Isabella said. 'It certainly didn't affect us in Bahia Blanca. It was a long way away.'

And that was that. They never discussed the Dirty War again but Louisa read more and more about the country of her birth. By the time she was ready to fly to Argentina, she felt she could easily do a South American studies course at university, rather than the economics degree on which she had enrolled.

What would she make of Argentina? What would she find there? What would she find out about her real parents and their families? She had grown up as a much-loved daughter to Isabella and Pedro but something gnawed at her gut; she needed to find out about her start in the world.

* * *

Louisa was slim, with thick, dark, wavy hair and a long neck. She had wide cheekbones and dark, dancing eyes. She and Isabella could almost have been sisters; they both wore tight jeans and light cardigans slung over their shoulders as they pulled their wheelie-luggage towards the taxis. Isabella's hair was tied with a coloured ribbon, but it was also thick and dark, and she swung her hips in the same easy way as her adopted daughter.

As the two women strode out to the taxi rank in the afternoon sunshine, Louisa already knew where she was going to go. By three o'clock that afternoon, while her mother rested in their hotel, Louisa was on her way to the Army headquarters to find out what she could about her father, Colonel Speta. Her clipped Castilian Spanish was markedly different from the slightly slurred local patois but the taxi driver immediately understood when she gave the address. In less than twenty minutes she emerged at the white marble building with the field guns outside and walked up the steps.

She was soon in the library, searching through the Army lists. She quickly found her father, Ignatio Florentine Speta, son of General Ernesto Speta and… Louisa sped through the documents. Married Consuela Bragatti in 1966. The colonel had been second-in-command at the Army base in Bahia Blanca, and there was a list of all his decorations. Finally the entry said: 'Both killed in a car crash in 1979'. There was no mention of any children.

For a moment Louisa panicked at not seeing her own name written down. If her birth certificate was to be believed, she was part of the Speta family. She put the list down and thought carefully, then went back a couple of pages to the entry for General Ernesto Speta and copied down his address and phone number. He'd probably moved, or was dead, but it was worth a try.

She was still looking blankly at the Army list when a young lieutenant passed by and asked if he could be of assistance. She wanted a telephone and he pointed to one. Before long she was drinking coffee with him, having tried and failed to get a response from the number. She resolved to try later from the hotel.

'They are very flirty, these Argentine men,' she said

with mock horror to her mother later that evening as they were having dinner. The lieutenant had asked her where she was staying and would she have dinner with him, if not that night, then tomorrow, or the next day. She laughingly told him that she would think about it and that she might see him the next day. She thought of Alfonse, her boyfriend of a few weeks at home in Madrid, and giggled to herself.

After dinner, she tried the number again from a call box. This time a women answered. At first, Louisa was tongue-tied but eventually she struggled out a request to speak to General Speta. The elderly woman on the other end of the telephone was patient and said that General Speta was no longer alive but had gone to the next world, and she would be joining him very soon.

'I'm so sorry,' Louisa stammered, 'but are you Señora Speta? I am your granddaughter, Louisa, the daughter of Ignatio and Consuela.'

The old woman was silent for a moment and then she said: 'But Consuela couldn't have any children…'

'But they had me.'

'You know my son and his wife were killed in a motor car accident.'

'Yes, I know. I was put in an orphanage and then I was adopted by … my … my adoptive parents.'

Again the old lady was silent for a moment, as if trying to collect her thoughts. Finally she said: 'Ignacio and Consuela adopted you because they couldn't have any children. When they were killed, we gave you to another orphanage. We couldn't look after you. That's all I can say, really.'

'But…'

There was nothing else to say. Louisa clung to the phone for a while, even after Señora Speta had replaced her receiver; eventually she put it down and rejoined Isabella, her lips clenched tightly to prevent herself from crying.

'What is it, darling?' Isabella asked when she saw her daughter. She took Louisa in her arms as the girl's tears spilled down her cheeks.

'Señora Speta said I was adopted *before* I went to the orphanage,' Louisa said. 'I don't understand.'

They talked as they walked back to their hotel, clinging together, chewing over the problem and trying to find a way through it.

'I knew there was something strange because your mother's name wasn't on the birth certificate,' Isabella said.

'But you're my mother anyway,' Louisa said quickly. 'I don't care about the Spetas or anyone else.'

They walked on, going over the same ground and coming to no conclusions. An ugly thought slipped into Louisa's mind, one she could not get rid of, and it festered all the rest of that evening and through the night. 'Do you think I could be one of the Disappeared?' It was the first thing that she said as they sat down to breakfast the following morning. 'I've been looking at the cuttings about Argentina that I collected at home. There's a special place in the city that can help you find out.'

'Do you think you are? Do you think that's where you

came from?'

'I don't know.' There were more tears in Louisa's eyes.

'If you are, darling, it is nothing to be ashamed of. We'll go later to this place and we shall see. I'll come with you.'

CHAPTER 36

The Commission for the Disappeared was housed in a brand new office block downtown, smaller than the original building but more suitable. The modern partitions gave more privacy to those who had things to confess or reveal.

It was just after ten o'clock when the taxi dropped off Louisa and Isabella. The two of them went inside, both feeling a degree of trepidation but determined to battle it out.

The building was almost empty; the crowds that flocked to the Commission in previous years had gone now. It had an air of quiet study; it was more like a library that anything else, Louisa thought, as they made their way to the reception area. There were helpful posters on the walls and literature on the table in front of the reception desk, all of which was completely new to both women. It was amazing, Louisa thought, how you could be completely oblivious to such events.

Within a quarter of an hour, Louisa was explaining her story to a couple from the Commission who were busy taking notes and looking up things in card index files. Every so often they dashed out of the room and along the corridor, returning moments later with a file or a newspaper cutting.

Jacob Van Haan looked intently at Louisa as she answered questions from his colleague, Susanna Michaels.

'It's interesting that you mention Colonel Speta,' Susanna said. 'We didn't – we don't – know that he took one of the disappeared children but we will certainly check it out. How long did you say you were staying in Argentina?'

'We are going to the waterfalls at Iguazu tomorrow and then down to Bahia Blanca. After that we'll be back in Buenos Aires for three days.' Isabella answered for both of them.

Jacob spoke for the first time. 'If you can give some blood before you go, we might have the results when you come back. We have built up a powerful database of people who are looking for children. If your DNA matches, we'll have our answers.'

It was Isabella who replied. 'But if Louisa's parents or grandparents are not on your database, the test would prove nothing.

'That is true. I'm afraid that we won't be able to help for the moment, although new people are coming forward every day just as you have. I am confident that we will get to the bottom of this before too long.'

Susanna made a phone call and arranged for Louisa to

go to the hospital next day to have her blood samples taken then Louisa and Isabella said their goodbyes and left. As they slipped into a taxi outside the building, Clara Silva was going through the doors on her regular weekly visit to check on the status of children who had been kidnapped by the State. There were fewer steps at this building than the previous headquarters but enough to slow Clara, so she paused at the doors to get her breath back.

Louisa and Isabella spent the day looking at the sights in Buenos Aires. The following day, after a nurse had filled half a dozen phials with Louisa's blood, they flew down to Iguazu to forget everything that had happened since they'd arrived in Argentina. If ever there was a place to forget the rest of the world, it was here. The magnificent falls plunged down the great gorge, throwing spumes of water high into the air. The noise was deafening but it cleared their minds of confusion, leaving them empty and calm.

Louisa and Isabella walked round the falls on a wooden walkway. They clung to each other, afraid that the supports might suddenly break and throw them into the deep. Every so often, as the wind whipped up, they were washed with spray.

They walked to the edge of the Devil's Throat, the highest point, and watched the water falling ninety metres into the pool below. Later, clad in raincoats and boots, they took a rubber boat out from a landing stage to the base of the falls, getting soaked as they did so.

At the end of the day, they walked back to their hotel for dinner and the thoughts which had been banished returned.

'Do you think I am being disloyal to you and to Gran?' Louisa asked.

'Of course I don't, darling. You are still the same person you were at home. Nothing has changed, except that you may find out you have a few more relatives than you realised.'

The next day, before leaving, they had their last look at the raging waters of the river cascading down the falls as it had done for thousands, perhaps millions, of years. Nothing had changed here except for building the vantage points and the hotel.

It was a long flight down to Bahia Blanca and, after checking into their hotel, they were anxious to get out and explore the town. They walked past the house where Louisa had grown up before leaving for Spain; they visited the park, the tea shop and the museum where she had gone with her mother and her father when he was not working.

All too soon, it was time to fly back to the capital. The first thing that Louisa did when they arrived was to phone the Commission to see whether her DNA results had revealed anything.

'Unfortunately,' Susanna said, 'the results are not back yet, but we are expecting them tomorrow. I will ring as soon as we know anything.'

That night, Louisa and Isabella went to the cinema to see a film about a piglet who turned out to be a whizz at herding sheep. They both laughed and cried and laughed again during the film. Afterwards Isabella told Louisa, 'It's all about finding your place in the world. And you will.'

* * *

Susanna was as good as her word; the following day she phoned Louisa with the news. 'Your DNA matches one of the records we have on file and we think we know who some of your relatives are. Could you possibly come in this morning?'

Louisa did not know whether to be happy or sad but, with Isabella holding her hand and trying to guess what was being said on the telephone, she agreed that they would go down to the Commission.

When she put down the receiver, Isabella was impatient for news. 'Well? What did they say?'

Louisa had tears in her eyes. She embraced her mother. 'I am one of the Disappeared.'

Isabella held her tightly, afraid she might faint. 'You mean you *were* one of the Disappeared. Now you are found.'

Within a few minutes, they were in a taxi speeding towards the Commission. They hurried up the steps and through the door, then they were running to reception. When they reached the door of Susanna's office, they were short of breath and panting. They paused momentarily then knocked and entered. The office was empty.

They looked blankly around the room. Just as they were about to leave, the door opened and Susanna, Jacob and a small, dark-haired woman entered.

Clara Silva, the colour visibly draining from her face,

stopped dead in her tracks as soon as she saw Louisa. 'I don't need the DNA results,' she said.

Louisa looked at her, not knowing how to react. 'You're – you're…' was all she managed to say.

'May I hold you, my dear?' Clara asked Louisa as she moved towards her. Louisa put out her arms and the two women embraced. 'You look exactly like my daughter did at your age. What are you, eighteen last month?'

'Yes, how did you know?'

'You're exactly the age my daughter's child would be,' Clara said. 'When was your birthday? I always thought that Caridad had a boy, but the likeness … it's incredible.'

Jacob made the introductions. He explained that Louisa had arrived in Buenos Aires recently; she had been adopted by Isabella in Bahia Blanca after her parents, Colonel and Señora Speta, were killed in a car crash. When Louisa got in touch with Speta's mother, the old woman had told her that she was adopted at birth by the Spetas and that when they died, she had put Louisa up for re-adoption.

Louisa hugged Clara throughout, almost oblivious to what was being said.

'We have nothing on Speta,' said Jacob. 'But he was a highly placed military officer. Louisa has a Buenos Aires birth certificate with only Speta's name on it as the father, which of course we now know is false.' He paused. Clara and Louisa were not even listening; they were simply hugging each other and crying.

Stranger things had happened. Jacob, Susanna and Clara vividly remembered the elderly couple who had tracked their twin grandsons for five or six years; when the supposed parents had made a trip back to Argentina from Peru, they had been arrested. The Commission and the grandparents were certain that the children were theirs but it was proved beyond doubt by DNA testing that they were not. Within a week, two more children were discovered who were the rightful heirs of the grandparents. For six years the grandparents had tracked one set of twins, believing them to be theirs, only to find another set of twins within days of losing the first set. An outsider might find it hard to imagine the roller coaster of emotion that a grandparent might feel when something like that happened.

Isabella could see Clara wilting under the strain. 'Sit down,' she said to Clara, pushing forward a chair. 'Was your daughter married?' she asked as Clara sat down, breathing heavily but unable to stop smiling.

'No, she wasn't,' said Clara.

'Do you know who my father is, or was?' Now it was Louisa.

Clara nodded and then she was crying again. She told Louisa about Guillermo, about how he had seen Clara at a demonstration and then worked with the Grandmothers to find a lot of stolen children. But then... Clara paused before she added, 'He simply disappeared. I mean, he went missing.'

Later, at their hotel, Louisa confided in her mother. 'I'm not sure if I want another grandmother. I'm not sure if I am ready for it.'

'You haven't changed, darling. You are the same person

you were when you came here. Only the details of your birth have changed and that was eighteen years ago. You can forget all about it, or you can embrace the past and accept it. It is entirely up to you.'

'I suppose so. It's just a bit of a shock.' Louisa clung to Isabella's arm. 'But they were very certain in the Commission, weren't they? They think I was born in that prison and that Clara is my real grandmother.'

'Don't you?'

'Yes, I do. Anyway, the DNA proves it beyond doubt.'

They had arranged to have dinner with Clara that evening and by the time they arrived at the restaurant, Louisa was quite calm. When she saw Clara sitting at their table, she ran to her and hugged her.

'It's a miracle that I have found you – or rather you have found me,' Clara said.

Isabella caught them up a moment later and also hugged Clara.

Louisa listened intently as Clara told her over dinner what a brilliant mother Caridad would have been. Louisa squeezed her new grandmother's hand and smiled.

Clara had brought a photo album and the three women pored over it. The likeness between Louisa and Caridad was uncanny. 'Here is your mother when she started at the university, not long before she disappeared,' Clara said. The large black and white photo stared back at Louisa: the same bright eyes, the same smile, the same flowing hair. 'And here she is as a baby … and here she is as a toddler.'

Now it was Isabella's turn to exclaim. 'Oh I can see

Louisa there,' she said, pointing to the three year old in the album. 'That is exactly how she looked when she came to us.' She dived into her handbag and produced a set of pictures of Louisa when she was a child.

There were other pictures, of Caridad with her parents at the beach, on her father's knee. 'Tell me more, tell me again,' Louisa asked Clara. 'Tell me about my father.'

'Caridad was very much in love with your father,' Clara began. 'And after she disappeared, he tried very hard to find her but he couldn't. That was the way it was in those days.'

'Who was he?'

'I've already told you,' she said. 'He was a brilliant young lawyer called Guillermo Haynes.' Clara paused, and then she added: 'He may be dead, we just don't know now.'

Louisa was confused but she could not put her finger on the reason why. 'But he knew where my mother had been taken?'

'Not then, no. Nobody knew. He asked everybody he could think of. He tried the Army – his father was in the Navy and his wife was from an Army family. Guillermo had very good connections. He also tried American and English diplomats to see if they could help, but each time he drew a blank. And then, after you were born, your mother, my Caridad was….' Clara could not bring herself to say the word. 'Caridad was…'

'She was killed, murdered!' It was Louisa who said it, quite bluntly. 'My God,' she added, as though only she understood the true horror of her birth. 'How she must have suffered.'

Clara missed Guillermo almost as much as she missed her own daughter and this was hard for her. After a while, though, she began again. 'After the war, after the fall of the military government, we had an election and your father came to the Grandmothers' Collective to help us. He was a lawyer, as I said, a wonderful lawyer. Together we searched for Caridad's baby and other children who had disappeared and we found many of them. But we didn't find…' She stopped for breath, for comfort, for something.

Louisa put her hand into Clara's and squeezed it. For a moment Clara was lost for words, as though she were desperately trying to remember something in the far distant past, which she knew had happened but which had fled from her memory. 'I don't know,' she said. 'Nobody knows. We just assume he hasn't "disappeared" too.' She said that word with weary emphasis and then added: 'But those days are supposed to be over.'

Isabella touched her hand. 'It's alright' she said. 'You can tell us more later. This must be very hard for you.'

'No, I must tell you now,' Clara insisted. 'Guillermo and I found a little boy who I was convinced was my grandson. Eventually it turned out that he was his parents' child, although the father had been involved with the Disappeared. He was the commandant of the prison where Caridad gave birth to you. We were sure of that.'

For the first time for years Clara was transported back to those heady days when she and Guillermo were hot on the trail of little Paulo, stalking his parents' every move, convinced he was their quarry. She had grown to love

Guillermo as she would have loved him if Caridad had brought him home as a prospective husband. She had got to know him and she loved him like the son she never had. She longed for the days she might have had with him and Paulo, living the rest of her life as a doting grandmother.

'Paulo's father was locked up for his crimes. But that was a long time ago; he is free now. We were so sure – Guillermo was so sure – and when it was proved that the child, Paulo, wasn't his it affected his mind. Guillermo became very distressed. He started drinking, he had a mental breakdown. He was married but his wife divorced him. I haven't seen Guillermo for twelve years now. He has disappeared. No one knows where he is, but I hope he is alive and will see you one day.'

CHAPTER 37

Louisa and Isabella were flying back to Madrid. They had said their goodbyes to Clara and resolved that they would see her soon; they had no idea when or where. Louisa had made a real connection with Clara and plans were made but Isabella, for one, could not be certain if they were escaping from a past her daughter wanted to forget about or flying to a future where the past would become the present.

On their last evening together, Clara presented Louisa with a present wrapped in gaily coloured paper and secured with a large bow. 'This is something I treasure very much,' Clara said, 'and I'm sure you will as well. It really belonged to both your mother and your father.'

Louisa unwrapped the pen which Caridad had given to Guillermo. 'Wow,' she said, and then later, 'Why did my dad give it away?'

Clara told her that he had left it in his office before he disappeared and that his secretary had given it to her.

'Thank you,' Louisa said. 'I will always treasure it.'

She and Isabella settled back in their seats as their plane took off and watched the city below getting smaller until it disappeared into cloud. They were flying in the upper atmosphere in the late afternoon, with blue all around them, and a lot to think about.

Louisa suddenly asked, 'Would you mind terribly if I went to university in Buenos Aires? I would still come home for the holidays.'

Isabella was surprised, shocked even, but she did not show it. 'You mean cancel your place in Madrid and apply again?'

'I may be able to transfer or I might change my course. I'm just thinking about it. But would you be upset, Mama?'

Isabella thought for a while before answering. 'I wouldn't be upset. You must do what you want to do.' And then she added, 'You will always be my daughter and I will always love you.'

'I would like to find my real father – and that means no disrespect to Papa,' Louisa said.

'Of course not,' Isabella replied. 'Your papa would have wanted you to know everything about your beginnings. He would have been proud of you.'

The scheme had come quite suddenly to Louisa and she wrestled with the pros and cons all the way home. It would be no problem to change her course or transfer, but she had no idea about the costs involved and how they might be borne. She didn't even know when the Argentinian academic year began.

By the time she arrived home, she was absolutely

determined. Somehow she would continue her studies in Argentina and she would find her father.

* * *

By the time she started reading law at the University of Buenos Aires the following February, Louisa had read every book she could lay her hands on about the country from its independence from Spain to the present day, but she had had little time to search for her father. There was so much to do, so much work, so much to absorb, so many new friends. In Madrid she had decided to study economics, not knowing that her birth mother had chosen that as her own subject. They had both figured it would give them the best chance of a job. But now Louisa wanted to do law, like Guillermo. Like my father, she thought, as she settled into a residence not far from where her mother must have studied years before.

She was nearly at the end of her first semester before she could address the search for her father but then she started in earnest. By the end of the second term, she had uncovered every detail of Guillermo's life until the time he disappeared.

With Clara's help, she located his first office and talked to old man Berruti and other members of the firm. She ran her fingers down the wooden panelling as she walked along the corridor, imagining her father sitting behind his huge antique desk, dictating letters or solving legal problems. She located Christina and quickly realised that here was a woman who had long been – and was still – in love with her father.

Christina was older than Louisa's mother but younger than Clara, and she could say things that the others might not understand. She and Louisa could be frank, sometimes brutally frank, with each other.

'You were a little in love with my father?' Louisa asked one day.

'Everybody was. He was a lovely man,' said Christina. 'But he was a naughty man; he had lots of affairs. I looked after him.'

One day Christina noticed the pen than Louisa was writing with. 'Is that Guillermo's pen?' she asked.

'Yes. Clara gave it to me.' And then she remembered. 'I gather you gave it to Clara. She gave it to me before I left Argentina that first time.'

'That and a picture of Caridad, your mother, were the only things he left in the office. He pretty much destroyed everything else.' Christina's eyes were moist.

Louisa visited Guillermo's mother on her farm and discovered a sad, lonely woman who was pining for her husband and her son, Horacio, and now for Guillermo as well. The frail old lady and her husband had no siblings so Guillermo was her only remaining living relative – and where was he? If only Louisa could answer that. She grew closer and closer to Guillermo's mother.

Louisa had more trouble with Pilar but the two women ended up with a mutual respect. Pilar was, in the end surprisingly kind; perhaps the anger she had felt years before had evaporated.

'Have you got any children?' Louisa asked her once.

'No, we never had any children.'

Louisa detected a sadness in Pilar but she did not press the point. Nor did she discover whether Pilar had ever had another relationship after she divorced Guillermo. She did not feel completely happy in Pilar's company but she discovered what she needed to and they parted on comfortable terms.

Louisa even contacted General Horloz, frail but still mentally alert and residing in a retirement home in the capital. It took him a while to understand who he was meeting in the garden at the home, but he was charmed by Louisa as everyone was. She had her mother's easy way and everyone was mesmerised. She continued to visit the general long after she had extracted every ounce of information he could give her, because he was old and lonely and in need of company. Pilar went to see him sometimes, but he no longer had the influence to attract her interest. He had always had a starring role at the centre of society but now he was cast as an extra, without a voice; the change of government had destroyed him completely. Horloz had not changed his views about the righteousness of the Dirty War, the necessity to uphold the Christian values of the *status quo*, but he bore no grudge against Guillermo – or at least none that he showed.

Louisa could paint an accurate picture of her father: a hardworking, hard-riding, womaniser who fell in love with a young student. She found out things about his search for Caridad that Clara had no idea about. Louisa tracked down Peter Tomlinson, Guillermo's old friend from the British Embassy, who had recently been posted to Madrid as ambassador. Louisa went to see him during one of her vacations, and was impressed that he spoke to her in perfect Castilian Spanish. But he could add nothing of interest, beyond remarking that he remembered Guillermo had been desperate to find Caridad.

She had more luck with Marshall Ingrams, the US counsellor who had tried to find Caridad through diplomatic channels. He could also remember Guillermo begging for help when every other avenue had failed, and how he could find out nothing about the girl Guillermo was looking for. He told Louisa, 'Guillermo was frantically looking for your mother. She must have been quite something.'

Ingrams had long been retired at his home in Wisconsin but over the telephone he told Louisa of his heartache for the thousands of Disappeared in Argentina. It was, he said 'a very, very bad time'. 'The CIA did some pretty awful things, in Vietnam and since. But I simply could not comprehend the sheer villainy of the Argentines at that time.' At the end of their conversation, Ingrams invited Louisa to 'drop by anytime'; he, too, was captivated by her charm.

Louisa spoke to journalists and academics writing histories of the period. Just before she took her finals, she met Jacobo Timerman who had been arrested and tortured by the military but had survived. After his release, he had written a famous book, *Prisoner without a Name, Cell without a Number*. Louisa had read the book when she initially began the search for her father in Argentina; she told a small untruth when she first spoke to Timerman on the phone, that she was writing an article for the university magazine about the Dirty War. In truth, of all the people who had been tortured he was the one she most wanted to meet, not so much to get information about her father but to understand the mentality of those who had tortured her mother. She never forgot the passive way Timerman described his torture and the way he preserved his strength and his sense of identity. After years living in Israel, he had come back to Argentina. Louisa tracked him down with her usual careful, dogged research.

'I remember Guillermo,' Timerman said suddenly, after they had been talking for about ten minutes. 'He came to see me. I remember him.'

'You mean my father,' Louisa said, almost unwilling to believe him.

Timerman was adamant. 'Yes,' he said. 'I remember him. He was a lawyer, I think, very bright, and he broke down and wept. He came to see me at *L'Opinion*, where I was the editor. No one, he said, could help him. I was his last chance.' He paused. Then he said, 'But I couldn't do anything; it was just before I was arrested.'

Louisa collected a cupboard full of files about her search for her father. She checked with the passport office and the driving licence authority and discovered that Guillermo had not tried to renew either document. She wrote to every home and hospital for the mentally afflicted, asking if they had anyone fitting Guillermo's description, sending photos and a résumé of his interests. Most had replied; she visited those that didn't, travelling to remote parts of the country at weekends or in the holidays. She eased her way past crusty matrons and unwilling doctors who, in the end, checked everyone present in case they were Guillermo, knew Guillermo or could give her any information about him.

Not long before Louisa was due to finish her course at the university, Guillermo's mother invited her down to farm to stay for a few days. 'You are my only grandchild,' she said. 'We should spend more time together.'

The two of them were sitting down after dinner when Sabrina Haynes said to Louisa: 'I have something for you. It is twelve years since Guillermo … went away. I still have some of his money in an account in the United States and I want you to have it. Perhaps you can use it to find out where he is. When I die, you will have this farm and anything else that isn't Guillermo's. Who knows? By then, he may be officially dead and you will be entitled to everything. But I want you to have this now.'

Louisa was overwhelmed. She had done her duty by her new grandmother but the two were not as close as Louisa was with Clara. But she could certainly use the money. For a start, she could arrange that every single person found dead in impecunious circumstances could be DNA tested.

Before she left, she arranged with the Grandmothers to continue following up every newspaper report that referenced a lost or ageing man, and she again placed adverts in every local newspaper in the country seeking information.

A generation after the end of the Dirty War, Louisa discovered that people were much happier to speak out but their memories were fading. She had found out everything she could have hoped, including details of Guillermo's life even he might not know about, but she had no idea where he was, or even if he were alive or dead.

* * *

By the time she graduated with a law degree, Louisa had become a firm friend of all the Grandmothers who toiled with Clara to find Argentina's stolen children. The number was going up very slowly now. Clara vowed to keep Louisa informed of anything which happened in Argentina which might affect the search for Guillermo. Louisa planned to widen the search via the internet and with visits to other countries.

Before she left, Louisa went to see Pilar to try and keep her onside, even though she knew Pilar did not spend much time thinking about her former husband.

CHAPTER 38

2005

Louisa was so thrilled at the news that she had to tell her mother but she could not do it over the telephone, so she and Bernardo were clinging to the ceiling straps on the crowded metro as they made their way through the evening rush hour to Isabella's house. She clung to Bernardo's arm as they walked from the metro station, so excited she could barely speak. Her life, she knew, would now be changed forever.

When her mother opened the door, Louisa flew onto her arms. 'You'll never guess,' she said immediately.

'Guess what?' Isabella said. 'You'll have to give me a clue.'

'Oh, Mama, come on. Guess, guess, guess!'

'I have absolutely no idea,' said Isabella and then, as though a light had been switched on she asked: 'Have you got news about your father?'

Louisa almost tripped over what she was going to say. 'No, I have not.' She was slightly embarrassed by the question. 'But I have other news. Bernardo and I are going to be married.' She beamed at her mother and then almost leapt into Bernardo's arms.

'That is wonderful! Come and give me a kiss, darling. When did all this happen?'

'Today.' Louisa was scarcely able to control her joy as she beamed first at her mother and then her fiancé.

'Maybe I knew before you did,' Isabella said.

'What do you mean, you knew? Did you ask her first?' Louisa looked at Bernardo, but he shook his head.

'No, no,' he said. 'I'm afraid I asked her today. I didn't want to lose you to some other guy.'

There was no 'other guy', of course. As soon as they had met at a party the previous year, there had been something between Louisa and Bernardo. Six months ago they had moved in together, or rather Louisa's flat sharer had moved out and Bernardo had squeezed in. Bernardo was a big man, six foot six tall and broad with it, but he was gentle and he was kind. Isabella had guessed his intentions a while before Louisa, and she had been crossing her fingers for weeks.

Bernardo was the ideal man for Louisa, at least according to Isabella. He was a recently qualified architect employed by a prestigious firm in Madrid and already working on large projects. Louisa had told him about Guillermo, Caridad and Clara early in their relationship. He knew the whole story because Louisa had told him the night they first slept together.

'You know I'm adopted,' Louisa said.

'What difference does that make?'

'Actually I was adopted twice. My real mother was murdered, by the Argentinian government.' Despite her calm tone, Louisa's eyes filled with tears.

'What? How?'

The whole saga came gushing out, like water from a tank where the bung has been removed and cannot be put back. Louisa confessed that she was still looking for her father.

At first Bernardo sympathised, even helping her with the search but over the months his feelings about the absent Guillermo changed. He began to feel that Guillermo was a bit a coward, a lot of a coward in fact, and chided Louisa about him. He was glad that, as their relationship deepened, Guillermo seemed to become less important. She rarely spoke of him, so Bernardo quietly put her absent father to the back of his mind.

'Well, come in. We must have some champagne.' Isabella ushered them through the hall and out to the terrace at the back; although it was tiny, it was dripping with flowers and catching the last of the evening sun.

'Bernardo,' Isabella said, 'you will find a bottle in the fridge and I will get the glasses.' She was not rich but she always kept a bottle of champagne or Cava in her fridge for 'special occasions'. It was a habit that Pedro had started early in their married life; Isabella remembered the night they had come home with Louisa and the bottle of *Baron B* was in the fridge waiting for them. Sometimes the bottle might be cooling for months before an occasion presented itself, but Isabella never failed to buy a replacement once one had been drunk.

Bernardo brought out the bottle with three glasses, and they sat on the terrace making toasts, laughing and reminiscing. At about nine thirty, they left the apartment and went to a local restaurant for dinner.

In the crowded room, Louisa did not hear her phone ring. When she finally listened to her messages at home, it was one in the morning. There was a message from Clara; she merely said: 'Call me, it's urgent.'

It would still be early in Buenos Aires and Louisa was desperate to speak to her grandmother – she knew Clara would be thrilled with her news. And anyway, Bernardo was already asleep.

Clara answered her phone almost immediately. 'Thank God you called!' she said before Louisa had chance to speak. 'You must come immediately. We have found Guillermo, but he is not well.'

Louisa was slightly tipsy and she struggled to understand what Clara was saying. It was six years, going on seven, since she had graduated in Argentina and returned to Spain; she had not been back since. She had continued to look for her father through the internet, the newspapers and occasional phone calls to people who might know something. Somehow, though, her sense of urgency had gone. She desperately wanted to find her father but she also desperately wanted to get on with her life.

Her head cleared immediately and she crashed back to earth, shaken by Clara's words. 'Where is he? How did you find him? Is he hurt?'

'A priest in the far south got hold of the

Grandmothers' Collective. Through them, he contacted me.'

For the rest of that night and half the next day, until she got on the plane, Louisa was in turmoil. She was confused again; those feelings of guilt she had felt when she discovered that she had been adopted twice, when she knew she was a disappeared child, when she found her real grandmother, when she started looking for her father, when she stopped looking for her father, resounded in her head. She had stayed close to Clara and they exchanged letters and the occasional phone call; she had grown even closer to Isabella. But falling in love with Bernardo had left little room in her heart for that part of her life that related to Argentina. It had taken second place to her new career and Bernardo. Now it was suddenly centre stage again.

Clara had explained to her that her father was dying of tuberculosis. In a moment of clarity, he had told the priest at the small mission house in Patagonia where he was hospitalised about Caridad. 'He kept calling for her,' Clara said, 'saying she had been killed by the government. He kept saying disappeared, disappeared.'

The priest had done some digging and eventually found the Commission for the Disappeared in the capital. When he made contact with Clara, she had tried to have a few words with Guillermo on the telephone but he had rolled in and out of consciousness. She could not tell him about Louisa.

'Will you come?' Clara had pleaded

'Of course I'll come, as soon as I can. Tomorrow. How

can I get down there?'

'I will have someone email you the exact address and instructions on how to make the journey. Come quickly. I am going down tomorrow morning with Guillermo's mother. Pilar is flying us down in a private plane.'

'Pilar?'

'Yes, she is doing it for Guillermo's mother. Since I was the one who told them both about him, they are allowing me to go as well.'

Louisa barely slept and was in her office before seven in the morning, sorting through her diary and shuffling appointments and commitments as best she could before others awoke. Even before she asked her boss for the time off, before she had worked out how she would pay for it all, she had booked her flight to Buenos Aires and on to Rio Gallegos, which was almost as far south in Argentina as she could go. There she would hire a car and drive two hundred miles to the tiny town of Brava, overlooking Lake Brava, where Clara said her that her father was being nursed.

The credit card was a wonderful thing, Louisa thought, as she tapped the number into her computer and booked the flights. There was no connection south until the morning after she arrived in Buenos Aires but the time change was on her side; she should arrive in Brava less than forty-eight hours after hearing of her father's sudden appearance.

* * *

There were tears in her eyes as she embraced her mother

before she left. 'I must see him,' she said.

Isabella agreed. 'Of course you must, he is your father.'

Bernardo was harder to convince; this was not the pattern of events he had planned for the first few days of his engagement. He argued with her at first, telling her that she had a responsibility to her mother, and to him.

'But he's my father,' Louisa cried desperately.

'Yes, and what sort of a father was he?' Bernardo responded. 'How long did he look for you? And where has he been since you were born? Nowhere!'

'Isn't that being a bit unfair?'

'I don't think so. You had a father, a good father – Pedro. I didn't know him, but I know your mother and I see the way you toast him at meals when I come over. He was your father, not some drunken Lothario who has now suddenly been discovered in Argentina.'

Louisa burst into tears. In some ways she knew Bernardo was right, but she could not abandon all of her past. She was torn between Guillermo and Pedro, between her Caridad and Isabella. The past plagued her; it always had, she thought, even before she knew anything about her origins. How could that be? All the time she was in Argentina studying, she had felt guilty for having abandoned Isabella; since she had returned to Madrid, she had felt guilty for losing interest in her birth parents.

'Please, Bernardo,' Louisa said at last. 'Please try and understand. I must see my father, talk to him, understand what ... well, everything. Before you know it I will be back and then we will go and choose a ring.' Louisa was not sure that she had convinced him. Nevertheless, she was now on her way back to Argentina.

Her father would have aged, she thought, but she would recognise him immediately. And he would certainly recognise her because she looked so like Caridad. She had been told that so many times.

As she sat in the aeroplane, half dozing, she thought about Guillermo falling in love with Caridad and her own conception. She imagined herself holding Guillermo in her arms and nursing him back to health. He would be thrilled that she was now a lawyer and that she was getting married, and he would love Bernardo just as she did.

She thought about Bernardo and wished he was with her. She deeply regretted the argument they had had before she left, the first real argument they'd ever had. She would have liked Bernardo to accompany her on this journey back to the very first days of her life. She could have introduced him to her father; she knew that would cement their relationship.

Then she remembered the disagreements with Bernardo over Guillermo; almost from the beginning it was a difficult subject. She recalled his stinging words: 'Your father was a serial philanderer. How would you feel about me if I behaved like him?'

'If he hadn't been a philanderer, as you call him, I wouldn't have been born,' she shouted.

'There are probably children all over Argentina that he has abandoned.'

Of the hundred and one things Louisa had not done before leaving, not asking Bernardo to come with her was the most serious. Now it was too late: she was going back to her roots alone. She wondered whether her relationship with Bernardo would ever recover.

Louisa thought about Pedro too, and how quickly his memory had been superseded by Guillermo. She felt guilty about that, more guilty than she had realised before. Pedro had been the father she had known, had loved, and he had loved her. Isabella always told her Pedro would not have been worried by Guillermo; he would have accepted Guillermo as her natural father and it would not have changed the way he loved Louisa. Louisa wondered now whether that could be true.

Louisa had wanted to ask Isabella if Pedro was always faithful. How would Isabella have reacted if he had not been? Pedro and Isabella had been good people but what if they had not been? What if they had done something in the past which she, Louisa, would have been ashamed of? What if they had been involved in the Dirty War? Would she still love them?

She wanted to know what she should think about Guillermo, whether she should really love him. She had never dared ask; she just knew that she could not abandon her real father now.

CHAPTER 39

Guillermo had tried many times to end his own life but each time he lacked the courage to pull the trigger, jump off the cliff, gallop into a wall, swallow the tablets, drive into a tree, just die. He had imagined every scenario, tried every method, failed every time.

When he had first gone AWOL, a doctor would have said that he was suffering from severe depression, nothing more. Years of careless living and sleeping rough, of itinerant work and wandering aimlessly from state to state, of fighting, drinking and not eating properly, had played havoc with his health. On many occasions he had been left in the gutter, crying and bleeding. After one particularly savage beating, heavy swipes from a metal bar had impaired one side of his brain permanently; thereafter he was frequently dizzy and disorientated.

Before, he had been able to forget that which he did not wish to remember; now his memory deserted him and only came back intermittently. The skills he had learnt as a young child stayed with him, so he never lost the ability to ride horses and could continue to scratch a living as a farmhand or gaucho, but the intellectual expertise he had acquired later in life was lost to him.

When he was asked how he had arrived in this or that place, he could never say because he simply did not know. Oddly though, Guillermo never forgot Caridad and that gave him permanent nightmares. She was always there, serene and beautiful then suddenly metamorphosing into a monster. She attacked him, bit him, pulled out his teeth and fingernails. She squeezed his testicles until they bled, drove her nails into his body and mocked him for his cowardice.

He knew he had failed her, abandoning her to her fate because he was not brave enough to stand up to her kidnappers. He had not done enough to get her released; he had rejected her because it was easier for him to live without her. He had gone through the motions but eventually he had retreated. He had maintained a sort of life with Pilar. And then, that fateful Thursday in the Plaza de Mayo her picture, carried proudly by her mother, had come back to haunt him.

Sometimes he could not remember why Caridad had gone away, nor who she was, but he knew that her image burned his brain like a branding iron on a cow's rump. Every day he paid the price of not finding her.

Now Guillermo was sure he was dying of TB and he could not even succeed in that. Some time ago a man, a doctor, he thought, had told him he had tuberculosis, and given him some pills. He had not taken the pills; why would he want to prolong his life?

He had been coughing up blood and mucus for a long time, as long as he could remember, and his chest hurt. His whole body ached and creaked. He knew he was thin and his grey skin was loose. He had lost a lot of his hair, and his feet and hands had apparently grown larger than they should have been. Or maybe they had not shrunk as the rest of his body had. He was stooped, he had no appetite, he sweated a lot and he could not sleep, although he was always dreadfully tired. He felt as though he were already in hell, lying on hot coals from which there was no escape.

He was not sure how he ended up in the Santa Cruz Mission, an old granite building which had fallen on hard times. Maybe the municipality had transported him here from the gutter; maybe the old priest, Father Pierre, had found him wandering.

Pierre lived alone in the mission most of the time except for his silent dog, a rather ramshackle but enormous Pyrenean mountain dog. Maybe the dog had taken a vow of silence before being admitted here.

The mission had been built about a hundred years ago at a time, Guillermo thought in his rare moments of lucidity, when God had been a frequent visitor to this land. Now He was not, Guillermo was sure about that. There were no celestial gates, no heavenly choirs, no green valleys and sparkling springs. Guillermo knew also that there was no hell beyond life. He was already in hell, and death would be the only way out.

Father Pierre did not seem sure about his faith; he

did not pretend to be very godly. Guillermo felt more comfortable in the mission, where at least it was dry, than he had done sheltering outside. The warm broth which Father Pierre gave him slipped down his throat and into his stomach, easing the pangs of hunger but making him want to throw up.

'Get this down you,' Father Pierre told him, as he spooned the liquid into his mouth. Pierre was large like his dog, with huge, gnarled hands and a bushy beard. His feet, thrust into old tattered sandals, were enormous too, with bony toes and horny nails all displayed from under his heavy wool cassock which didn't quite reach his ankles. For all his size, he was surprisingly gentle as he held the spittoon up for Guillermo to be sick into, or when he helped Guillermo to the lavatory or, more often, lifted Guillermo out of the bed after he had wet himself so that he might change the sheet.

Guillermo had no idea how long he had been in this room, in this bed, but now he was surrounded by his mother, his former wife and… Surely that was Caridad? Sometimes he could distinguish her, see her quite clearly; a moment later she was hazy, incomplete. Sometimes she was talking to him, but only occasionally did he understand her.

The sad party of three women arrived at the mission at about two o'clock that afternoon, squeezing out of the car after a lengthy flight from Buenos Aires and a long drive.

Pilar had met Guillermo's mother in the executive lounge in the private area on the far side of the airport. A moment later, Clara arrived. 'I am so grateful that I can

325

come with you,' Clara said to Pilar. 'I know it must be difficult.'

'There is room.' Pilar was cool but polite; this was not the time for histrionics. She had put to the back of her mind that it was her, Pilar, who had started this tragedy by delivering Caridad to the police. Did she regret that now? No, she did not. Guillermo had started it by falling in love with a young girl, breaking every rule that her society lived by. She might have put up with his occasional affairs but no, she did not have anything to be contrite about.

Pilar recognised Clara from the images of Caridad she had seen in newspapers over the years, but specifically from a large picture Christina had brought when she returned the things left in Guillermo's office after he disappeared. As soon as Christina had left, Pilar smashed the photograph and frame and threw them in the waste bin. She had no wish to be reminded of Caridad. Now she saw Caridad in Clara: the two of them looked so alike.

Clara had a warmer reception from Guillermo's mother, a woman more her age. Clara knew that Señora Haynes had suffered the loss of her husband and one son already; there was a sadness in her eyes which matched Clara's.

'Your son did a lot for me and for all the Grandmothers before he disappeared,' Clara said. 'We owe him a lot.'

Clara sat on her own in the Lear jet, thinking about the children that had been found since she had worked with Guillermo: the little boy Fernando; the twins Ernesto and Christa; Maria, Consuela and Joachim. There were Gabriela, Sophia, Lucia, Bruno, Javier, Rafael and later

Caridad's daughter, Louisa.

Clara had never found Caridad's body and that would always trouble her. Perhaps her daughter had been flung from a military aeroplane over the sea, a fate usually reserved for the almost dead as a final torture; or perhaps her grave was in some hidden place, yet to be discovered.

Clara's agony was not over but in a few hours she could embrace Louisa again, and that would remind her of Caridad. Louisa had promised that this time she would fix Clara up with a computer and a magical invention called Skype so she could see Louisa when she telephoned her. One day she would be able to see Louisa's babies.

It was Louisa who had made sure Clara had a mobile phone. At first Clara was reluctant to use it but now it was always in her handbag. Not that she used it often, but it was always there, and every night she charged it religiously so it would be available the next day. Now she could call Louisa from wherever she was, although down in the south reception was poor and she could not always get a signal.

'Bless you all,' Father Pierre said to them as they entered the mission, his huge, silent dog by his side. 'Come in out of the cold and warm yourselves. I will show you where Guillermo is. I have to say, you're not a moment too soon.' He led the party up the stairs to Guillermo's room. 'He is barely conscious. I fear he has not much time left.'

They trooped silently into the tiny room. Guillermo's mother approached him, stifling her tears and grasping his hand. Pilar and Clara held back.

The priest brought chairs and they sat down.

Occasionally Guillermo opened his eyes and stared at one or other of them, then closed his eyes again. He tried to speak but no words came out. His cold, bony hands sometimes gripped whichever hand was holding his, though the effort seemed to exhaust him. His breathing was heavy and uneven.

As gently as they could, each of them tried to engage him in a dialogue, though even when he was conscious he did not understand what they were saying. 'Why?' they kept asking him. He did not know the answer. It was 'why' to everything: why had he left them, why had he given up his job, why had he left the capital, why had he not been in contact, why…?

Guillermo had asked himself those same questions. And in the far distant past, he had had other 'whys' to ask. Why had they arrested Caridad? Why did Pilar denounce her to the police? Why had he been such a coward?

He is dreaming, or is he remembering? He is riding a small pony through the long grass with Horacio. He is cradling a foal but the foal is dead. He is lying down on the sofa in the house at Tigre with Caridad. There is a huge explosion and water rushes through the rooms. Caridad is screaming and he is drowning. He is walking round the Plaza de Mayo with a crowd of women wearing white headscarves. He is looking at Clara, who is carrying a picture of Caridad. He is aware of someone holding his hand. Is he still dreaming? Is it Caridad, holding his hand and speaking to him? 'Will you marry me, Caridad? I want to leave Pilar, and marry you?' Guillermo cannot hear her reply. He strains his ears, but he can hear nothing.

'I don't know if you can hear me.' This time it was Clara. 'We are all here.' She took his hand in one of hers and stroked it. 'We want you to get well.'

'Will you marry me, Caridad? I love you.'

For the most part, Pilar stood at the end of the bed and let Guillermo's mother and Clara do the talking. But she heard his muttered words and she was angry.

Guillermo is not sure who anyone is. He cannot answer their questions but then he has been unable to answer anything for a long, long time. Pilar is screaming at him; Caridad, Bollini, the police, everyone is screaming at him. The pain is intense, his head is on fire. His brain is fogged but, in a moment of coherence, he recognises Pilar standing near him.

'Why did you tell them?' he shouted. 'How could you do that? Why?' he shouted again and then retreated into his blackness.

'What do you mean, Guillermo?' asked Clara.

'Why did you? Why?' Guillermo made an effort to sit up. The three women saw his arms and his shoulders move but the effort was too much for him. He slumped back down but he was obviously angry.

'It was a long time ago,' Pilar said quietly.

'What do you mean, Guillermo?' Clara asked again.

'Why?' he managed to exclaim again, and Clara thought she could see his face redden.

'He is talking about one of his mistresses,' Pilar said flatly. 'I reported her to the police.'

Guillermo could hear two women speaking but they were now in another world and he was a silent witness. He tried in vain to mouth the question again: 'Why?'

Father Pierre intervened. 'I think,' he said, holding up his hands, 'I think you are tiring him. Perhaps two of you should wait outside and one stay for a while.'

His mother stayed and Pilar and Clara went outside. As soon as the door was closed, Clara rounded on Pilar and asked her: 'What did you mean?'

'I told you, I reported one of his mistresses to the authorities in an effort to save my husband.'

For a moment Clara was confused, then transfixed, then angry. 'You did what?' She was incredulous. 'It was Caridad, wasn't it? My Caridad that you shopped to the police?'

'Yes, it was. At that time I wanted to save my marriage and my husband.'

For a moment Clara struggled make sense of what Pilar had admitted. She tried to form sentences; her mouth moved but no sounds emerged. She was crying now and reached into her handbag for a handkerchief to dry her tears. Eventually, she said: 'You told the police. You denounced Caridad...?'

'Yes I did!' Pilar was not proud of herself but she fought a valiant defence. 'I had no idea she would be…' She could not finish the sentence. 'I wanted to save my marriage. You might have done the same if your husband was screwing everything in a skirt! I was sick of his womanising.' She looked away, down the hall, down the stairs, up at the ceiling, wishing that she had not agreed to take Clara with her, that she had allowed Guillermo's mother to fly down on her own in a commercial jet.

Clara was now sobbing uncontrollably. Pilar turned

and started down the stairs. 'How could you?' Clara shouted after her 'How could—?'

Pilar turned to face Clara; she was defiant now. 'I'm surprised Guillermo didn't tell you.'

'He never did. I should think he was too ashamed of you to mention it.'

Pilar looked away. She was surprised when Clara ran towards her. She had stopped crying and looked straight at Pilar. 'Didn't you realise what might happen to Caridad?' she demanded. 'What might happen to Guillermo?'

Pilar spoke very quietly. 'No, I didn't, I really didn't. My brother told me about … about your daughter. I just couldn't bear Guillermo being unfaithful all the time… I thought it would teach him a lesson.'

Clara fought to control her anger. 'You must have known what would happen to her,' she said bitterly. 'You must have.'

'I did not, I swear I did not.' Even now did Pilar refuse to recognise the full repercussions of her action. She continued to excuse herself by saying that Caridad might only have been warned. Pilar had no idea that she would be killed.

For Clara, though, the effect of Pilar's admission was immediate: like a punch to the solar plexus, it made her double up. The colour left her face and she felt faint. Holding onto Pilar's arm, she steadied herself. 'To do that…' She clung desperately to her dignity. She steadied herself and walked past Pilar down the stairs and outside before bursting into tears again. She sobbed uncontrollably for several minutes. She had had sympathy for Pilar but that had now evaporated.

Clara had grown to love Guillermo, despite his faults. She was not sure how she would have dealt with him had he been her husband, but he was not; he had come to her searching for the same life, the same child, that she was looking for. Now he was dying; there was no point in pointing out an affair that had ended over a quarter of a century ago. Now that bloody woman had told her how she had betrayed him and Caridad, Clara realised that, for the first time in her life, she could not forgive. She thought about Louisa; she would know how to deal with this situation. She wished Louisa was here already and they could sit down together with Guillermo and pray for Caridad.

Later, much later, when Guillermo was conscious again, he found Clara once again sitting next to him. 'Did you know we have found Caridad's child? Your child?' she said, holding a handkerchief to her eyes, still red with tears. 'Her name is Louisa and she is coming here now.'

Guillermo tried to reach out to Clara but he could not lift his head. He could not comprehend what was being said, nor who was saying it. Some time later, it could have been hours or the next day, for Guillermo had no notion of time, he awoke again and recognised Clara through his half-closed eyes. She was holding his hand and she had been crying but now she was smiling at him. He could not make out what she was saying; he knew she was speaking but no meaning could pass the fog in his brain.

'Louisa will be here soon,' Clara said. 'She is flying all

the way from Spain. You would be proud of her. I am. She is a very clever lawyer, like you.'

Clara lifted Guillermo's almost lifeless hand, as though she was drawing comfort from it as much as she was desperately trying to pass comfort to him. It felt desperately fragile, as though lifting it too far would tear it from his arm.

'It's all because of Louisa that we have found you.'

CHAPTER 40

As soon as she touched down in Buenos Aires, before the plane had finished taxiing and come to a standstill, Louisa switched on her phone. There was a message from Clara: 'Come as quickly as you can,' the message said. 'He is very, very weak.'

Louisa tried to phone Clara back but all she got was a number unobtainable sound. Perhaps mobiles did not work that far south; perhaps the signal could not get over the mountains. She tried again first thing the next morning and again before she got on the plane south but still there was no reply.

She phoned Bernardo and Isabella to tell them she had arrived safely in Argentina, but also to check that no messages had been left there; none had. She was still sad that Bernardo had taken such exception to her wanting to see her father; he sounded gruff on the telephone, claiming it was late at night.

'I miss you already,' she told him.

'Good,' was all he said, and then, as an afterthought, 'don't be too long.'

'I wish you had come with me.'

'Well...' Bernardo started, as if to reveal something comforting, but then he added, 'I think it's better if you sort this out on your own, then get back here.'

It was not the response that Louisa wanted. A moment later, when she spoke to her mother, Isabella was more comforting. 'Don't worry about Bernardo,' she said. 'He will be fine.'

'I'm not so sure,' Louisa replied. 'I'm not sure I haven't made a big mistake.'

As she whiled away the hours in the airport waiting for her connection, Louisa worried about Bernardo. Here was an otherwise perfect man who could not understand why she needed to go to Argentina to see her father. Her father's blood flowed in her veins; but for him, she would not have been born.

Just before she got on the plane she tried Clara again and this time got through. The news was not encouraging. 'He is very weak and not conscious for long. I'm not sure he understands what we are saying.'

'I am coming,' said Louisa. 'I will be there as soon as I can. Does he know about me? Have you told him?'

'Yes I have,' Clara told her, 'but I'm not sure he understood. Come as quickly as you can.'

The plane journey south to Rio Gallegos was cramped and bumpy and Louisa was feeling the effects of her journey to Buenos Aires. She flew almost directly over Bahia Blanca, where Pedro and Isabella had found her, adopted her and loved her ever since, though she was too high in the sky and too lost in her thoughts to realise. For almost the whole way she appeared to be over the sea, a vast, grey sea with nothing between her and New Zealand, on the other side of the world.

As soon as she arrived, she was on the phone again but once more heard Clara's voice asking her to leave a message. She waited for her luggage and was walking out to the hire car desk when suddenly her phone rang. She snatched it up but it was a message. 'Hurry,' it said. She tried to phone Clara back without success.

Louisa made a quick call to her mother, who was sympathetic, and then to Bernardo, who sounded bitter. 'Haven't you got there yet? How long are you going to be away?'

Louisa was in no mood for a fight, so she let Bernardo go. He did not tell her he loved her and she did not say that she loved him. She thought about that a lot as she drove on.

For the first twenty or so miles Louisa drove on a good tarred road at breakneck speed towards Brava, the wind buffeting the car and the low sun, when it appeared, nearly blinding her. But then sanity overtook her; what was the point of killing herself? She slowed down a little but cursed herself for having slackened her search in recent years; she had been so close. Guillermo had been in Argentina, most recently holed up on a remote farm, and she had not been able to find him. Now, when he had been found and she was on her way to claim him, he was almost dead.

The road gave out after a hundred miles and from then on Louisa drove on dirt, with occasional passages of tarmacadam as she went through villages. There was an incredible number of birds; some she recognised and some she had never seen before. Periodically she passed small herds of guanacos, which looked like llamas but were slightly smaller. She ignored them all, still focused on her time in Argentina and the period after she left the country. She should have stayed on after her studies and continued the search. She gripped the steering wheel in desperation, at one point nearly turning the car off the road. Why? she asked herself. Why hadn't she stayed and continued looking?

It was cold, raining and dark by the time she arrived in Brava and found her way to the mission. The building was in darkness, apparently empty, with no cars outside. She sat for a moment then forced herself out and knocked loudly on the front door. Soon she heard footsteps and the bolt being drawn back; the heavy door was pulled open by an elderly priest, who was guarded by a massive dog.

He smiled and beckoned her inside. 'It's Louisa, isn't it?' he said. 'Come inside. Don't worry about Jo-Jo. Señora Silva is still here.'

The old priest led Louisa through the entrance hall and closed the door. He said: 'I am afraid that your father has already gone to the other side, about an hour ago. I'm so sorry.'

Louisa could not speak for a moment. She had run from the car to the door; she had expected to grasp her father in her arms and wish away the sins of the past.

Now she was… What was she being told? 'What do you mean?' she said at last.

The priest took her arm to steady her. 'He has passed,' he said. He offered no explanation, no solace, just the simple fact.

Louisa started to cry. Tears ran down her cheeks and she clung to the priest. 'He can't have! He can't… He can't…'

But he had. He had died before she could tell him anything.

Clara appeared at the top of a short flight of steps. She came down and put her arms around Louisa. 'I'm so sorry you missed him,' she said, as Louisa turned to embrace her. 'I am so, so sorry.'

They were both crying now. 'It is wonderful to see you, Clara,' but even as Louisa said it she was pulling away, anxious to see her father. 'Where is he?'

'Come with me, my dear, I will show you.' It was the priest, and he led Louisa up the stairs to a tiny chapel. A stretcher lay between two chairs with Guillermo's body laid on it. A white sheet was drawn up to his chin; it was as though his body was lying in state.

'He died about an hour ago,' Clara said. 'His mother is already making arrangements for his burial, although you may have some thoughts about that.'

Louisa was scarcely listening.

'I will leave you for a moment,' the priest said, as Louisa walked gingerly towards the stretcher. She looked down at Guillermo's face, thin, gaunt and now lifeless. Did he know he had a daughter? Had anyone told him she had been found?

A patterned wool rug had been placed on top of the sheet. Apart from his head and neck, nothing of his body was visible; Louisa could not hold his hand. She bent down and kissed his forehead and it felt cold to her lips. She looked around for a chair to sit on by the coffin.

The priest understood without being asked and he fetched a chair from the side of the chapel. 'He spoke to me a little,' he said, 'before he died.'

'What did he say? Did he tell you why he was here?'

'He was obviously a troubled man, very troubled. He kept calling out for Caridad Silva and then he told me about the Grandmothers Collective. That's how I got in touch with Clara – through the Grandmothers. I'm sorry you didn't have a chance to see him alive.'

He paused, waiting for a reaction from Louisa, but she remained silent. 'I wanted to give him absolution but he told me he could not accept it. He said he did not deserve it. Then, when the others arrived, he was mostly unconscious and I did give him absolution. He has gone to meet his maker in peace.'

Louisa sat down and leant on the side of the stretcher, gazing at Guillermo's body. The priest held his hand against her head for a moment, as if saying a prayer, then silently left the chapel.

Louisa sat in silence. She had imagined every conceivable scenario for her meeting with her father except this one. She had imagined her father galloping across the *campo* and sweeping her up in his arms; she had wanted to canoe down the Iguazu River or sail across the

Rio de la Plata Bay with him or laze in the warm evening sunshine at Tigre with an *asado* slowly cooking. She had longed for him as she might have longed for a lover. Now she had found him: a shape on a plank of wood, wrapped in a carpet and wearing a death mask.

She was too late to tell him that she had passed her law exams at the top of her class and was now a lawyer, just as he had been. She was too late to tell him about how she had found Clara and what a wonderful relationship she had with her natural grandmother. She could not tell him about Pedro and Isabella and how he would have loved them if he had known them. She would definitely have related her fears about Bernardo, about how confused she was about her husband-to-be; she would have confided that she wanted lots of children and for Guillermo to be a grandfather to them.

But, as she stared into the waxen face, she regretted most that she was too late to say that she loved him, even though she had never known him, never embraced him, never held his living hand.

* * *

In 2012 General Videla, who had led an Army coup against President Isobel Peron and was then in charge of the military junta in Argentina, was sentenced to fifty years in prison for his part in the kidnap and murder of the Disappeared. He was accused of being the main architect of what became known as the Dirty War. He was originally found guilty of murder, torture and other crimes in 1985, but freed in 1999 by President Carlos Menen.

In 2010, the Argentine Supreme Court upheld a Federal Court decision to overturn his pardon. Eight months later he was found 'criminally responsible' for the torture and deaths of thirty-one prisoners and jailed for life.

He died in prison of natural causes in May 2013.

ACKNOWLEDGEMENTS

This book has been inspired partly by Señora Estella Carlotto, the head of the Grandmothers of the Plaza de Mayo, who began searching for her daughter and grandchild in 1977. She knew the then president, General Videla and when her twenty-two-year-old daughter, Laura, was suddenly disappeared by the State, Estella begged Videla to return Laura's body so that she might be buried decently. Eventually the body was unceremoniously dumped on Estella's doorstep with a bullet wound to the stomach and the face smashed in. Laura had given birth to a son while in captivity. Last year, Estella's grandson, then aged thirty-six, presented himself for DNA testing. He was eventually reunited with his eighty-year-old grandmother.

When I made the first documentary for the BBC about the Disappeared in 1982–3, which broke this terrifying story in Britain, I met Estella Carlotto and was immediately struck by her mix of compassion and steely determination. So far she has led her organisation to find nearly 120 of the estimated 500 children born in captivity and farmed out to new families.

I have turned the story into a novel which I hope you, the reader, will find both exciting and thought provoking. The work has started and stopped over a long period of making documentaries for television and has been read and revised by a number of people. In particular I would like to thank my wife, Pam, and son, Stefan, for their invaluable work when the book was finally in a state to be read; Fred Emery, with whom I made that first film in Argentina; Stewart Binns, John Stevens and Subniv Babuta who made extremely valuable suggestions and comments, most of which I took on board; Penny Ebden and Luis Parada who corrected a number of points about Argentina, a country in which I have spent a considerable time over the years; Susan Phillips, who proofread everything. And lastly Karen Holmes, who edited the final manuscript prior to publication.

David Wickham
Limpsfield Chart
August 2016

ABOUT THE AUTHOR

David Wickham has worked all over the world as a writer and television director and producer on news and documentaries, factual entertainment and drama programmes. He has won numerous international awards in London, New York, Banff and Monte Carlo and also earned a Royal Television Society award for his work.

He first came across the story of Argentina's stolen children while working on a documentary about the sinking of the *General Belgrano*, after the Falklands War. He has since made two documentaries about the children (one for the BBC and one for ITV) which inspired him to write *Stolen Children*, a fictional novel based on the story.

David is married and currently lives in south east of England.

Lightning Source UK Ltd.
Milton Keynes UK
UKOW05f1846081116

287183UK00024B/821/P